RED DRAGON-
WHITE DRAGON

Gary Dolman

REYNARD PRESS

RED DRAGON-WHITE DRAGON

This edition published in 2015 by
REYNARD PRESS
HG4 2NP
First published in the United Kingdom in 2013 by
THAMES RIVER PRESS
An imprint of Wimbledon Publishing Company Limited.
LONDON.
SE1 8HA

© Gary Dolman 2013-2015

The right of Gary Dolman to be identified as the author of the work has been asserted by him in accordance with the Copyright, Designs & Patents Act, 1988.

All Rights Reserved
No part of this publication may be reproduced, stored in a retrieval system or be transmitted, in any form or by any means, without the written permission of the publisher, nor be circulated in any binding or cover other than in which it is published and without similar conditions being imposed on any subsequent purchaser.

All the characters and events portrayed in this novel are imaginary, and any similarity with real people or events is coincidental

Cover: © GentianMedia.
Image: © Witthayap, Dreamstime.com - Sun Rays Photo

ISBN: 978-0-9934208-2-5

RED DRAGON-
WHITE DRAGON

Also by Gary Dolman:

The Eighth Circle of Hell

The Satyr's Dance

RED DRAGON-WHITE DRAGON

Dolman has penned a great novel, which lays an icy grasp around the reader. The period details and language are both spot-on, and the sense of madness driving the murderer on is truly haunting.

-CRIMESQUAD.COM

I was impressed with Red Dragon-White Dragon. Gary Dolman's novel had just the right mixture of realism and Arthurian legend to keep me guessing at every turn. And the ending—amazing! Just when you think you know what's going to happen, even if you've guessed the villain already, there is a huge twist that completely blindsides you.

-THE MAD REVIEWER

I was greatly impressed by this book and would recommend that anyone who likes a great mystery with a historical slant, checks this one out.
You won't be sorry that you did!

-READFUL THINGS

*And oftentimes, to win us to our harm,
The instruments of darkness tell us truths,
Win us with honest trifles, to betray's
In deepest consequence.*

> -Macbeth, Act I, Scene 3,
> William Shakespeare

CHAPTER ONE

The Edge of the World.

That was what they called this place; this vast, rocky promontory, which lay across the kingdom of Northumberland like a slumbering dragon. It was here the Emperor Hadrian had chosen to build the great wall that marked the very edge of the Roman Empire, making use of the natural barriers of cliffs and crags in his bid to keep out the barbarians beyond.

He stood on the Edge of the World and gazed out over the bleak, rock-strewn moorlands, pinched into ridges and escarpments like the waves of some ancient, petrified sea.

It was to that country he was bound. His work for this day, given to him by the Fates themselves, was done, and he could go back now to his cool and silent vault, hidden deep in the crags and rocks of the Northumbrian fells. There he would tell this tale to his Lady and to Lancelot, his one-time companion-in-arms, as they slept their eternal sleep.

He smiled at the thought of his Lady and felt the spilled blood on his face bristle and crack. She was his love, his only true love, and he imagined kissing her smooth, white brow, taking her limp fingers in his own and telling her of the killing.

Ah, yes – the killing. His smile spread wide and the mask of gore tightened and pulled. With the memory he became aware of the familiar weight of the sword hanging, always ready, at his side. Instinctively he reached down and touched the cold metal. Perhaps his Lady was not his only love after all.

He allowed himself to luxuriate in the recollection of the long, elegant blade sliding so easily into the Gypsy's body and stilling the heart inside. He remembered how, with the tip of that blade, he had searched out the place where the ribs ended and the soft, yielding flesh of the belly began, how he had sliced deeply into the intricately embroidered waistcoat and watched the flesh beneath it part obediently before the steel. And then, because this was a gift, he had carved open the flesh for a second time and formed the broad 'X' of a *crux decussata*.

The apex of that cross had gaped wide and beckoned him to the viscera within. It had gaped wide enough for him to push in his hand, wide enough for him to reach into the ribcage and wide enough for him to tear out the heart.

He glanced down to the clod of bloody flesh still grasped in his hand. It was cold now, cooled by the chilly dawn winds. He would wait until he was back with his Lady before he devoured the rest of it. It seemed only right to do so. She would know then, that in this final reckoning, he truly was the victor.

CHAPTER TWO

Atticus Fox gently drew aside the parlour curtains of Number 16, Prospect Place and gazed out across the Stray – the two hundred acres of open pasture which opened out the very heart of the bustling, fashionable spa town of Harrogate in the West Riding of Yorkshire. Its elegant avenues and walkways were filled with the cream of European and Oriental society taking the 'Cure', that curious mix of light exercise and hydrotherapy for which the town was world-renowned. It was a sight of which he would never grow truly tired but in truth, he was bored and he was restless. After all, there was only so much tea one could drink and so much chess one could play.

"Tea, Atticus?"

He throttled an inner sigh and turned to smile his thanks to his wife. Lucie Fox was already pouring milk from a dainty, porcelain jug into dainty, porcelain tea cups. She glanced across at him as he dropped into an armchair opposite and instantly read his mood.

"The Post Office messenger boy has just called with a telegram for us, Atticus. It's a commission."

"What is it?" Atticus asked sullenly, "Some old dowager's lapdog has got itself lost down a rabbit hole? Or perhaps a hotel has had another silver teaspoon go missing?"

Lucie lifted the lid of the big teapot and inspected the contents.

"Neither, Atticus; it concerns a murder."

"A murder?"

Lucie nodded.

"Yes, a murder; you'll find the telegram on the tea-tray if you'd care to read it."

Atticus, his woes vanished, plucked the slip of paper from the salver and stared at it with an increasingly incredulous expression.

"It's dated today, Lucie: Wednesday, 4th June, 1890. *'To A. & L. Fox, Commissioned Investigators. From Colonel Sir Hugh Lowther, Shields Tower, Northumberland. Wish to engage your services. Investigation of a brutal murder. Please come forthwith.'*"

He stared at the paper once again.

"A murder!" he repeated at last, "But why would anyone engage us to investigate a murder? We are only private enquiry agents; murders are constabulary business."

His wife shrugged.

"I have really no idea, Atty. It's a great pity that Colonel Lowther didn't give us any more detail, other than the murder was brutal, of course."

Atticus drummed his chin with his fingertips as he chased down a memory.

"Now I come to think of it, there was a very peculiar death reported a few days ago – in the *Daily Chronicle,* as I recollect. It was in Northumberland, on an estate near Hexham. A Gypsy man was found stabbed to death, but not only that, he'd been mutilated and beheaded.

The paper was speculating as to whether or not it might have been the Whitechapel Ripper at work again, although I'm quite sure it was not."

He passed the telegram to his wife.

"What do you think, Lucie; shall we take up this commission?"

She smiled at his expression – like a dog with its leash.

"Of course we shall," she said brightly. "It is a murder enquiry. How often is it that we get one of those?"

Atticus beamed.

"In that case, I'll fetch a telegraph form and advise this Sir Hugh Lowther that we shall be taking the first train north tomorrow morning. *Quo Fata Vocant*, Lucie, 'whither do the Fates call us, eh?"

CHAPTER THREE

Quo Fata Vocant.

The Fates were calling for him again. They were calling for him from the secret place beyond the Wall, and he could not help but to obey. They would mock him, he knew. They would fling scorn at him and torment him as they always did. But this time, like opiates to the wounded, they would help him too. This time, they would grant him relief from his pain.

They had promised.

Because now was the End-Time. Now, at last, the hour appointed to avenge the abominations of the past had arrived.

CHAPTER FOUR

The next day was sunny and bright and very warm for the early hour. It was just half past seven in the morning but already the streets were bustling with the Ailing, who were roused promptly at seven to begin their Cure.

The Foxes' luggage had been sent-on to the railway station together with their bicycles and Atticus had only his big leather investigations bag and unusually thick, pewter-topped walking cane with him as he and Lucie stepped out into the morning to take the short walk across town.

Harrogate Central Station was a designated 'floral' station of the North Eastern Railway. The Foxes stepped onto the east-bound platform, already very warm under its delicate, iron canopy, and Atticus inhaled deeply. His stomach fluttered. That smell: the heady mix of perfumes from the magnificent floral displays overlaying the lingering odours of oil and smoke was the scent of adventure, the precursor to an investigation, and it was nothing short of wonderful.

The hands of the platform clock twitched from 7:54 to 7:55 precisely and they heard the shrill whistle of their own train as it appeared on the tracks of the station approach. It puffed slowly along the length of the platform and then, with a hiss of steam and a clattering of couplings, drew gently to a halt.

The stationmaster, resplendent in silk top hat and tailcoat, stood by a large, brass bell. He peered along the line of glossy, maroon-painted carriages, his hand gripping the clapper-chain, ready to peel the arrival of any important visitors to the town. Atticus took Lucie's arm and shepherded her through a ribbon of steam and up into an empty first-class compartment.

They changed onto an express train at the busy station at York and duly settled into their seats for the long journey up the East Coast Main Line to the north.

As the train slowly gathered speed through the suburbs and outskirts of the city Lucie pulled a copy of the *Lancet* periodical from her handbag.

"Is there anything of interest in there, my dearest?" Atticus asked, opening his own, much larger bag and lifting out a travelling chess set.

"There's an article on modern nursing practice I am especially interested in," she replied without looking up. "I know I've left the profession now, but I do like to keep abreast of new developments. They seem to happen so quickly these days."

Atticus nodded and turned back to his chess. He had a particular aversion to all things medical and most especially if they happened to involve any amount of blood or gore. In their profession of reuniting errant pets and straying spouses it was, thankfully, uncommon but it was still very much an area he left to Lucie, who by contrast seemed to positively revel in it.

Atticus Fox believed very strongly in the need to keep his brain in first-rate order. It was, after all, the principal tool of his profession. In addition to drinking several large glasses of the iron-rich, Harrogate chalybeate water each day, he often played against himself at chess. By so doing, he was convinced that he was training his mind to be completely objective and dispassionate in all respects. After all, that was what he was obliged to do each time he switched between the black and the white chessmen.

As their train snaked inexorably northwards, the farms and villages of the rural Vale of York began to give way to the chimneys and manufactories of the industrial north-east of England and a dramatic view of the bridges over the River Tyne eventually heralded their arrival into the city of Newcastle. Once there, they changed again, onto the final leg of their journey, the Newcastle to Carlisle railway line, which, Atticus had promised, was to be spectacularly scenic.

Lucie reminded him sharply of his promise as she dotted her handkerchief with French perfume and held it tightly against her nose whilst the train skirted the foul open sewer that was the Tyne. Very soon however, it began to gather speed over the gently-curving iron bridge at Scotswood and the rows of mills and factories, along with their attendant slums, ceased. The stench faded, the vista opened out once again and the train began to climb imperceptibly into the rolling hills of south Northumberland.

It seemed no time at all before they came to the small but bustling village station at Bardon Mill. Just beyond

Hexham, this was the nearest point of the railway to their final destination of Shields Tower.

CHAPTER FIVE

The Fates: Urth, Skuld and Verthandi. Like clamouring ravens they call for the old man's spirit.

He owes them it, and more – seven times more. He owes it because they have pledged him a gift. It is the gift of his lady, pure and whole once again, and there could be no gift more precious.

But he is bound by honour to give in return, and in return they have demanded a *wergild* – a man-price – seven times over.

The old man's life is to be the second part of that *wergild*.

And lo! He spies him – the old soldier, victor of a thousand battles. He, who once led whole legions of men, is alone now, slumped in his chair by the lake.

"*He is sleeping,*" Verthandi cries exultantly.

He cringes. Surely she has woken him.

"*By God, you have the luck of the Devil,*" Verthandi continues, "*He might be an old dog now but were he awake, he could still teach a young puppy like you a trick or two.*"

"*He certainly taught your woman a trick or two,*" Urth quips and they both cackle with delight. "*And his powder charge never went off before even he put the ball in.*"

The cackles become mocking peals of laughter, a cacophony that grows louder and louder and louder.

"*Pay no heed to them.*" Skuld cuts across them and their laughter ceases. He is grateful. She at least understands how deeply their words cut into him.

"*Kill him,*" she urges, "*I do not care who he is.*"

Quo Fata Vocant.

Striding forwards, he pulls a broad ribbon of silk from his pocket.

CHAPTER SIX

When Atticus and Lucie Fox alighted onto the platform at Bardon Mill, they stepped down into a bustle of industry and a mass of people going about their daily business just as they had been in Harrogate. They were, perhaps, a degree less fashionable, a little less affluent than their counterparts to the south but what they lacked in sophistication was more than compensated for in the warmth of their faces, in the cordiality of their smiles and in the richness of the backdrop of the South Tyne Valley.

A tall, strikingly handsome man in the uniform of a footman complete with felted top hat and, despite the heat of the day, a great, black cape-coat stood waiting for them on the platform. He lifted his hat and looked enquiringly in their direction. Atticus tipped his own in response and took out one of their thick, embossed calling cards. He said, "Mr and Mrs Atticus Fox of Harrogate," and the footman bowed smartly, clicked his heels and took the card respectfully between his white-gloved fingers.

The required protocols being satisfied, he cleared his throat and read: "'A. and L. Fox, Commissioned Investigators,'" then twisted the card slightly to read the smaller, italicised script beneath: "'*Quo Fata Vocant*.'"

Looking up, he grinned as he translated easily: "Whither the Fates call."

Atticus was both taken with the footman's reading of the Latin in his broad and lilting Northumbrian accent, and taken aback by the ease of his translation.

"You speak Latin very well," he remarked.

The footman laughed. He had very white, very even teeth.

"Aye, well I really don't, sir, begging pardon. My father didn't think it worth the penny a term it cost to learn Latin and Greek at the Bobby Shaftoe. That's the school in the next village, Hayden Bridge, where I did my letters. No, sir, I've served a time in the Northumbrian county regiment, the Fifth Regiment of Foot, and by coincidence *Quo Fata Vocant* was our regimental motto."

He laughed again.

"Welcome to Hexhamshire, Mr and Mrs Fox. My name is James and I've been sent by the Colonel, Sir Hugh Lowther, to fetch you back to Shields Tower. Follow me, if you please."

He bowed again and then led them across the railway tracks to a large square of open ground adjacent to the stationmaster's house. There, a glossy black carriage stood aloof from the carts and waggons of miscellaneous freight that filled the yard. It was harnessed to a team of four perfectly-matched bay horses, whose sleek coats were curried to perfection. The coachman, dressed identically to their escort, stood in his seat and raised his top hat as they approached and several onlookers turned to see who the important personages might be.

"That is taken from Sir Hugh Lowther's coat-of-arms, I presume?"

Atticus nodded towards a large and crisply detailed crest painted across the lacquered panel of the carriage door.

"It's the Lowther family crest, yes, sir," replied James, pinching the brim of his hat. He pulled the front of his cape-coat to one side and bared an identical device embroidered on the breast of his jacket. It was a white dragon. "The Colonel uses it for his household livery too."

"Dragon, passant, argent," murmured Atticus.

"I beg pardon, sir?"

"White dragon, passant – it's the heraldry of the crest. Do you see that the dragon is walking to the left with its right forepaw raised? One cannot live in Harrogate and not be completely fascinated by the subject of heraldry."

Lucie coughed suddenly.

"The motto is interesting too," Atticus continued: *"Magistratus indicat virum* – *The office shows the man."*

He grunted, considering the words.

"I'm not sure I wholly agree with it, though."

"No, sir," said the footman.

After a moment Atticus said: "James, we have come all the way up from Yorkshire today. We've been sitting for hours in all manner of cramped railway compartments, so while we recover ourselves," he glanced back to the still-stationary train, "And whilst we wait for the porter to fetch us our bicycles, pray, what can you tell us about Sir Hugh Lowther?"

The shadow of what might have been panic chased away the laughter from the footman's face. He hesitated.

"I'm not at all sure it would be my place to make comment about the Colonel, begging your pardon, Mr Fox."

"Oh, come now, James," Lucie purred, "My husband isn't asking for your opinion of Colonel Lowther, only for a little bit about him as a gentleman. It would be a great help to us in our enquiries."

James regarded her dubiously, but his resolve had clearly broken.

"Aye, well…I suppose as you've asked me directly, and as my orders are to render you every assistance, I could try."

He stood straight and tall, almost as if he might have been back on the regimental parade ground at Spital Tongues.

"Well, first off I should say that Sir Hugh Lowther is a British officer in every proper sense of the word – a very fine and valiant, first-line soldier and the colonel of the 'Fighting Fifth'. That is the Fifth of Foot, ma'am, or the Northumberland Fusiliers as they're called these days. He has fought with the greatest honour all around the Empire, just like his father and his grandfather before him, and I can truly say that he's the bravest man I have ever known.

"I served with him myself. That was back in the fifties, during the Indian Rebellion."

He paused, a smile lingering on his lips, lost suddenly in his own recollections.

"And I could tell you a right tale or two about that."

"I imagine so," said Atticus.

"Sir Hugh is all but retired from the army these days though. He has been since his father, Sir Douglas Lowther, fell ill a twelvemonth or so ago. Sir Hugh is his only son, you understand, and he had to take over the estate. He also has interests in a number of coal mines and iron works across Northumberland and he owns one of the biggest tanneries in Hexham. As you might imagine, he is a rich man; he's a very wealthy man indeed."

"Shields Tower is a large estate?" Atticus asked.

"Aye, sir, very large, several thousand acres in total, mainly tenanted out except for the home farm, which is called Shields Tower Farm. Sir Hugh isn't especially interested in the management of the estate and he leaves the running of it pretty well entirely to a land steward, a gentleman by the name of John Lawson. Besides, with all his other interests, he's much too busy. I declare, we see less of him now than we did when he was away fighting with the army."

"Does he have any family?" Lucie asked, "A wife or children?"

"Oh aye, Mrs Fox, aye he does. He has a son; Master Arthur, or Master Artie as we all generally call him, a tall, strapping young gentleman of twenty-one, and a very beautiful daughter; Miss Jennifer, who is Master Artie's younger half-sister."

"Half-sister, so Sir Hugh has been married more than once?"

James nodded.

"Yes, ma'am, he's been married twice now. Lady Igraine, the first Lady Lowther, vanished one day from the

Great Whin Sill. That is a high ridge that stretches right across the county as far as the coast at Bamburgh. It was around a year after Master Artie was born. She was presumed to have got lost and perished on the moors, though they never found her body."

In spite of the heat of the day, he shivered under his coat.

"It can be terribly bleak up there, you know. There are supposed to be wolves on the fells…and worse."

His gaze drifted past them, towards the steep hillside beyond the village, and he shivered again.

Atticus and Lucie glanced to each other and waited in respectful silence until James' thoughts returned once more to the here and now.

"Sir Hugh married a young widow-woman soon afterwards. Lady Victoria Lowther died in childbirth whilst bearing Miss Jennifer."

"Oh poor Sir Hugh; how very unfortunate he's been," Lucie cried, "Losing not just one, but two wives. I'm very sorry for him. But Lady Igraine, what a beautiful, romantic name that is."

"Aye it is, ma'am, it's a very beautiful name for a very beautiful lady. We all utterly adored her. I myself had the honour to serve as her footman in my younger days. She was vivacious and charming and full of passion, with never a day of sadness or a day of sickness in all of her short life."

"It's a very unusual name too." Atticus said, "Arthurian, unless I'm very much mistaken."

"You're quite right, Mr Fox, it is. You see, there are a great many old legends about King Arthur and his

Knights of the Round Table hereabouts. Sewingshields Castle, up on the moors not far from here, was the site of one of King Arthur's castles and his final resting place. Many people locally are named for characters from the Arthurian tales and Igraine was the name of King Arthur's mammy."

"That's it," Atticus exclaimed, "Igraine was the wife of King Uther Pendragon, King Arthur's father."

"Which is why Lady Igraine Lowther named her son Arthur I imagine?" Lucie added.

"Exactly, Mrs Fox, she insisted on it by all accounts, even though Sir Hugh wanted to call the lad Douglas after his own father and the Colonel usually gets his way. But Arthur did seem so natural and fitting."

"Didn't Sir Hugh's father mind?"

"Not at all, Mr Fox; Sir Douglas adored Lady Igraine too and with him she could do no wrong. He thought her the most beautiful woman in Christendom."

He chuckled.

"He always used to say that she was lovely enough to eat."

His broad grin froze.

"Aye and he was right too. Lady Igraine was born here, in Bardon Mill village, but she left to become an actress and a dancer in Newcastle. That was where Sir Hugh first met her – in the Theatre Royal there. She was very beautiful, with long auburn hair and a kind of wildness, a bit o' mischief in her eyes that meant he fell instantly in love with her. We all did in fact, meaning no disrespect to the Colonel."

"There must have been some who considered it a rather unsuitable marriage though," Lucie ventured, "That he married beneath himself perhaps?"

"Aye, and that's right enough, a canny few did but the Colonel would hear naught of it. He said he was fated to be with her and married her anyway, in the great Abbey at Hexham."

He nodded past them.

"And at last, here are your bicycles."

James chuckled as he glanced significantly once more at the slope leading up to the village of Bardon Mill and the much steeper hills beyond.

"If I might be so bold, Mr and Mrs Fox, the lanes of Tynedale will require some canny-hard pedalling."

The carriage swayed slightly on its big, iron leaf-springs as the heavy bicycles were passed up to the roof, and it rocked again as James clambered up to join his companion up front.

"All set, Mr Grey," he called, and the coachman duly urged the team forward into a brisk trot. They glided through the open gates of the station yard towards the village itself. Along the road, dozens of children seemed to have appeared from nowhere and they stood shyly in front of the low, heather-thatched cottages that flanked it to watch as the elegant coach-and-four swept past. Lucie, feeling rather grand, smiled and waved to them through the windows and almost immediately, the whole village seemed to be waving back.

The four bays leaned into their harnesses as the lane steepened and they soon left the long ribbon of houses and the village pottery works with its tall, square chimneys far below. Green hedgerows became dry stone walls, and lush meadows, bleak grassy moorland and scrubby trees hunched against the wind.

Lucie was utterly entranced.

"Atticus, isn't this the most romantic country you've ever seen? You can almost imagine King Arthur and his gallant knights galloping across the fells."

Atticus grunted.

"Oh, and is that the castle James mentioned, Sewingshields Castle, over there?"

She pressed a finger against the glass of the carriage window. Atticus leaned across her and peered out. A cluster of low, stone ruins were pressed into the grass of the moors just below them.

A tiny hatch slid open in the roof above their heads and they looked up to see James' earnest face framed in the square.

"I beg your pardon, Mr and Mrs Fox, but to your left you can see the remains of the old Roman fortress of Chesterholm. There were a canny few Roman forts built around here with it being so close to Hadrian's Wall an' all. There's another up on the Wall itself called Housesteads. It's much more complete." He sounded like a sixpenny tour guide.

"Oh, I see. Thank you, James," Lucie replied. Then: "We thought it might have been Sewingshields Castle."

"No, ma'am," the footman explained patiently, "Sewingshields is up on the high moors, up beyond the Wall. If ever you wanted to go there, it's out to the north-east of Shields Tower and a little way east of the Broomlee Lough.

"That's one of the small lakes there are around here," he added.

Lucie smiled, thanked him again, and settled back into the plump, buttoned-leather of the seat.

CHAPTER SEVEN

He steps forward to where the short, sheep-grazed turf drops steeply away. With a soldier's instinct, he senses the point at which the jagged lines of the edge would be broken by his silhouette and he stops. It would not do to be spied from the black carriage creeping steadily along the lane below.

There is a woman in there. He has glimpsed her through the lens of his spy-glass; a beautiful, dainty woman with long, dark hair, who puts him so much in mind of his own lady, sleeping as she is, in the womb of the rock beyond the Wall.

Looking down, the hillside is steep but not quite sheer. It is terraced, striped like the belly of a nursing mother, where the clinging soil has slipped and slumped into scars. He longs to scream. He needs to leap down those scars, as if they are nothing more than the steps of some gigantic stairway, to fall upon that carriage and carry her away.

But no! He presses his eyes tight shut and waits for the urge to pass. There will be time enough for that in the days to come.

His breathing is ragged. His pulse is racing so that his mind feels strangely light, as if he might have fallen to opium or hard liquor. And then he realises that he is indeed intoxicated; he is drunk with the elation of the kill.

The killing was the second part of his gift. It has been made and it has been sealed, and all the Fates, even Verthandi, even Urth by God, have been fulsome in their praise of him.

The hatch in the carriage roof slid open once more and Atticus and Lucie Fox glanced up again into James' beaming face.

"We're approaching Shields Tower now, Mr and Mrs Fox; you can see it ower the estate walls on Mr Fox's side."

They looked.

Butted to the end of a long, perfectly-straight avenue of neatly clipped yew trees, Shields Tower was not at all as they had speculated it might be during the long hours journeying north. True, it was built just below the high moors, just out of the teeth of the Northumbrian gales, but it was neither grim, ancient fortress nor modern Gothic recreation. This was a classic country house, such as those they knew from their own county of Yorkshire, with two elegant wings flanking a larger central portion built in the Palladian style.

To the south, the dark curve of a carriage-way led to a cluster of low buildings which would almost certainly be the stable block and carriage house. To the north was only bleak moorland.

As the coach clattered out of the avenue and into the wide turning-circle in front of the house, the two leaves of the doors parted and a tail-coated butler stepped through. He stood dutifully, waiting for James to bow them down the carriage steps and then bowed himself as they approached.

"Good day, sir; good day, madam," he greeted them crisply.

"Good day to you. We are Mr and Mrs Atticus Fox of Harrogate."

Atticus held out another of their calling cards, which the butler took and regarded impassively for a moment.

"Quite so, sir. Welcome to Shields Tower. The master is expecting you of course. Please, follow me."

The broad Geordie accent seemed somehow at odds with his impeccable formal dress and affected, somewhat pompous manner.

Atticus and Lucie followed him through the doors, through a surprisingly deep archway, and then both gasped in awe.

The splendour of the approach had in no way hinted at this. Rather than a sumptuous and modern interior, they found themselves instead inside a vast and ancient hall. Walls of brute, heavy stone towered high above them, up to a vaulted ceiling gathered around a large, glass oculus. Directly in front of them a stairway climbed to a galleried, first floor landing and by the foot of this stairway was a dais of rough, black stone on which stood an exquisitely detailed, limestone sculpture of three mythological figures. The statues seemed almost to glow with a golden aura as light streamed onto them from a large, round window set high into the front wall of the tower. The afternoon sun caught the stained glass perfectly, illuminating the rich golden-yellow of the Lowther coat of arms and contrasting it sharply with its device of an inverted triangle of six black rings.

"*Or, six annulets in pile, sable*," chanted Atticus looking round to the source of the light, "Crest, as we have seen already: *dragon passant, argent*."

"Indeed, sir. If you and the lady would care to be seated through here, I will fetch you some tea and daintycakes. Sir Hugh will be informed of your arrival directly upon his return."

The butler showed them through the hall into a large and spacious library, two walls of which were lined from floor to ceiling with shelves filled with all manner of books. A third wall was given over to a large portrait, hung rather low, of some gallant military officer.

Lucie settled herself happily into one of several comfortable, leather reading chairs whilst Atticus scrutinised the bookshelves.

"These are mostly military books," he announced after a while, "Historical battles and regimental histories; descriptions of arms and armour, that sort of thing. There are quite a number of books and poems on Arthurian legend too. Exactly what one might have expected, I suppose, given what James has told us."

"Is there anything that might interest me while we wait?" Lucie asked him. "War doesn't appeal to me in the least, and I'm much too tired for poetry."

Atticus shrugged and glanced across the rows of titles.

"What about this one? It's called *Herbal Physic*."

He pulled a good-sized volume down from its shelf and opened the front cover.

"'To my darling Jennifer on the occasion of her eighteenth birthday,'" he read, "'From your adoring father, H.D.L'. This might be the very ticket. It says it is: '*A guide to the preparation of medicines to cure most ailments from commonly-found plants together with easy recipes for sleeping draughts, banes and poisons.*'"

"Charming," observed Lucie drily, reaching up and plucking it from his grip.

It was then that Colonel Sir Hugh Lowther burst into the room. He was followed by his butler, clearly struggling to maintain his affectation as he scurried along in his wake carrying a glittering, silver tea service.

Even in the generous space of the library Sir Hugh seemed formidable, like the dragon passant of his crest. He was well above middle height and broad in proportion, with piercing blue eyes, greying dark hair and large, bristling whiskers. Somehow he seemed to fill every inch of the room with his presence.

"My dears Fox," he roared, "Welcome to Shields Tower and thank you for coming all this way so promptly— Good God in Heaven!"

He stopped short, standing open-mouthed for several seconds as he stared between Lucie and the book on her lap.

Then he remembered himself.

"I do beg your pardon, ma'am, please forgive me. I was just a little taken aback, that's all. I was…I was expectin' two gentlemen, do you see: 'A. and L. Fox'? But never mind, never mind. I am Colonel Sir Hugh Lowther, Fifth of Foot; how do you do?"

He bowed, formally and straight-backed, to Lucie, who stood and curtsied elegantly in response, and offered his large, tanned right hand to Atticus. It was covered in thick, black hairs.

"We are very well, Sir Hugh, thank you."

Atticus grasped the hand and bowed, wincing as he felt his own being suddenly crushed. "I am Atticus Fox and this is my wife and fellow investigatrix Mrs Lucie Fox. How do you do, sir?"

"Never better, never better, I thank you." Sir Hugh hesitated as he glanced sideways at Lucie. "Blow me but I'm not sure that this is women's work, Fox. Investigating a killing and particularly one as, forgive me, bloody and gory and damnably perplexing as this, is surely a task you'd only want to give to a man."

Atticus sensed Lucie's hackles rising.

"Have no fears on that score, Sir Hugh," he assured him quickly, "My wife was once a nurse. Blood and gore are second nature to her."

Sir Hugh grinned.

"In which case, bully for her! There's been enough blood and gore to satisfy any nurse. Now then, let's take this tea and I'll tell you both why I've summoned you here."

He shuffled restlessly as the butler poured the tea and handed around the cups. Then, like an actor about to enter upon some grand stage, he took a deep breath, composed himself, and began.

"We had a labourer employed on my home farm by the name of Elliott, Samson Elliott, a Romany Gypsy as I recall. Very early on the morning of Saturday last, he set off in his little caravan to visit the Gypsy Horse Fair at Appleby-in-Westmorland. That, as you may know, is held every year and always in June. We're quiet on the farm at that time of the year so Lawson, my land steward, generally allows him to go and meet up with his two brothers to do…well, whatever it is that Gypsies do at the Appleby Horse Fair.

"I'm afraid that Elliott never even got so far as the boundary walls of the estate. Lawson found his body later that same day, lying at the edge of one of the moor-side fields. He'd been run-through with a sword; he'd had his guts sliced open, and he'd been beheaded. Expert swordsmanship it was too, by the by, and I should know! His horse was filling its belly on the headland, a little way away, still in its harness.

"We immediately called for the police and a detective came out directly from Hexham with two of his constables. He examined Elliott's body and the circumstances of his death, but he could make nothing of it, the bloody imbecile."

He grunted under his breath and muttered: "You must forgive me, Mrs Fox but this is a military house and we are wont to use military language.

"Anyway, I did his damned job for him. I practically told him who the killer was – a madman who lives in an estate cottage not twenty yards from where the body was found.

"He went through the motions of interrogating him, of course. He did that for most of the next day. But he discovered nothing – absolutely nothing. As I say, the man's a rank fool."

Sir Hugh paused and looked directly at Atticus and Lucie in turn.

"It is clear beyond any shred of doubt that the madman was responsible for that murder. He was an accomplished swordsman before he went insane and he has a sword – a great two-hander – in his cottage. I told the detective as much. Unfortunately neither he nor his constables could find any trace of it when they searched his cottage, and he refused point-blank to search the moors or the lakes, even at my own personal request. Bloody dereliction of duty if you ask me, by God!"

He pounded the leather arm of his chair with his fist and swore again.

"I'm frustrated, Fox – damned frustrated – by the lack of progress. Elliott, for all he was an imbecile, was a labourer on my estate and I feel honour-bound to ensure that the greater justice is served and a culprit punished. That's why I'm engaging you both. I want you to find someone to hang for Samson Elliott's killing, and I declare you'd do well to begin with our madman."

Atticus felt the maw of irritation nibbling at his guts. He was always fiercely independent-minded when it came to the disposition of any investigation and he said: "Very well, Sir Hugh, thank you for your suggestion. However, I must insist that we approach this commission as we do every other: with a completely open mind. We follow a tried and tested method, which always begins with an examination of the crime scene itself."

He was conscious of Lowther staring at him with his intensely blue eyes.

"Is it possible we may do so now please?"

"Yes of course, Fox." Lowther continued to stare.

"May we do so directly? The case is already five days old and time, in any manner of investigation, is very much of the essence."

"I don't see why not; I'd intended to take you there myself."

Sir Hugh leapt out of his chair and strode across the room towards the low-hung portrait of the military officer. There he produced a key from his waistcoat pocket and prodded it into a hole in one side of the heavy, gilt frame. A hidden lock gave a gentle click and the frame drifted ajar, which Lowther caught and wrenched wide on its hinges to reveal a large, hidden closet recessed into the immensely thick wall behind.

Sir Hugh's broad frame almost filled this cavity as he leaned into it, all but obscuring a heavy, cast-iron safe on top of which sat a row of handsome journals, all identically bound, and each held shut by its own delicate silver clasp. He reached behind these and lifted out an ugly, black handgun.

"My service revolver," he said by way of explanation, "Webley Mark I, Break-Top. I keep it hidden behind my first wife's old diaries."

He broke open the gun in one expert motion and noted with a grunt of satisfaction that the chamber was full.

"Just in case of trouble," he added with a grin below suddenly blazing eyes. He looked very much as if he might relish any chance of trouble there might be. Tucking the gun securely into the pocket of his jacket, he led the way out of the room and back into the vast cathedral that was the great hall.

"Lucie Fox," exclaimed Sir Hugh loudly and suddenly as they passed the dais at the foot of the stairs.

"Yes, Sir Hugh," Lucie replied.

Lowther turned to stare at her, the full, black circles of his eyes darting across every detail of her face. The golden light from the window tinged his own skin and in those moments he seemed like some grotesque, somehow carnivorous appendage, to the statue behind him.

He hesitated for a moment longer and then asked: "Mrs Fox...Do you...How do you like Shields Tower?"

"I like it very much indeed, Sir Hugh," Lucie assured him, "And I adore Northumberland."

"Good...That's damned good," he muttered and smiled.

"I confess that I was a little surprised by this hall," Atticus said. "Magnificent as it is, it is quite a—"

"It is quite a deal different to the outside of the house, eh?" Sir Hugh finished his sentence for him. He laughed harshly. "That is because Shields Tower is actually two houses in one."

He swept his arm around.

"What you see here is the original. The Kingdom of Northumberland, Mr and Mrs Fox, has seldom been at peace and this part is nothing less than a fortress – a castle. My grandfather built the newer part around it, like a smart overcoat, and added the north and south wings. My father, Sir Douglas Lowther, rebuilt the stables and the carriage house."

"That explains it admirably," said Atticus, "And also the immensely thick walls. I like Shields very much too, Sir Hugh."

Lowther did not reply but led them out through the front doors and down the gently curving lane that connected Shields Tower to its stable block. It was a route that took them through a scattered audience of hideous grotesques and fiendish beasts carved brutally in stone and perched on columns of various heights. They seemed to be following their progress through their blank and sightless eyes.

Ahead of them, a couple emerged from the shadows of a carriage-arch beneath the stables' clock tower. It was a young man and woman.

The man was tall and lean with hair the colour of rich copper. The woman, they could see even at that distance, was exquisitely beautiful; slender and elegant, with white-blonde hair swept casually back from her face. She was wearing the new 'rational' clothing of which Lucie was so fond; a divided skirt and no bustle, which allowed for a far greater freedom of movement. They were walking arm-in-arm and both were in gales of laughter.

Sir Hugh halted as they approached. He stood tall and straight and said: "Mr and Mrs Fox, I should like to present my daughter: Miss Jennifer Lowther, and Master

Arthur. Jenny, Arthur; Mr and Mrs Atticus Fox are the privately-commissioned investigators I told you about. They are here about the murder of the Gypsy and they shan't be leaving until they have found us someone to hang."

Artie bowed his head and said: "We are very pleased to meet you, Mr and Mrs Fox," and Jennifer bobbed a graceful curtsey. There was a second or two of awkward silence before Atticus advised them that, as a routine of their investigation, they might wish to speak with them both in the course of the next day or so.

"Yes of course, Mr Fox," Artie replied genially. "We'd be only too pleased to help in any way we can."

"And we can tell you who was responsible for Samson Elliott's death," added Jennifer earnestly.

"What the blazes! Who?" barked Sir Hugh.

"We're quite sure it was King Arthur himself, awoken from his slumbers, Papa," Jennifer replied.

Sir Hugh snorted.

"Arrant, bloody nonsense! King Arthur indeed, whatever next? Preposterous! You sound like an ignorant villager from Bardon Mill, Jenny. In any event, introductions are over; we mustn't hold up Mr and Mrs Fox's examination of the facts." He laid heavy emphasis on the word 'facts'. "We don't have all day. Time, as Fox here has only just reminded me, is of the essence. Let us proceed."

As they passed through the carriage arch, both Atticus and Lucie were stopped short by the panorama that opened out suddenly before them. Beyond the rails of the white-painted fence that stretched along the boundary of the stable yard was a broad mosaic of lush meadows and grey, dry-stone walls. Then stretched mile after mile of rolling, grassy moorland, punctuated only by the bright azure waters of the loughs the footman had told them about and the black rocks of the Great Whin Sill. Then rose the great Northumbrian Pennine hills, shimmering blue in the distance through the haze of the summer sun.

Sir Hugh stopped too and pointed ahead into the middle distance.

"Do you see that white cottage there?" he asked, stabbing the air with his fingertip. "That's where the madman lives. The square field next to it is where the Gypsy was killed."

Atticus and Lucie peered along the line of his finger and Sir Hugh explained: "He was ambushed as he took a short-cut through that field, no doubt on his way to join the public lane, which you can just see to the left of it."

"I'm no farmer, Sir Hugh," Lucie conceded, "but I notice that that field is a different shade of green to the others. Might it perhaps be growing a crop of some kind?"

"You have a wonderfully keen eye, Mrs Fox – Lucie – and yes, you're quite correct. I'm no farmer either and normally I would leave the running of the estate strictly to the peasants. But this year I'd insisted to Lawson, my land steward – the Peasant-in-Chief – that that field be ploughed and sown with wheat. It was by way of an experiment to see if these high pastures could be a little more productive than they are at present in supporting a few scraggy cattle or sheep. Lawson tells me the early signs are disappointing and heaven knows it was devilish difficult to plough it up in the first place. There were only a few inches of dirt under the grass, d'ye see, and more stones than Hadrian's Wall, but I dare say that for all that, it was more than worth the attempt."

He grinned defiantly under his fine growth of whiskers and set off once again. As they walked, Sir Hugh asked: "Tell me, Fox, are you any relation to the owner of the Leeds Forge, Samson Fox? He's from Harrogate too, I believe."

Atticus replied that he was a cousin.

"Brilliant man of course," Sir Hugh went on, "in spite of his humble birth. We use his inventions in our own factories. I hear he's something of a philanthropist?"

Atticus was piqued.

"He is an extraordinary man, thank you, Sir Hugh and a great philanthropist. His birth, if I may say so, is neither here nor there."

Sir Hugh bristled.

"Now you're the one talking nonsense, Fox, never mind my daughter. I've no time for all that deuced egalitarian claptrap. Officers are born, not schooled, and breeding, good or bad, will always come out in the end. We Lowthers are warriors and we do our philanthropy on the battlefield. Civilising the world is our good work and that is just about big enough for us."

He began to tell them of the ancient and noble history of the Lowther family and about some of the more illustrious of his forebears. As he spoke of the Anglo-Saxons and of the reach of the Domesday Book, Lucie suddenly noticed again just how beautiful the

Northumberland moors were, and how spectacular the yellow gorse. Indeed, it was rather like the gorse thickets on the Stray that they could see from their own window at home.

They arrived, at last, at the gateway to the little field Sir Hugh had pointed out from the stable yard. As they had seen at a distance, it was roughly square in shape, with a second gateway punctuating the wall directly opposite them. The two were linked by a broad, grassy headland, which tracked around the northern edge of the field close to the madman's tiny cottage. The rest of the field was filled with stunted, chlorotic wheat and the warm breeze was blowing dapples across it like the waves of the lake that sparkled in the sun a few hundred yards upwind.

Atticus swung his heavy bag onto one of the massive stone stoops which carried the gate and glanced around, gauging his bearings. As he twisted, he felt a cold bead of sweat trickle down his skin, where the bag's strap had lain a moment before.

"Elliott's cottage was where, Sir Hugh?" he asked.

Sir Hugh turned and pointed across the horizon to a short terrace of cottages.

"His was the farthest to the right of those."

"And the lane you say he was intending to join?"

"Is just on the other side of that." He nodded towards the gate on the farthest side.

Atticus pulled gently on the hairs of his whiskers as he considered. "Did Elliott always take this route?"

Sir Hugh nodded.

"Most folk do whenever they're heading over to the west. It saves a long detour down the valley."

"Good, then that gives us at least a starting point to our investigation. Now, Sir Hugh, where exactly in this field was Elliott's body found?"

Lowther led them some two thirds of the way around the headland path, to a point just beyond the cottage. Here, he indicated a number of dark stains still just visible on the lush sward of the grass. The area was humming with dozens of flies and bluebottles.

"It was here he died, Fox; you can still see his blood on the ground, although he was first attacked back there, next to the madman's cottage."

"You say he was riding on a Gypsy caravan?" Lucie asked.

"Yes he was." Sir Hugh regarded her thoughtfully. "As I've told you already, he was a Gypsy himself. He spent hours back-aching over that caravan; painting it, scrubbing it and whatever."

His piercing, blue eyes became ice.

"When he first came to settle on the estate, he would often take it over to the moors and spend the nights there, even though we gave him a proper cottage to live in. It was his roving nature, I suppose, his lack of civilisation."

Atticus asked: "Where is his caravan now? Has it been destroyed yet?"

"Destroyed? Why no, of course not. Why should we want to destroy it? We put it into the barn at the request of the detective superintendant. He wanted to preserve any evidence there might have been on it – not that he found a great deal by all accounts."

"Detective superintendant!" exclaimed Atticus. "Bless me, but they have certainly brought the big guns to bear on this case. But that's excellent news because Lucie and I can examine it at first-hand. There is a very good chance we might find something the police have missed."

He pointed through a narrow gap in the dry stone wall. It was a style, just large enough for a man to pass through.

"The cottage there is where your lunatic lives, you say? Tell us more of him."

"And why," Lucie added, "you allow him to remain living here, on your estate, if you believe him to be a murderer?"

Lowther turned and stared at the cottage for several long seconds before he replied.

"Yes, that's where the madman lives, if living is what you can call it. I'd call it more of a day-to-day existence myself; just one step up from the cattle Lawson keeps in the fields yonder.

"Why do I allow him to remain in the cottage, Lucie?"

He shrugged.

"That is to do with the repayment of an old debt of honour my family owes him – which I owe him."

He turned back to face them.

"You see, many years ago, our madman served in the Royal Navy. He was a midshipman on board the justly-celebrated ship, HMS Shannon. The *Shannon*, and consequently he, was involved in the relief of Lucknow during the Indian Mutiny back in 1857. My father and I also fought at Lucknow but we were with the army, with the Fighting Fifth, the Northumberland Fusiliers. It was there that our mad friend rendered my father a very great service. He single-handedly rescued him from a large number of Sepoy mutineers.

"Shortly after he returned to his ship, his feeble mind finally gave out and he went insane. He was discharged from the Royal Navy as unfit for duty and given an almshouse by the Greenwich Hospital Trust, which owns a lot of property hereabouts. As time went on, however, he became more and more mad, and it wasn't long before even they threw him out.

"My dear father, hearing about it all, allowed him that cottage *gratis* for the rest of his life, together with sustenance and a small allowance in gratitude for saving his skin. My housekeeper, Bessie Armstrong, delivers a food parcel to him twice each week as she visits a…a lady-friend she has living up on the fells. If he didn't live there with alms from the estate, I have little doubt he would either be dead or locked up in a lunatic asylum just as his doctor insists he should be. But for my father's sake, Lucie, until he is proved beyond doubt to have committed the murders, on this estate he will stay."

"Then you are to be commended on your judiciousness, Sir Hugh, but tell me: in what respects is he insane?" Lucie's question was intense with professional interest.

Lowther laughed, briefly and without mirth.

"His real name is Britton, Michael Britton, but he calls himself Uther. You see, Lucie, Michael Britton firmly believes that he is actually King Uther Pendragon and the father of King Arthur."

The long silence that followed was shattered by the harsh cawing of a raven silhouetted on the ridge of the cottage.

"Does he indeed? Then he must be suffering from what is called severe, delusional madness. James, your footman, mentioned that this part of Northumberland is steeped in Arthurian legend and his delusions are clearly linked to that."

"Ah yes, James, my footman, my faithful, angel-faced fart-catcher. But James is correct. The court of Uther Pendragon – the real Uther Pendragon – was supposedly just south of here at a place called Mallerstang. King Arthur's court Camelot, again by local supposition, was no more than a mile away from this very spot at the site of the old Sewingshields Castle."

"How fascinating; I should very much like to visit Sewingshields Castle before we leave."

For several long, discomforting seconds, Sir Hugh was completely silent. Then he growled: "I've no doubt of it. I know how you ladies love the romance of King Arthur and his Knights of the Round Table.

"I'm afraid there is very little to see there these days. Sewingshields Castle is gone, barring a few overgrown earthworks and a stagnant old fishpond. But, as you are so fond of the tale, let me tell you of another part of the legend of King Arthur and Sewingshields Castle; the part that tells how King Arthur and his queen, Lady Guinevere, lie in an enchanted sleep, deep in a hidden vault, very near to the castle. They lie there ready to be awoken at such time as Britain is in great crisis and once again has need of them. Needless to say, Britton is convinced that they are already risen."

"That's as may be, Sir Hugh," returned Atticus, "But deluded or not, why do you consider Britton to be dangerous?"

"Because he is mad of course; he's quite as mad as the proverbial hatter." Lowther laughed very loudly and added: "Quite literally so, and I should know, since I own a hat manufactory myself."

His laughter died as if throttled.

"But that's why you're both here isn't it; to prove his guilt?

"Consider a murder in which the victim is not only run-through with a sword but is carved open and beheaded. Do those sound like the actions of a sane man? And it happened just yards from the door of a confirmed madman; a madman who believes himself to be a Dark Age king and who keeps a great medieval sword by his bed."

"You may very well be right," Atticus conceded, "but proper method is proper method. If we are going to send a man to the gallows, the very least we can do is build a case against him founded on something more substantial than circumstance and likelihood, however damning the circumstances and however strong that likelihood may be.

"I don't believe there is much more to be gained here today. May we move on to your barn now, Sir Hugh?

We need to examine this caravan of Elliott's for any vestiges of evidence."

Sir Hugh looked at him and a black shadow passed over his face.

"Aren't you going to examine this field a little more thoroughly first, Fox; properly earn your fees? A fellow is due his full sixteen annas-worth, after all. Aren't you going to look for footprints or suchlike?"

"Not today. The light is wrong for one thing. For another, we find it always to be most effective if we first look at a case *in toto*. After that, we can begin to delve more precisely into the minutiae. So please; on to the barn."

CHAPTER EIGHT

The barn in question formed one full side of the farmyard of Shields Tower Farm. It was a long, low, single-storey affair, built ruggedly of stone and rubble under a heavy, stone-flagged roof.

Sir Hugh said: "This is it." He cast a glance to Lucie. "It's built of the stones we took from the ruins of Sewingshields Castle, Mrs Fox." His eyes flashed and he beckoned them through the great black square of the doorway, into the looming shadows within.

"There it is," he said, pointing into one corner, "That's Elliott's caravan."

Atticus grimaced.

"It will be almost impossible to properly examine it in here; it's much too dark. Can't it be drawn outside into the sunlight?"

Lowther stood still for a moment. Atticus was about to repeat his request when the colonel winced.

"I'm sorry. I'm so sorry. I didn't think," he mumbled.

"I'm so sorry, Fox," he repeated, his voice stronger now, "I should have realised. Please forgive me. I've been deuced thoughtless. I'll arrange for it to be done directly."

He bowed and took his leave, chiding himself under his breath as he strode away.

Lucie made a face and whispered: "He seems a little on-edge, Atticus."

Atticus nodded. The light was poor but his expression might have been one of bemusement.

"He's a military man. He needs everything to work like a Swiss clock."

After many minutes of uneasy silence, save for the occasional scuffling of rats in the shadows above their heads, they heard the sound of heavy hooves moving across the cobbles of the farmyard outside. Sir Hugh's broad silhouette appeared in the glare of the doorway, moved away, and was replaced almost immediately by that of a short, thick-set man dressed in a jerkin and billycock hat. He was leading an enormous, jet-black shire horse.

"Mr and Mrs Fox, this is John Lawson, my land steward. The farm men are all out in the fields so to save time Lawson has brought the horse himself."

Atticus lifted his hat. "We are obliged to you, Mr Lawson."

Sir Hugh grunted and said: "Lawson, this lady and gentleman are the privately-commissioned enquiry agents I've engaged to look into the Gypsy's death. As I told you, they'd like to examine his caravan outside, in the daylight."

Lawson pinched the brim of his billycock and said: "Good afternoon to ye both, Mr and Mrs Fox."

He guided the horse into the corner of the barn; its wide, feathered hooves clattering loudly on the hard-packed stones of the floor, and backed it expertly between the caravan's shafts. A few minutes later, the harness was buckled up and they followed the giant horse and the little, green-painted caravan with its white, calico-covered top into the afternoon sun, sun that was almost unbearably bright after the thick gloom of the barn.

While Lawson unhitched the horse, Sir Hugh stepped forward. He patted the smooth-worn wooden slats which formed a seat for the driver in front of the high front arch.

"Here is where Elliott was sitting when he was run-through."

He scowled at something unpleasant on his fingertips, and then reached over and wiped them across the gathered material of the hood. Atticus opened his mouth to protest, but the sudden realisation of what the lumpy, brownish streaks on the calico must be stopped his mouth.

Lucie stepped forward now and began to inspect firstly the seat, and then the painted boards of the caravan's door, which was set into the arched front wall behind.

"There is a reasonable quantity of blood here and here, Atticus."

Lucie's finger darted between a number of thick, dark blotches pooled between the slats and another: a single stain, marled and mottled, on the timber of the door.

"And do you see this indentation?"

She pointed to a deep puncture in the planks of the door.

"That is likely where a sharp instrument has passed completely through Elliott's body. Gracious me! It must have been struck with some force.

"There is more blood-staining here on the footrest. Do you see it? It looks very much to me as if Elliott pitched forward from his seat onto that, before sliding to the ground."

She straightened.

"But if you recall there was much more blood on the grass where his body was discovered. Therefore, I would think it almost certain that, exactly as Sir Hugh described, the beheading and mutilation was done there, as the body lay on the grass, but very shortly after he was stabbed. That must have happened as he was sitting here, on this seat."

Lucie stared for a few moments longer at the guilty puncture mark in the door, ringed as it was with a sagging, marbled halo of blood.

Then she turned to the land steward.

John Lawson was regarding her nervously, gently stroking the horse's broad muzzle with the backs of his fingers. Lucie wondered for a moment if it was more soothing to himself or to the big horse beside him.

"Mr Lawson, Sir Hugh tells us that you were the one to actually find Mr Elliott's body. Can you recall exactly how the body was lying, and in particular where Mr Elliott's head was in relation to his torso?"

Lawson's fingers stopped moving and the horse's ears pricked forward, almost as if it too was waiting on his answer.

"Aye, Mrs Fox, I surely can; I expect I shall remember it until the day I die. The body was just lying there, in the grass. It didn't look like a human being at all, if truth be told; it looked more like a…a great wax doll. I could see all the blood, so I knew right enough that something terrible had happened, but I didn't realise that his head had been chopped off.; least-ways not until I got close up to him and tried to lift it up. It came away in my hand."

He sobbed suddenly and Sir Hugh scowled.

"So his attacker must have used a very sharp blade to decapitate him and the blow must have been both swift and accurate."

"I said it was expert swordsmanship, ma'am,' Sir Hugh reminded her.

"Was there any cadaveric rigidity, did you notice?" Lucy continued.

Lawson looked at her uncertainly. He glanced nervously towards Sir Hugh before he said: "Cadaveric rigidity? I'm sorry, Mrs Fox, but I'm not quite sure what that is."

"Forgive me, Mr Lawson, it is a medical term. I meant was there any stiffness of the body? In other words, did you notice if *rigor mortis* had set in?"

"Ah, yes." Lawson nodded his comprehension. "Yes, Mrs Fox, it had. I tried to fold his arms over his chest as is proper but I couldn't move them."

"And when did you find the body?"

"It would have been around the middle of the afternoon. I went up there directly the Colonel asked for a report on the progress of the crop."

Lucie turned to Atticus. "So the likelihood is that Mr Elliott was killed earlier that same day, although we can't be certain as to the precise time."

"I've already told you when it was," Sir Hugh growled irritably.

"Rigor mortis sets in usually around two to four hours after death," Lucie continued, "and lasts for between one and two days. After that, the body becomes flaccid once again and begins the process of putrefaction."

Atticus grimaced and leaned forward to examine the deep, blood-ringed indentation in the door. He filled his lungs with the warm, fragrant moorland air and held it there. The images being formed in his mind were hellish.

Lucie said: "Now, Mr Lawson; what can you tell us about Samson Elliott, the man?"

Lawson removed his hat and glanced to Sir Hugh, who nodded.

"Well, Mrs Fox, I would like to say first off that Samson was a good man."

Sir Hugh snorted and said: "Of the dead say nothing but good."

"Although you must not hesitate to do so in this case, Mr Lawson," Atticus returned. "Horace, whom Sir Hugh quotes, was not, after all, conducting a murder investigation."

Lawson fingered the brim of his hat.

"I dare say he wasn't, Mr Fox. Samson was a good man though, alive or dead. What can I say of him, Mrs Fox? Well, he was around middle height, well formed, with a swarthy but kindly appearance. He was not what you would call well educated but I always found him quick to learn with a ready wit. For that he was a very great favourite with the farm men, and the women come to that.

"Before he was settled permanently on the estate, Samson was a true, roving Gypsy, living the whole time in this caravan here. He called it his vardo. I believe he has two brothers who still live that way. In those days he would come and take employment by-the-day, helping with the harvest and with clipping the sheep and suchlike. He always applied himself well to his work, never drank, never thieved and hardly ever quarrelled.

"When the first Lady Lowther, God rest her soul, was having the Tower's gardens re-laid, he stayed on to help. He made such a good fist of it that she helped secure him a permanent position on the farm. That was when he left his vardo and moved into one of the tied-cottages."

Atticus asked: "How long had he been in the cottage?"

Lawson's work-worn fingers were twisting now at the brim of his billycock.

"Let me think on it, sir. He'd been coming here as an itinerant for around five years. After that he would have lived on the farm for mebbees two- or three-and-twenty years. Yes, it must have been about that, because he moved into his cottage a year or two before Master Arthur was born. I'd say he'd been working here for nigh-on thirty years all told."

He hesitated.

"Mrs Fox, Samson was a good man and I'm truly not just saying that because he's dead."

He glanced timorously to Sir Hugh.

"He was good craic, a good worker and I, for one, will sorely miss him."

"Which is why," Sir Hugh countered, "I have fetched these sleuth-hounds all the way up from Harrogate. You can rest assured that justice will be served."

"Well said, Sir Hugh," Lucie said, "But one last question, Mr Lawson, if you please: How old would Mr Elliott have been when he died?"

Lawson smiled.

"That no-one knows for sure, ma'am, not even Samson himself. Around his middle forties I would reckon."

Lucie cast a glance to Atticus, who reached up and lifted the little iron latch that held the door of the caravan shut. Rather eerily, it drifted open of its own volition and they peered inside.

"How quaint!" exclaimed Lucie, "It's just exactly like a dolls' house."

Still smiling, John Lawson drew a short ladder from beneath the caravan's chassis and fitted it between the shafts.

"Take a look inside if it might be of interest to you," he said.

Lucie needed no second invitation. She scuttered nimbly up the steep steps and through the narrow doorway. Atticus clambered up behind her.

The gaudily-painted interior of the Gypsy vardo was indeed very much like a doll's house with, "a special place for everything," as Lucie remarked.

It was dominated by a large, wooden-framed cot-bed, which stretched across the full width of the farthest end. It was neatly made-up with the bed covers turned back, seemingly still waiting for a man who would now sleep eternally elsewhere. Along one side was a line of intricately decorated wardrobes and Atticus and Lucie began to open each in turn. Nothing seemed out of place there either. The closets appeared to be full of the ordinary stuff of life, albeit of a life now snuffed out in a most extraordinary way.

Lucie pulled at the flimsy wooden doors of the last of these closets and, as they parted, she turned her head from the sudden, pungent stench of sulphur and mothballs. She peered inside. Hanging in the cramped compartments within were three suits of traditional Romany clothing. The first; a fine silk shirt with a pearl-buttoned jerkin, was evidently for a man but in the spaces adjacent were two extravagantly embroidered skirts and brightly coloured, cotton blouses.

Lucie was captivated by them.

"They're so beautiful," she effused, lifting out one of the blouses and smoothing it against her front. "Do you see? This would fit me perfectly."

She lifted out the shirt.

"Even the man's clothing is gorgeous. Such gay colours. But I imagine that you might require a gusset, Atticus."

"I should look like a music hall turn in that," Atticus retorted, then: "Lucie, something isn't quite right here, although just what that is, I can't place at present."

It was then that he noticed Sir Hugh glaring up at them from the foot of the ladder. He said: "We have gathered a great deal of information for our consideration, Sir Hugh. I propose that Mrs Fox and I bicycle back down to Bardon Mill village. We've taken a room in the Bowes Hotel there and we can discuss the establishment and the basic facts of the case before we then determine the best way to proceed."

Sir Hugh shook his head emphatically.

"Nonsense, nonsense, I won't hear of it, Fox. You will stay here at Shields Tower as our honoured guests. Miss Armstrong, my housekeeper, has already prepared a room for you both and I'll arrange with James for your luggage to be fetched up from the Bowes. You'll be more comfortable here and much closer to the task in hand."

Lucie beamed and Atticus had no choice but to accede. He said: "Very well, Sir Hugh, thank you. We accept your offer with pleasure."

As they picked their way back down the tiny steps of the vardo, Lawson coughed. It was a timid cough, such as a schoolboy might make before his headmaster.

"Excuse me, Mr and Mrs Fox. Before you go, there is one more thing I ought to mention."

"What's that then, Lawson?" Sir Hugh barked.

Lawson was blushing deeply and twisting the brim of his hat now as if he might be trying to throttle it.

"Sir, Elliott did mention to me that he had been rather fearful of late…" He hesitated for a moment, "On account of his belief that he was being haunted."

"Haunted?" Atticus was incredulous.

"Yes, Mr Fox, haunted; that was what he said. The day before he set off for Appleby, he told me he believed he was being haunted by the ghost of a knight – a knight in armour. He claimed to have seen it a good few times over the past month or so. Each time it just stood and watched him awhile before it disappeared back into the rocks up by the Roman Wall."

"Poppycock!" boomed Sir Hugh, although his face betrayed just the merest trace of amusement. "Everyone knows there are no such things as ghosts. Lawson, I'm surprised at you."

The land steward coloured yet more deeply.

"Begging your pardon, Colonel, but that's what Elliott told me. I thought I should mention it. He was quite glad to be getting away from the farm, if truth be told, if only for a while."

"Did Elliott describe this supposed apparition to you?" Lucie asked.

"Apparition, be damned!" growled Sir Hugh.

"Yes he did, ma'am," Lawson replied. "He said it was enormous and that sometimes it was on a great, black charger and sometimes it was on foot. It only ever appeared late at night or early in the morning, and it always came from the direction of the Sewingshields Crags. He believed it might be the ghost of King Arthur, awoken and abroad once more."

CHAPTER NINE

The large guest chamber to which Sir Hugh Lowther personally escorted Atticus and Lucie Fox quite took away their breath. Despite the fact that it was within the very ancient part of the house, it had been decorated fashionably in the new Liberty style with its flowing, natural lines. The exquisite walnut furniture was inlaid with a vibrant marquetry of vines and twining plants, a theme continued in the gaily-coloured stained glass of the window tops and the moulding of the plasterwork.

Most strikingly of all however, and painted directly onto the wall above the bed-head, was a large and wonderfully detailed mural of a fiery, red dragon. It had a long, exuberantly coiling tail and a head which, although fearsome and bestial, somehow possessed an expression of fragility and angst that was almost human. It was curled around as gaoler, or protector, or perhaps even captive of a beautiful, naked, copper-haired maiden.

To Atticus it seemed unsettlingly familiar. Both maiden and yes, dragon, he had seen before – but where? In another picture perhaps? The fresco was especially suggestive of Blake's work but—

"What a very modern room, Sir Hugh!" Lucie exclaimed, interrupting his thoughts.

Lowther did not reply immediately.

"Modern? It is hardly modern, Lucie. Would you believe that the decoration of this room was conceived and laid out well over twenty years ago? No? Well this was the room I shared with Igraine, my first wife. She personally designed and commissioned everything here."

He smiled and a sudden pain haunted his eyes.

"Igraine was something of a 'free spirit', shall we say, and she wanted the house and gardens to reflect that. That picture over the bed was painted by the madman, Michael Britton, before he went insane for the final time. My second wife Victoria restored the house to the classical style – all except this room. I forbade her to change anything in here because it somehow represented the very essence of Igraine and I needed something to remember her by.

"After Victoria died, I moved into the farthest room of the north wing myself – the one at the eastern corner. The room is by no means as grand as this one but it is handsome enough and I am afforded a wonderful view of the moors and the loughs from my window.

"So this house is an amalgam of my two wives' characters do you see, Lucie? My own humble contributions are a new garden room, and the sculpture of *Die Schreiberinnen*, or 'The Writing Women', at the foot of the stairs."

"The three figures from Norse mythology?" Lucie asked.

"Bravo, my dear. I'm very impressed!" Angst forgotten, Sir Hugh clapped his hands together in delight, "Norse and Teutonic actually, but yes, the very same. The

Writing Women are also known as the 'Norns' or the 'Sisters of the Wyrd,' and they are to us and our Anglo-Saxon ancestors what the Fates were to the ancient Greeks. They have the task of carving the deeds of our pasts, our presents and all our futures in mankind's great *Book of Destiny*."

He smiled grimly.

"Whither do they call us, Lucie Fox; whither do they call us?"

"I have to confess I was a little unnerved by the statue of the crone pointing up the stairs," Lucie admitted. "It seemed as if she was pointing directly at me – just as if she were accusing me of something. Her eyes seem to be following me every time I look at her."

She turned and glanced down the stairway to the dais at its foot.

"Look there! Even now, she stares at me still."

Sir Hugh was silent for a moment before he replied.

"The Norns see all things, and yes, they are exceedingly well sculpted – almost as if they might be alive. I commissioned the piece from Mr John Taylor, a rising star in the world of art, and it cost me a small fortune. It is worth every single farthing though and it suits me much better than the suits of armour it replaced. They weren't even authentic, just a pair of reasonably good reproductions my father had made.

"But do not worry, Lucie Fox, the Norn watching you now is Urth – *That Which Is*. She is concerned only with the deeds of our past, unless of course there is something in your own past which might give cause to trouble her."

His gaze lingered on Lucie for a while, as St Peter's might rest on a fresh-dead soul at the Gates of Paradise.

"But I think not.

"Verthandi, the figure that is depicted as embracing the entire household is the 'Present,' or *That Which Is Becoming*. She examines our current deeds.

"My Lady Skuld, or *That Which Should Become*, the youngest and most beautiful of the Norns and my own particular favourite, the one who writes and directs all our futures, faces, well she simply faces out towards the moors. All of our futures are like bleak moorland, do you see, a wilderness, where there are no roads and no paths, where we all need direction lest we lose ourselves…and perish."

He closed his eyes as if in supplication.

"*Quo Fata Vocant*," he murmured at last, "Whither the Fates call. It is the motto of my old regiment. It is also what attracted me to commission your own services. You use the same, do you not? *Quo Fata Vocant*. You hear them too."

Atticus chuckled. "Yes, I suppose in a way we do. My two great passions in life are chess and reading. A writer called Arthur Conan Doyle has just had a story, *The Sign of the Four*, serialised in *Lippincott's Monthly*, which I take for its scientific articles. Mr Doyle created a detective character called Sherlock Holmes, whose methods I very much admire. Of course I understand that Holmes is merely a figment of imagination, whereas we, quite clearly, are very much flesh and blood, but Holmes' pen-and-ink companion

Dr Watson supposedly served in your own regiment: the Northumberland Fusiliers. I knew of the motto from there, and Mrs Fox and I decided to adopt it as our own. It seems somehow so appropriate to this profession."

Sir Hugh grinned wearily. "Then bully for the both of you; it is a first-rate choice." He pulled a handsome half-hunter watch from his waistcoat pocket and glanced down at it.

"I'll leave you to have your palaver now. Bessie Armstrong, my housekeeper, will call on you shortly to see if there is anything you might need to make your stay here more comfortable. We might not have the grand facilities of Harrogate here at Shields but we are, in our own way, just as hospitable. I'll see you both at dinner."

As if to cue, there was a sudden, loud rapping on the door.

"Come in, Bessie," boomed Sir Hugh.

Atticus and Lucie turned to see a broad, rather mannish looking woman in middle-age filling the doorway. She stepped obediently into the room, bowed deeply, and introduced herself as the housekeeper. Addressing Lucie, she asked if there was anything they might require. Lucie replied politely that everything in the room appeared to be just-so and quite in perfect order.

"If there is anything you would like, anything at all, you have only to ring down." The hint of a smile broke the cast of Miss Armstrong's face and softened the gruffness of her voice by just a degree.

Their room was situated at the front of the ancient fortified tower, on the first floor. It had a large, mullioned window, which not only made the room very airy and light but also afforded them a wonderful view of the long, straight avenue of yew trees that drew their eyes continually to the hills and fells beyond it and to the chameleon Northumbrian sky.

Atticus settled into the deep, leather cushion of the window-seat and gazed out at this panorama. Part of Skuld's wilderness, he mused, before he gathered together his thoughts and brought them back again to the matter in hand.

"So, Lucie, we've had a most interesting first afternoon here, have we not? The case is quite as intriguing as I'd hoped it would be, and a good deal more engaging than our usual fare."

Lucie had freed her long, brown hair from its ribbon and let it tumble down onto her shoulders. She began to brush it out.

"Perhaps so, but the long-lost cousins and the straying husbands pay the housekeeping, Atticus, never forget that. Notwithstanding that, yes, it was a particularly brutal and bloody murder and if we should happen to find the murderer before the police do, it would be an enormous feather in our cap. It's sure to be in the London newspapers."

"Was it actually a murder though?" Atticus asked. "To approach the enquiry in the proper manner, we need first to ask ourselves whether Elliott might have been killed in some other way, by accident or by suicide perhaps."

"Oh, Atticus, that would be ridiculous. It has to be murder. Elliott wouldn't have beheaded himself, would he?"

She giggled suddenly in spite of herself.

"I suppose not," Atticus conceded, a little testily, "In which case we can inform Sir Hugh that that is our starting supposition."

Lucie stopped brushing and pursed her lips. "I'm not sure that would be such a terribly good idea."

Atticus turned away from the window, the low rays of the sun accentuating the lines of puzzlement on his face. "But we've just agreed it, haven't we?"

"We have, Atticus. It's just that I am not sure Sir Hugh would be too delighted if, after having spent most of his afternoon showing us around the trail of evidence, he is told we have educed that his Gypsy was murdered. I think he's probably come to that conclusion already.

"I know, I know," she continued as Atticus opened his mouth to protest, "I know it's all proper method, but I still feel it would be much more prudent to say that we have some early theories which require the further gathering of evidence."

"I suppose you're right," Atticus admitted. He turned back to his window. "So, what are these theories to be, other than it's the work of Sir Hugh's madman, of course?"

Lucie paused for a moment as she carefully inspected her hair in the dressing table looking-glass.

"I would much prefer it if you didn't use that term, Atticus. 'Madman' is such an awfully derogatory word, as if he is some kind of drooling beast or something."

Atticus shrugged. "It sounds as if he might well be."

"Even so, I should much prefer it if you called him 'lunatic' or 'insane'. As you very well know, most people who are mad look no different to you, or to me for that matter, or to Sir Hugh, himself."

"Or to Miss Jennifer," Atticus added drily. "She must have been either mad or joking when she suggested that Elliott's killer was the risen King Arthur."

Lucie frowned.

"That's just it: I'm not so sure it was a joke. She seemed deadly serious about it to me."

She twisted in her chair to face him.

"There was something else about Jennifer and Artie that seemed a little bit out of the ordinary too. I just can't quite put my finger on it."

She stared past Atticus and through the big window as her mind played through their brief meeting.

"I know what it was! They were close – intimate even – far too close for a brother and sister, even for a half-brother and sister. They seemed to me to be…to be more like sweethearts."

"*Sweethearts!*" Atticus gasped, "But surely that can't be possible?"

"As you always take care to remind me, Atticus Fox; anything is possible."

"And I suppose it is too," he admitted, "But sweethearts? Mercy me! We must make certain to speak with them again tomorrow and see if you get the same impression. I should like to re-examine the murder field tomorrow too, but at very first light, while the sun is still low over the horizon."

He pulled his old Wehrly watch from his waistcoat pocket and glanced at the face.

"For now, I suppose we ought to change for dinner. It wouldn't do to keep our patron waiting."

CHAPTER TEN

"You are giving her to me? But how can that be? She is another man's wife."

He feels the panic and the dread he has been holding back these many long hours break suddenly free.

"You promised to give *my* love, *my* own lady, back to me."

"*BE SILENT!*" The voice seems to emanate from the shadowy, black walls of the vault itself. "*Do you doubt we know very well what we promised you?*"

He falls to his knees in despair and deep obeisance, and presses his cheek against the chilly rock of the floor.

"My Lady Urth, I am sorry. Forgive me. I was thoughtless. I meant no disrespect."

The voice crackles with scorn and derision.

"*Sorry, sorry, sorry. Always you beg, and always you are sorry. You are a craven abomination to man; do you know that?*"

"Yes, My Lady." He does know it.

"*That is why your wife ran to the arms, and to the bed, of another.*"

His eyes creep along the floor, to where the figure of Lancelot sits, motionless, in the shadows, the light of the lantern flickering across the plate of his armour. He knows that is the truth too.

"*Let me tell him, Sister – let me be merciful.*" His heart leaps. It is Skuld.

"*Be careful, Skuld.*" Verthandi's acid tones hiss around the vault. "*Do not be too indulgent with him. The mortal already yearns to fuck you.*"

He cringes and the voices of the three Sisters of the Wyrd, even Skuld's, dissolve into peels of mocking laughter.

And then Skuld, who reminds him so much of his true love, of his lady as she was before the bad times, before he put her to eternal slumber in this very vault, speaks to him.

"*Your lady will wake. Once your tasks are complete and the blood-gift is sealed, by our power she will be awoken and by our power her spirit will take the body of the other woman yet living.*"

He opens his eyes. The ripples and fissures of the whinstone floor dance orange in the lantern-light.

"She must take the body of the other woman?" he asks, puzzled now.

"*She must,*" Skuld replies. "*The natural balance of order must be maintained. If her spirit is to take its place once more in this world, then another's must be removed. We have written that she will assume the body of the woman Lucie Fox.*"

He feels the cold seeping into his skin from the black stone beneath it and he sobs. He understands now, and he sobs in gratitude for their wisdom and for their great and boundless mercy.

CHAPTER ELEVEN

Although she chided herself for being silly, that she was a grown woman after all, Lucie Fox felt an inexplicable but overwhelming sense of discomfiture as she sat in the grand dining room of Shields Tower. The reason for her unease lay in a row of three large and very life-like portraits which were hanging on the wall directly opposite her place at the table. They were all of men, all in full military uniform and all bore varying degrees of likeness to Sir Hugh Lowther. Mounted on the wall beneath each was an officer's regimental sword.

"Those portraits, Atticus, they seem to stare at one so," she finally whispered after Sir Hugh, purple-faced with fury, had snapped his apologies and stormed out to personally fetch Artie, Jennifer and Sir Douglas Lowther, his father. All three had, for some reason, failed to respond to Mr Collier's dinner gong.

Atticus stood and turned to examine them.

"First the statue of the Norns watching you and now these portraits," he chuckled. "I declare, Lucie, you'll be quite as insane as Uther Pendragon by the time we've concluded this investigation."

"Atty!" hissed Lucie as the door all but exploded from its frame and Sir Hugh, still ruddy-faced and as blown-up as a bullfrog, re-entered the room. He was followed meekly by Jennifer and Artie.

"I apologise for our tardiness, Mr and Mrs Fox," Artie explained sheepishly, "But Jenny was feeling a little… unwell. She was sleeping and I didn't like to wake her."

"Didn't like to wake her; didn't like to wake her, by gad! There's nothing amiss with my daughter that a plate of good, hearty, Northumbrian fare won't mend." Sir Hugh glared him into silence as he took his place once more at the head of the table. "She is a Lowther after all!

"My father is nowhere to be found though," he added after a moment. "Collier tells me he went up to the loughs after luncheon. He seems to spend most of his time loitering around Broomlee these days. Fallen asleep in his chair, I expect. In any event, Collier has sent angel-faced James the fart-catcher to seek him."

"My wife and I were just admiring these portraits, Sir Hugh," Atticus remarked, glad to be able to switch the conversation. "I presume by the likenesses that they are ancestors of yours?"

A broad grin swept away the scowl on Sir Hugh's face.

"Two of them are, Fox, yes: my father and my grandfather." He stabbed towards each of them in turn with the handle of his soup spoon. "The third one is actually me, in my younger days. We're all in the uniform of the 'Old and the Bold' of course, and those are our regimental swords beneath."

"They are noble blades, Sir Hugh. May I?"

Lowther nodded affably. "Please do."

Atticus gently lifted the farthest sword, that of Sir Hugh himself, from its mount. It was a rapier and, even with his untrained eye, he could see that it was a very handsome weapon with a long, slim, razor-sharp blade and finely-wrought hand guard. It was also plainly a true fighting sword. Atticus curled his fingers round the grip and made a gentle, experimental lunge into fresh air.

"Do be careful, Atticus," Lucie warned.

Sir Hugh chuckled and hammered his spoon on the table in glee.

"Bravo! You have the makings of a fine swordsman, Fox. If ever you give thought to enlisting, be sure to come to the Fusiliers first, won't you? I won the British Army fencing championship with that sword. In fact I won it thrice in a row, which is to say I was the finest blade in the country, as was my father before me."

"Now, Papa, don't be boastful!" Jennifer admonished him, giggling.

"By God but it's true nevertheless, Jenny." Sir Hugh was chuckling too; Jennifer's laugh was infectious.

"It's all about speed, do you see, Fox; speed of the eye, speed of the arm, and most importantly of all, speed of the brain. I have the reactions of a viper."

He became suddenly serious.

"And you need a first-rate sword too, of course. My father swore by the Shotley Bridge blades, made just over the hill towards Durham. But not I; I had one as a boy and I found it to be damned shoddy. I use Sheffield steel."

"Does your own son intend to follow you into the Fusiliers?" Atticus asked him.

A sudden and oppressive silence settled over the table and Sir Hugh and Artie exchanged sharp, resentful glances.

"There is almost nothing in this world I would love more," Artie said.

The ticking of a great brass garniture clock steadily ratcheted up the tension in the room, ticking and ticking until it became almost unbearable.

"I have forbidden it, Fox," Sir Hugh growled at last. "I have set him to work in the commercial businesses instead. Commerce suits his…character and constitution much better than ever a life in the army would."

"Papa, that's just not true," Jennifer retorted indignantly, "I've told you over and over that Artie would make a brave and perfectly gallant Fusilier officer."

Sir Hugh coloured.

"Our family motto: *Magistratus Indicat Virum*; 'The office shows the man'. The man must therefore be worthy of the office, Jenny, and Artie quite simply is not. I will not be shamed. My mind is made up and it is immovable. Now let me be whilst I tell the Foxes something of the history of the fighting Lowthers."

One full hour later, even Atticus was beginning to lose interest in the conversation. The arrival of thick, syrupy, Abyssinian coffee, which Sir Hugh explained, he had taken a great liking to during his time in the Sudan, provided a welcome opportunity to change the topic.

"While I remember, Sir Hugh," said Atticus, "Would you have any influence with the coroner in this case? Mrs Fox would like to go through Elliott's post-mortem necropsy report tomorrow – assuming of course that one has been carried out. I imagine the cremation has not yet taken place so it would be helpful for her to examine the corpse too."

"Your wife wishes to examine the Gypsy's corpse?" repeated Sir Hugh incredulously.

"If that is possible, yes she would. It is an important part of our investigation and, as I said to you earlier, she has a far stronger stomach than I for such things."

Sir Hugh looked bemused.

"I suppose it is courageous of you to admit to that around the dinner table – you might wish to take note of that, Artie – but there really is nothing to fear from the dead, Fox; they have already paid their debts in full to the Fates.

"But in answer to your questions: yes, I do have some little influence with the coroner, and yes, of course I'd be pleased to use it on your, or rather on your wife's, behalf. In fact she's in luck; a warrant for an inquest has been issued but I don't believe any autopsy has yet taken place."

At that moment the door crashed open for a second time and Collier burst into the room with James at his shoulder. Propriety and affectations forgotten, they both wore identical, horror-struck expressions that shrieked that somewhere, something diabolical had happened.

Collier bent by the Colonel and panted something into his ear.

"He's dead? How do you know he's dead?" Sir Hugh thundered.

"He is, sir." James seemed to be struggling for breath. "I found him up by his chair at the Broomlee Lough. He's been throttled to death with a piece of cloth and—"

"Who is it? Who's been throttled to death?" Atticus cried.

"It's Sir Douglas, the Colonel's father." James' answer was no more than a croak. As he turned towards Atticus, the sunlight caught a dark stain, slick and wet, across the shoulder and front of his cape-coat.

"Where is he now?" Sir Hugh was suddenly on his feet.

"We left him in the scullery, sir. I carried him back but Mr Collier didn't think it wise to bring him through the house, not with the ladies here and all."

"Show me," Sir Hugh commanded and strode from the room.

Above stairs, Shields Tower was grand and imposing. Below them, it was dark, cramped and labyrinthine. Endless corridors twisted this way and that, more of a lair for monsters than a large, comfortable home. But James and Collier led them unerringly and all at once they had passed through a stricken, sobbing crowd of servants into a sudden billow of ferocious heat and found themselves in the scullery.

It was a very large scullery, as was surely necessary to provide for the wants of such a grand house as Shields Tower. Or perhaps it was Grendel's kitchen because the scene within was monstrous.

They gathered, silent but for Jennifer's sobs, muffled by Artie's shoulder, around a large, scrubbed-top table which stood in the centre like some sacrificial altar and stared at the offering upon it. It was what once must have been a man, an old man certainly, but a living, breathing human being nonetheless. Now it was a lifeless husk, part-covered with a blood-peppered tablecloth and the manner of its transformation must have been terrible.

Its glassy, lifeless eyes were protuberant, bulging still from the bloated, ruddy face. Two thick lines of blood, drawn from the nostrils, were coagulating and crusting above the mouth, a mouth that retched and gaped in a never-ending death scream.

But it was the throat above the crisp collar that drew the stare of every person there. Bound tightly around it, and banded above and below by angry, purple stripes, was a cloth. It was a golden-yellow cloth that had been twisted into a tight rope and knotted fast below the ear.

Lucie was the first to react. She bent to examine the knot pressed deep into the bulging flesh and then reached for a scullery knife. Cautiously and with infinite care, she sliced through the weave, peeled it free from the skin and laid it onto the table next to its victim. Carefully unrolled and smoothed flat, it became a crumpled strip of golden silk, perhaps eighteen inches in length by three in breadth. It was finely woven and had, in some inexplicable way, a feeling of great age about it.

"Death by strangulation," murmured Lucie, voicing the terrible thoughts of every person in the room and Atticus nodded.

She began to examine the head and the neck, and the marks around the throat, frowning as she did so. Then: "Hallo! Atticus, look at—"

"What is it?" Sir Hugh cried.

In response Lucie pushed her fingers deep into the gaping mouth and pulled out a long strip of something hard and black that reeked of vomit.

Atticus turned away and retched.

Lucie held it up between her fingertips, where it hung down like something unholy.

"What is this?" she asked.

James the footman it was who replied. "I believe it is biltong, ma'am."

Lucie peered into the corpse's mouth.

"There's more of it, lots more. Biltong did you say it was? What is biltong?"

"It's meat, ma'am, dried and cured. We saw a lot of it when we were out with the regiment in Africa. Once it's cured, it lasts almost forever."

Lucie laid it onto the table top next to the silk strip. She carefully wiped her fingers dry on a corner of the table cloth and then, pursing her lips tight, she lifted it back. As she did, she revealed completely the cause both of the mottling of blood across the white linen, and of the wet slick on James' shoulder.

Sir Douglas Lowther had been cleaved almost in two below his ribs, the greying flesh of his viscera clearly visible in the long, blood-soaked gashes across his waistcoat front. The gashes were in the form of the flattened 'X' of a *crux decussata*.

"Just like Sam Elliott!" James gasped, and Atticus retched again.

"Pull yourself together, man. What's the matter with you?" Sir Hugh snarled.

Lucie stared at the footman.

"Elliott had wounds like this?"

James nodded. "Yes, ma'am."

Sir Hugh took command once more.

"Collier," he snapped. "Use the telephone in my study and call for the police. Tell them the madman has struck again. Do it directly."

He pointed to the strip of cured meat lying by his father's corpse.

"Many years ago, Lucie Fox, when the madman lost his mind for the final time, we used to send biltong meat up to his cottage. It wouldn't go bad if he didn't eat it directly, do you see? Well, let me tell you something about that meat lying there: it is old – very old. In fact, it could well be a good twenty years old…"

He left the sentence hanging and a crescendo of whispered murmurings rose from the gathered servants at the door, a sound augmented by an indignant stirring of insect wings as Lucie waved away a cluster of blowflies that were crawling in the corpse's wounds. She bent close and began to examine the gashes minutely.

"How very curious," she muttered after a little while.

"What is curious?" Atticus blurted. This scullery was suffocatingly airless.

"The position of these wounds for one thing. The deepest is right up against the ribcage, and it seems to have been struck from below. It has quite cut through the diaphragm and carved open the chest cavity."

Atticus took a great breath and held the air in his lungs as he considered Lucie's words.

"So must we educe that Sir Douglas was lying on his back when he was attacked?" He glanced awkwardly at Sir Hugh, who was staring back impassively.

Lucie shook her head. "That was my first assumption too, but then his waistcoat is soaked in blood below the wound. That would suggest he was upright – standing or sitting perhaps. Sir Hugh, you remarked that he spent much of his time sitting by the lake."

"He did," Lowther confirmed, "He kept his old campaign chair up there."

"James said he found him by his chair," Atticus reminded them.

"And then there is this second wound. It's much lighter – almost superficial, in fact."

"Perhaps he tried to evade the first blow and that light wound was all his attacker could manage," Atticus suggested.

Lucie shook her head once more.

"No, I don't think so. It looks almost as if it were…carved into the skin. Besides," She pressed the lips of the deeper gash together with her fingertips, "It was made after the deeper cut opened him up – not before. Do you see how the line doesn't quite meet when I push these edges together?"

Atticus cast a brief and horrified glance.

"Yes, I see, but why throttle him, and then choke him, and then inflict injuries like those? Any one of them would have been sufficient to kill him. Why murder him thrice over?"

"I really have no clue, Atticus." Lucie tried to lift Sir Douglas' hands across towards his belly. They were stiff and unyielding. "Perhaps the autopsy will reveal something."

Atticus nodded. Please god Lucie was almost done here. "Let us hope so."

It was easier to look at the silk than the corpse and Atticus reached over and lifted it, rather gingerly, by one of its ends.

"This is an unusual material, Lucie."

"Yes it is. It seems very old."

"It is tablet-woven silk."

"I've never heard of that," Lucie admitted.

"Tablet weaving was a technique, very popular in medieval times, used to produce long, narrow strips of cloth."

"So you believe it might be medieval?"

Atticus nodded.

"I believe it could very well be." He paused to reflect. "Which, along with these rather singular wounds, is highly suggestive of an association with this business of King Arthur. The deaths of Sir Douglas Lowther and Samson Elliott are clearly linked, Lucie and there can be little doubt that they were murdered by the same person…or persons."

Collier was suddenly standing by Sir Hugh's shoulder.

"Well?" snapped the Colonel.

"I've spoken with the police superintendent, sir. He sends his compliments and his condolences and asks that you keep the body safe until first light. He intends to come over then."

Sir Hugh bristled like a bulldog.

"Do you see, Fox?" he roared. "Do you see? Now you know why we sent for you both. The Hexham police couldn't catch the pox in a quayside whore-house."

CHAPTER TWELVE

The scene that confronted Atticus and Lucie Fox as they left Shields Tower shortly after dawn the following morning was surreal, almost phantasmal.

They stepped down from the great carven doors and waded into a low shroud of amorphous white mist that completely smothered the ground and seemed almost to glow as it was illuminated by the low, flat rays of the early morning sun. They might have been angels walking through the clouds of Heaven but for the fact that, here and there, the veil was ruptured by bushes and trees and by the malevolent presence of the grotesques standing erect from its mass to cast long, dark shadows across its surface.

Atticus adjusted the shoulder strap of his bag as he and Lucie rounded the corner of the great south wing. There was no sign yet of the Hexham detective but the relentless swelling of the dawn meant that they could wait no longer. They began to retrace their steps of the previous day, along the sweeping carriage-way that led to the stables, and beyond, to the moor-side field where the horrors of Samson Elliott's nightmares had taken form and substance and so brutally overwhelmed him. After that, James had described in detail how they might find the lakeside spot where Sir Douglas Lowther had met his own equally bloody and violent end.

By the time they reached the field adjoining the lunatic's little, white cottage, all vestiges of the dawn mists had been burnt away to leave only a sprinkling of dew on the yellow, stunted leaves of the wheat.

They found the guilty, dark stains once more on the headland path and Atticus crouched low, hanging for support on the thick, pewter grip of his cane. He squinted across the surface of the ground, towards the great square stones that footed the dry stone wall.

"Hullo!" he cried almost at once, "See here, Lucie".

He waited until his wife had stooped down next to him.

"Just as I'd hoped; with the sun still so low in the sky, we can readily see any marks and indentations in the ground."

He pointed.

"So do you see that line of footprints leading from the style in the wall?"

"Good gracious!" Lucie exclaimed, "They're huge. They must have been made by someone enormous."

She stepped over towards the nearest of them.

"They are an odd shape too, Atty, don't you think – very long and narrow? Shall we see if there are more on the other side of the wall?"

"Presently," Atticus replied. "First, if I am able, I would like to try to take a cast of one of them."

He spent some minutes in examining and comparing each of the peculiar footprints. Then, once he had satisfied himself that he had identified the sharpest and most complete of them, he reached into his bag and lifted out a tin-plate box. It was full of very fine plaster-of-Paris powder. Carefully adding water scooped from a puddle in the sodden ground around the base of the wall, he vigorously mixed the plaster before slowly, and with great care, decanting it into the impression.

"The plaster has an orange tinge to it," he remarked as he studied its smooth, creamy surface. "It can only have come from the puddle water. Perhaps it's a bloom of algae from Mr Lawson's spreading of fertiliser for the wheat. Hullo! There are little bubbles of gas forming in it too. How queer! I hope it is not so contaminated the plaster doesn't set properly."

He shrugged.

"Well it's done now. No doubt we shall see when we return. So, Lucie, whilst it cures, we have a perfect opportunity to investigate to where these footprints lead."

Countless generations of Northumbrians had spent their lives labouring to spread the vast network of dry stone walls across the breadth of their county, often advancing no further than a stride each day. It was brutal, exhausting work that kept them as lean and spare as the land they worked. Those men could never have imagined that one of their fellows might ever grow fat and they built their styles accordingly. It was with difficulty therefore that Atticus squeezed through the narrow gap between the upright stones. He jumped down heavily to the other side and turned to offer his hand to his wife, who slipped through with ease.

They did not need the sun to find the same narrow and peculiarly long footprints pressed deep into the sodden, yielding turf on this side of the wall. The trail led directly and brazenly in the direction of the tiny cottage, where, to the Foxes' great frustration, it disappeared as the turf yielded way to the black rock of the Great Whin Sill.

"Atticus, look!"

Lucie's hand clamped onto his wrist.

"The door of the cottage – it was open a moment ago, but when I glanced over, it shut tight. There was a face at the gap, I'm sure of it. Atticus, the lunatic; I think he's seen us."

"Has he indeed." Atticus stared towards the door. He hoped his wife couldn't feel the sudden pounding of his pulse. "He is up at a good, early hour and that's a fact. This is very convenient for us, Lucie and we might as well take full advantage."

With that, he took Lucie's arm, gripped the handle of his cane tightly, and strode along the trail of footprints towards the cottage.

As they approached, and the nails in Atticus' boots began to tick on the naked rock, something on the door itself caught their eye: Across the shabby, blistered planking was painted the profile of a large and vividly red dragon with wings outstretched. Several large, black flies were crawling across its surface and they were both reminded sharply of the blood-soaked grass in the field beyond the wall. Atticus exchanged a quizzical glance with Lucie and then rapped briskly on the timber with the pommel of his cane.

There was no reply. The cottage remained silent save for the sudden buzzing of the flies and the lazier drone of a bumble bee foraging somewhere near to them.

From a distance, the little heather-thatched cottage nestled snugly on the cusp of the moors had seemed quaint and pastoral, almost like the pictures on the chocolate boxes Lucie used for her keepsakes. Close-to however, they could see that it was mean, neglected and shabby. The lime-wash on the rough, cobble walls was cracked and flaking, and the thatch on the roof, old, thin and bleached almost white by the sun. Its only concession to luxury was a short length of rusted iron gutter fixed just above the door from which a large, black raven was regarding them inquisitively.

Atticus knocked again, harder this time. The raven sprang, croaking in alarm, into the blue of the sky and a single flake of rust fluttered down to their feet.

Lucie put her hand on Atticus' arm and gestured towards the grimy lattice that served the cottage as a window. Atticus looked, and as his eyes began to interpret the shapes and shadows within, he could distinguish the outline of a man. He was a tall and slender man, standing quite still and facing the windowless wall opposite. His arms appeared to be wrapped tightly around his head.

Atticus stepped up to the window and peered through its marbling of dust. He tapped several times on the glass with the tips of his fingers. The man started violently and peered round at them. His expression might have been that of a poacher caught at the end of a gamekeeper's shotgun.

"We would like to speak with you, Mister...Pendragon," Atticus called, loudly and slowly, through the glass.

Pendragon – the man they took to be Michael Britton – was motionless for a moment. Then, very slowly, he lowered his arms to his side and began to shuffle reluctantly in the direction of the door.

An age later, the latch clicked and lifted and the door retreated a few inches. A grimy, bearded face filled the gap.

"Mr Pendragon, Mr Uther Pendragon?" Atticus ventured.

"Yes," the word was a croak, barely audible. The voice that spoke it sounded as if it might not have been used for a very long time.

"May we come in and speak to you for a moment please?" Lucie asked gently.

Pendragon looked from one to the other. Then, with an expression somewhere between defeat and resignation, he pulled the door wide.

If Michael Britton's cottage seemed mean and small from without, from within it was positively claustrophobic; the low, timber-beamed ceiling festooned with cobwebs and rotten plaster making it seem all the more so. An old, cast-iron kitchen range filled one side of the space and the only items of furniture they could see were a battered table and four equally shabby chairs. This table was littered, as was every other surface in the cottage, with a mulch of charcoal and pencil sketches. Even the grubby, lime-washed faces of the walls were crowded with painted frescoes like the tattooed arms of a fairground wrestler.

One of these latter stood out in particular. It was rendered on the plaster of the rotting partition that separated the living area from what they presumed must be a bedroom and it might have been a scene taken directly from the poetry of Mr William Morris. Here was an ethereal beauty clothed in a flowing, blue gown. It must have been a wedding gown because her face and her long, auburn hair were hazed in a veil of lace. A large, fiery-red dragon was curled around her, seeming to guard her from all peril. It was a reworking of the scene from their room at Shields Tower and, like its twin, its characters too seemed disconcertingly familiar.

Atticus spoke in a loud, slow and patient tone.

"Mr Pendragon, my name is Atticus Fox. I am a privately-commissioned investigator and this is my wife and fellow investigatrix Mrs Lucie Fox." In an effort to make himself understood, he pointed firstly to himself and then to his wife.

"Mr Fox, I am not completely witless. You may speak to me plainly. Why does everyone always take me for an imbecile?" Britton's tone was quiet, more beseeching than indignant.

Atticus was mortified.

"Mr Pendragon, please forgive me. I really meant you no offence – none whatever." When Britton nodded in weary acknowledgement he went on, "We are here on Sir Hugh Lowther's instructions to investigate the recent deaths on his estate."

Uther Pendragon stared at him with emerald-green eyes, startlingly bright against the grime of his face. His hands shook slightly as he reached between the tattered edges of his trouser pocket and pulled out a filthy, crumpled rag that once might have been a pocket-handkerchief. He wiped it across his mouth and whispered: "Deaths, so there has been another murder then? Who is it this time?"

"Do you not know about Sir Douglas?" Lucie asked.

Uther turned sharply towards her, his eyes brighter yet with horror and astonishment.

"Sir Douglas – Sir Douglas Lowther you mean?"

Lucie nodded.

"Yes, Sir Hugh's father. He was murdered beside the Broomlee Lough sometime in the afternoon of yesterday."

"How was he murdered?"

"He was throttled, and choked with biltong meat."

Uther closed his eyes and began to sway slowly to-and-fro.

"So it's started once again. I am truly sorry for Sir Douglas. He was always kind and generous to me, in spite of my madness. At least he can be with his wife again, in Heaven. That is, if she is in Heaven. They say suicide is a sin."

"What do you mean by 'it's started once again'?" Atticus asked, interrupting him.

"I mean that there have been other deaths – most of them many years ago now. The first were the three gin smugglers; they had all been horribly mutilated and thrown off the crags up yonder." He inclined his head in the direction of the moors. "Then an officer from over Hexham way went missing. That was just before Igraine – the first Lady Lowther – disappeared too. Her body has never been recovered either."

He closed his eyes for several, long moments.

"And then there was another – just the other day. Saturday I believe it was. Three policemen came to talk to me about it."

"We know, Mr Pendragon; that was one of the deaths to which my husband refers." Lucie's tone was patient and soothing in a way that Atticus, try as he might, could never quite manage. "A Gypsy, a Mr Samson Elliott, was found, stabbed and decapitated, beside his horse and caravan. It was in the next field, just over the wall from here, and we are curious as to whether you heard or saw anything that day."

Uther considered for a moment. "What day is it today?" he asked.

"It is still early on Friday morning."

Uther shook his head emphatically.

"Then no. As I told the policemen, I was out around Sewingshields for most of the day last Saturday." His hands began to tremble violently and he wiped his mouth with his rag.

"I heard the sound of the bugle over the moors and I dared…that is to say, I went out to investigate."

"The sound of the bugle," Atticus repeated.

Uther nodded.

"Yes Mr Fox; I'm certain it was King Arthur's bugle again. It was early in the morning. Even though I searched the marshes and the crags around the castle for the whole day, I found nothing, just as I always find nothing, and I returned home shortly after nightfall."

He stared suddenly at Atticus and the huge circles of his eyes betrayed what might have been raw fear.

"I've told the policemen all of this already. Upon my life that is all I know."

"The castle you mention being Sewingshields Castle?"

Uther nodded.

"What is King Arthur's bugle, Mr Pendragon?" Lucie asked.

Uther turned his gaze onto her and his eyes all at once became shining and animated. He began to speak very quickly.

"Good King Arthur and his queen, Lady Guinevere, together with several of the Knights of the Round Table lie slumbering in an underground vault somewhere near to the ruins of Sewingshields Castle. They will sleep there until 'The End of Days', which is a time when there will be a great need for them to rise once again."

He held up a grubby forefinger.

"Then will they be awoken.

"They sleep with a knight's garter, a sword and a bugle horn. To wake them, one need only to draw the sword, cut the garter and sound a note on the bugle."

Uther took a breath and lowered his head, conspiratorially.

"One day, many years ago, a shepherd sat knitting as he tended his flock on the common land close by Sewingshields. By chance, his ball of wool rolled away from him and fell down into a cleft in the rocks. Climbing down in order to search for it, he discovered a hidden cave. It was full of toads and newts and suchlike creatures and bats flying in and out, so he made sure to be quick to retrieve his wool and be gone. But then, just as he was about to clamber back out, he noticed the light of a bright blue, magical fire flickering far away in the depths. Summoning all of his courage, he followed it and eventually came across a great, cavernous vault where King Arthur and Lady Guinevere, together with their knights and hounds, lay in a deep, enchanted sleep. With them were the sword, the garter, and the bugle horn spoken of in the legends.

"Remembering them, the shepherd drew the sword and used it to cut the garter. As he did so, Arthur, Guinevere and the knights all began to stir and awaken, and the poor, simple shepherd took fright. He thrust the sword back into its scabbard and fled the vault without blowing the horn, which would have woken them fully. Guinevere and the knights immediately fell back into their slumbers and only Arthur remained awake."

Here Uther leaned in close towards Atticus and Lucie and the stench of his unwashed body caught them almost like a physical blow.

"King Arthur cried these words after the shepherd:
'Oh, woe betide that evil day,
On which this witless wight was born.

*Who drew the sword, the garter cut,
But never blew the bugle horn.'*

"Mr Fox, on the morning of the Gypsy man's death, I heard the note of a bugle calling across the moors. I am no witless wight like the shepherd, so I set off immediately through the mists and the rain to discover the source. Where the bugle sounds, there shall I find my son King Arthur. But after many hours of searching the crags, and the fells around the castle as far as the shores of the Broomlee Lough, I found nothing, so I returned here to my cottage."

"You surely can't think the legend is real?" Atticus asked incredulously.

Uther shrugged and wiped his mouth.

"I believe it is the truth, Mr Fox, yes; of course I do. The shepherd's story has a ring of truthfulness about it and in any event, King Arthur and his Lady Guinevere have visited me here, in my cottage, on many occasions. That is why I have a red dragon, the standard of Pendragon, always freshly painted upon my door. Arthur sees it and recognises the red – the blood-red. He knows that he will always find a welcome from his father here.

"Do you think that King Arthur would leave us all unprotected, Mr Fox? Do you, Mrs Fox? Of course he would not, and in any event, you cannot deny that the sound of the bugle horn was real enough."

Atticus searched for a moment for some way in which to reply to him. Finding none, he said: "You might have observed that there are a number of long, deep footprints in the soft ground around the site of the murder. They lead through the style, to the area around your cottage.

Mr Pendragon, they are footprints which might well have been made by a large man such as you."

Uther looked at him, puzzlement creasing the thick mask of grime on his skin.

"There were no footprints when I left that morning that I can recollect, although I'll admit it was very misty, and when I returned it was already dark. I have not been able to leave my cottage since then, except to go round to the back, to my fresh-water pump, so I'm sorry, I cannot assist you with that. Upon my honour though, I have never noticed any such footprints."

"Very well, so tell me this: Do you possess a sword – a sword, or any other instrument with a long and exceedingly sharp blade?"

"Oh yes, there I can help you because I do have a sword; I have a very fine one."

Uther wiped his mouth.

Atticus and Lucie exchanged sharp, uneasy glances.

"May we see it?" Atticus asked.

"I'm sorry but that will not be possible. It has been taken from me."

"Taken from you? Stolen do you mean? When did this happen?"

"Whilst I was out searching the moors on the day of the Gypsy's death. I expect that King Arthur took it. He always threatened he would. He said it was the sword Excalibur."

Atticus glanced to Lucie once again but her eyes were still fixed on Britton.

"From precisely where was…Excalibur stolen, Mr Pendragon?" she asked.

Uther's hands gave a violent spasm.

"Please do not say that it was stolen, Mrs Fox. Excalibur is Arthur's own sword, his to take should ever he wish. He took it from the wall by the side of my bed, where I kept it in case…in case I had need of it."

"Had need of it for what purpose? Not for protection, surely?"

Uther bowed his head.

"Forgive me, Mrs Fox but I do not wish to say."

"Very well, we shan't ask more, for the present anyway, but tell me: where did you get the sword from?" Atticus asked.

"Now you're beginning to sound like the doctor, Mr Fox." There was a sudden sharp edge of agitation to Uther's tone. Then he shrugged, helplessly.

"I had a proper naval cutlass from my time on the *Shannon* – HMS Shannon that is. I spent time in the Royal Navy, you see. My physician, Dr Hickson, confiscated it. He said that I might have it back when I could properly be trusted with it and not before. But Sir Hugh gave me another sword – the one Arthur told me was Excalibur. He said that whatever our differences, he'd be damned if a fellow military man would be left without a sword for his honour, particularly one who had served in the Uprising and rendered his family such a service as I had."

He sighed.

"And what would Sir Hugh be doing with Excalibur?" Lucie asked.

"It's quite obvious if you take time to think on it," Uther replied curtly. "Excalibur was cast into a lake – a lough – by Sir Bedivere, who was one of the Knights of the Round Table. Sir Hugh's family has owned the land around the loughs for generations. So it's really not surprising at all that it should have been in his possession."

He glanced between Atticus and Lucie.

"Why do you ask about it?"

"Because Samson Elliott was killed by something very much like a sword blade!"

Uther cried out as if he had been struck and his hands began to shake uncontrollably.

Lucie put a cautioning hand on Atticus' arm.

"This is becoming too distressing for you. Let me get you a glass of water. Where might I get it from?"

"Thank you, Mrs Fox," Uther answered with a sob. "There is a draw-pump around the back of the cottage."

"Never mind draw-pumps," Atticus said, "I have some Harrogate water here in my flask, first-rate chalybeate water that you may have with pleasure. Chalybeate water is full of iron, which is good for the mind and the Harrogate waters are recognised generally as being the best healing waters in the world."

"Thank you, Mr Fox. That is extremely kind of you and at least it won't be orange."

Atticus regarded him sharply. "At least what will not be orange?"

"At least the water won't be orange. There is an orange tinge to the water from my pump. There has been for years now. I think it must be the peat washing down from the moors into the well beneath it."

"How very singular! But now that you mention it, I took a plaster-of-Paris cast of what I hope will be the murderer's footprint before we came here. The water I took from a puddle to mix the plaster, which might well have been from the overflow of your pump, did have a slight but definite orange discolouration."

Atticus took a slim, silver hip-flask from the pocket of his jacket and reached for a glass tumbler from a shelf above the cooking range. There was a thin but distinct film of gingery dust on the tumbler bottom which broke up when Atticus wiped it clean with his pocket handkerchief. He emptied his flask into the tumbler and held it out to Uther who took it gratefully. Uther held the clear water up to the light streaming in from the window, whispered, "A willing foe!" and drank deeply.

Atticus regarded him uncertainly.

"What did you mean, 'A willing foe'?" he asked.

"Nothing, nothing," Uther replied, "It's just an expression, a naval one, from the wardroom. I mean you and your beautiful wife no harm."

Lucie smiled, perhaps a little self-consciously, and said: "Now, if you are feeling a little stronger, would you be so kind as to show us where your sword was kept, before it was…taken?"

Uther shrugged clumsily. "Of course, if you think it will help."

He led the Foxes through into the second room of the cottage. Their surmise that this would be a bedroom proved correct; it was filled almost completely by an old and much-tarnished, brass-framed bed, littered by paintings and drawings on almost every size and type of paper imaginable.

But Atticus and Lucie barely noticed these. Instead their attention was drawn irresistibly to a singular group of objects clustered in one corner, where there were no sketches and no dirt. It reminded Atticus somehow of a shrine his mother had kept for a time to his long-dead father.

Here was a large, imposing and highly polished suit of medieval armour. Nothing could have looked more out of keeping against the shabby, mouldering walls. On the breastplate of the armour was a large, scarlet emblem of a dragon and above that, on the flat top of the great helm, the figure of another red dragon crouched, as if ready to leap out at any moment to devour them.

Resting against the shoulder plate, and extending up through a neatly cut circle in the rotting lathes of the ceiling, was a spear, or rather a lance. It was a long lance, half as tall again as Atticus, with a razor-sharp and lethal-looking iron tip that glinted in the columns of sunlight pouring in through the worn thatch of the roof.

Their eyes crept down the length of the shaft to the floor, where next to the greaves – the shin guards – was a good-sized block of stone. It was very similar to the stones used to found the dry stone walling just outside the cottage, with the very same patination of moss and lichen. Side-by-side on the top of this were a platter and a goblet. Both were plain, wrought without ornamentation from bronze, and both appeared to be exceedingly old.

After several long seconds of staring in stunned bemusement, the meaning of the collection hit Atticus with a force that almost knocked him to the ground.

"Upon my word!" he exclaimed, then: "Is that armour authentic?"

Uther shook his head.

"It is one of a pair of reproductions that Sir Douglas Lowther had the blacksmith make for a fête in Hexham, many years ago. It was to re-enact the prophecy of the Red Dragon and the White Dragon. This armour, with the emblem of the Red Dragon – the Pendragon – was given to me by Lady Igraine. It was as a token of her appreciation for a mural I painted for her down at the Tower. The other, with the emblem of the White Dragon, sits on a whinstone dais at the foot of the grand stairs there…along with a replica that Igraine had the blacksmith make to replace this one. Sir Hugh was very angry at her for giving it to me. I heard he struck her, several times, over it."

"And the spear, goblet and plate?"

"Are completely authentic, Mr Fox, of course."

Atticus stared at him. "So what are you saying – that these are the Hallows, the lost Hallows of Arthur?"

"Yes, sir," Uther said simply, "I am honoured to have been entrusted with them and I clean and polish them each day I am able."

Lucie was biting her lip.

"What are they, Atticus?" she asked, "Whatever are the lost Hallows of Arthur?"

Atticus turned to his wife and his expression, even to her, was unfathomable.

"The Hallows are a legendary collection of sacred objects, Lucie. Once brought together, they are said to render their possessor invincible. King Arthur and his Knights of the Round Table supposedly undertook a great quest to seek them all out. Two of them you will have heard of already; they are the Holy Grail, the chalice used at the Last Supper of Christ, and the sword Excalibur."

Lucie nodded, wide-eyed.

"But there are also two others, rather lesser-known," Atticus continued: "The Holy Lance, or the Spear of Destiny, supposedly the very spear that pierced Christ's side at his crucifixion, and the Holy Platter, the dish used by Christ's apostles at the Last Supper. Our friend here evidently believes them to be the genuine relics."

"Oh they are, Mr Fox," Uther said with utter conviction. "I know they are genuine because it was King Arthur himself who brought them to me."

For probably the first time in all of his thirty-six years of life, Atticus Fox was struck completely dumb. He stared, thunderstruck, at Lucie, who was regarding Uther with something akin to fascination.

"When did he bring them to you, Mr Pendragon?" she asked at last.

"Oh, all in this past twelvemonth," he replied earnestly. "There are times when I do not sleep, when I cannot sleep, and it was during one of those times, very late one night around a year ago, that I heard the sound of the bugle horn calling.

"I always take care to wear my armour when I go up to the moors, Mrs Fox and I hurried straight away to put on the breastplate; there was no time to put on more, you see. At least it has the Red Dragon emblem upon it so King Arthur will not mistake me for an enemy. I searched and searched all night but there was no sign of him. Eventually I returned home disappointed. He must have gone back to his vault.

"I began to feel very low. I went down and down, overwhelmed, as I sometimes am, by the blackness. But then something wonderful happened: King Arthur himself came here, to my cottage, accompanied by his beautiful queen, the Lady Guinevere. It was broad daylight or I should have thought it a dream. He knocked on my door and came in, shouting my name and calling me 'Father'."

Uther's eyes began to glisten, suddenly wet with tears as he spoke.

"From that day on, they began calling upon me regularly. Sometimes they would bring me food and sometimes physics and medicine. They seemed to sense somehow that I had an illness. Then they started to bring the Hallows to me too. The Holy Grail was the first; Guinevere had it hidden in the pretty wicker basket she often carries. The Platter was next and finally the Spear of Destiny. The Spear I found outside my door one night after I heard the bugle call very close-by and I went out to investigate."

"You say you had the sword already?" Atticus prompted.

"Yes, I had," Uther replied. "When I asked King Arthur about the last Hallow; the sword Excalibur, he told me that it was the sword Sir Hugh Lowther had already given to me. He showed me the inscriptions etched into the blade to prove it. They were runes and he explained to me their meaning. On one side they read *Take Me Up* and on the other *Cast Me Away*. But then he warned me he might have to take it back from me...for my own good."

He pointed to a pair of stout, iron pegs that had long ago been driven into the mortar of the wall next to the bedstead. A long, heavily soiled and greying cloth like a bandage hung from one of them and trailed through the plaster-dust on the floor.

"It was usually hung from those hooks. When I returned home from the moors the day the Gypsy was killed, I was feeling very angry. I couldn't bear it any longer and I came in here for Excalibur. It was then that I noticed it was gone."

"What is the cloth?" Atticus asked.

"I use it to wrap Excalibur's blade, Mr Fox."

"May I see it?"

Without waiting for an assent, Atticus reached down and gently lifted it from the peg.

"Hullo, Lucie," he murmured after a moment, "Aren't these bloodstains?"

Uther coloured deeply behind his great, matted beard. He began to shift uncomfortably; clasping and unclasping his hands as they once again began to tremble.

"Those are just rust stains, Mr Fox," he whispered, "Only stains of rust."

Atticus passed the cloth to Lucie, who took it and examined the marks closely.

"It does look very much like blood to me," she said gravely.

"Very well, yes, it is blood, I admit it." Uther grabbed two fistfuls of his hair. It was flecked with silver; the dying embers of a once fiery red. "I nicked myself – just by accident, hark ye – a few days ago."

Atticus frowned. "There seems to be a very great deal of blood on that cloth to have come from one accidental nick. Nevertheless…"

He took a breath.

"Mr Pendragon – and please forgive my indelicacy in asking you such a question, but you will understand that we are investigating no fewer than two murderous attacks – are you aware that you are insane?"

"Atticus!" exclaimed Lucie.

"It is fine, Mrs Fox, it is fine. There is no escaping the fact. Yes, Mr Fox, I do know: I am mad – quite mad."

Atticus grunted and Lucie, with a scowl to her husband, asked: "How exactly is your…insanity manifest?"

Uther let go his hair and grabbed his own forearms, hugging them tightly against his body.

"As I believe I've told you already, I often suffer from the blackness – from the long periods of melancholy. They are the worst. But then, sometimes, I become alive – more alive than you can possibly imagine. It is then that I feel truly mad. It is then I must sketch."

"You must sketch?"

"Yes, I must. I cannot eat, I cannot sleep. All I can think to do is to sketch, or to draw, or to paint. Everything is so vivid, do you see? I have to draw it. I cannot stop. I am compelled to. It is then that I am a true artist."

Atticus glanced around. He was treading deep water here, he knew.

He said: "Well you certainly have been busy. There must be hundreds of sketches and drawings here."

"These have been done over many years. When I see something that catches my attention, I sketch it."

Lucie picked up a roughly-torn square of butcher's paper from the bed beside her.

"But surely you can't have seen any of these around here? This is a dragon."

"Dragons are what I see the most. I see them everywhere: in the reflections in the windows; in the clouds; even in my dreams. You see, Mrs Fox, a dragon follows me all of the time, and one day, it will kill me."

"Dragons are just make-believe, just creatures from folklore and nursery tales," Lucie countered. "They aren't real. Besides, don't you believe yourself to be Uther Pen-*dragon*? You bear the name of the dragon; you have its emblem upon your breastplate. Why should a dragon wish to harm you?"

Uther reached down and picked up a second square of paper. It was a charcoal sketch, a depiction of two vividly detailed dragons entwined as if in combat. One was lightly shaded, the other, much bigger, more fearsome, and with an expression out of Hell itself, was not. He placed his finger on this latter and said, a little huskily: "These are the two great dragons: the white and the red. This one, the White Dragon, will torment me to my grave. I must always, always, be on my guard against it." His finger trembled against the paper and he began to breathe in short, asthmatic gasps. "But it will all be in vain. The White Dragon will kill me at the last. It can only be defeated by another – by my son."

Lucie lifted the trembling paper from his hand.

"Hush now. Try not to upset yourself. Have you always suffered from this terrible insanity, or did it strike you later in life?"

Uther shrugged, bleakly and hopelessly.

"It is only now, when I look back across my life, that I can see that I've always suffered from the same long periods of hopelessness – from the blackness – even when I was a boy. But because I knew no better, I accepted it as normal. For years my father tried to thrash it out of me and then, when he found he could not, he would taunt me, and call me pathetic and weak.

"When I grew older and finished my schooling I enrolled in the Royal Navy. It was mainly, I admit, to escape from Father and his constant bullying. The friendships and comradeships I found at sea, and the way I could throw myself completely into my duty helped me a very great deal. I became – dare I even say it – almost like a normal man.

"But then came 1857 and the Sepoy Rebellion – the Indian Uprising. I was with the *Shannon* at the time and I was detailed to be part of the naval brigade."

He shuddered.

"Cawnpore, Lucknow, the Secundra Bagh – dear God, the Secundra Bagh; they are probably just names from a history book to you. To me, and to hundreds like me, they were Hell itself."

"Tell us what happened at the Secundra Bagh," Lucie invited.

Uther stared at her in horror.

"Tell you about it? Do you really wish to know?"

Lucie nodded. "I think it might help."

Uther wiped his mouth and then he closed his eyes, and shivered.

"Very well then, I will tell you. We were…we were part of Sir Colin Campbell's relief column making our final approach to relieve the British residency at Lucknow. It was the sixteenth of November, 1857, a date that will stay with me until the day I die.

"As we were passing along a sunken road through the city itself, we came under very heavy fire from Sepoy mutineers holed up in a big villa. They called it the Secundra Bagh. We were trapped, Mrs Fox, pinned down, and I admit I have never been so afraid in all my life. Even the officers thought we were done for. But then the Bengal Horse managed to bring some of their field guns to bear and we turned the tables on them."

He sobbed.

"We fought our way in. Dear God forgive us, but we slaughtered them to a man – over two thousand of them shot or bayoneted in there. They were screaming to us for mercy, Mrs Fox, screaming to us. But everyone was shouting 'Remember Cawnpore!' and 'Remember Delhi!', and we gave them no quarter. We killed them all.

"I refused though. When the assault became a massacre, I threw down my rifle and turned my back. I said I would have no part in it. The army wanted me court-marshalled for that. Cowardice in the face of the enemy they called it. But before they could, Sir Douglas Lowther, who was one of those besieged in the residency, led a flying column out into the city to try to disrupt the Sepoys' defence. He became separated from his men in the melee and finished up surrounded by mutineers.

"Fortunately, I managed to fight my way through to him and pull him back to safety, and so he had all charges against me quashed.

"I am no coward, Mr and Mrs Fox, whatever the army might tell you. But that expedition lasted for twelve months and in that year I saw things that no civilised man should ever see, things that get between me and my sleep to this day.

"Shortly after we got back to the *Shannon*, I fell ill once again and I was discharged into a charitable institution. But then Sir Douglas Lowther heard about it all and he fetched me back to stay here, in this cottage, where it is quiet and peaceful.

"I discovered painting here and sketching and eventually even true love. I recovered my health and I was almost completely well for a while. But then one day, my sweetheart, my future wife, disappeared without trace from the high moors beyond the Roman Wall and I succumbed once again.

"Now I feel that every day, I am slipping further and further down the slope to complete madness. My hands are the worst; they keep shaking so much these days. They never have before, even when I was at my maddest, but now, try as I might, I can't stop them."

He spread his trembling fingers and stared at them in despair.

"When they first began to shake, they prevented me from being able to paint. I used to paint a great deal. It helped me with the demons in my head. The frustration almost drove me to kill myself, but now, I find that if I sketch with a pencil, or with charcoal if I have no pencil, then I am able to hide the tremors in the detail."

"You mentioned your future wife – your fiancée. You said she disappeared from the moors?"

"Yes, Mrs Fox, she was taken by the White Dragon. Two children, who were out collecting bracken on the moors that morning, said they heard two awful screams from the direction of Sewingshields, one after another. They were the screams of a woman."

He rolled his eyes and his agony bled out.

"But Sir Hugh's first wife was also lost from those moors!" Atticus exclaimed, "Around twenty years ago, as I understand it. When was your fiancée's disappearance?"

Uther bowed his head.

"The same."

Atticus frowned towards Lucie and asked: "So what did the police make of it all? Had they no clue what might have happened to her?"

Uther shrugged.

"The police of twenty years ago were not what they are now."

"How truly awful for you, to have to cope with all of that," Lucie said, "Did you never see a physician?"

"I used to do, very frequently. Dr Hickson called upon me most days, if only to say his greetings and then to go again. But then he stopped. It was just before my love disappeared. There was – there still is – little point in him wasting his time on me because there's truly nothing that can be done. This is what I am and I stand condemned to be like this always."

He cast his eyes to the ground.

"Dr Hickson has begun to call upon me again of late. Sir Hugh Lowther insists on it by all accounts but I don't know why. He keeps trying to persuade me to go into a lunatic asylum at Morpeth or Gosforth. He is just trying to get rid of me, of course. I'm incurable, you see. I'm just a drain on his precious time."

He snorted derisively.

"In any event, I have no time for him. He called regularly when I was well but then stopped when I was at my lowest, when I really needed his help. Now it is all too late."

"But couldn't treatment at an asylum still help you, Uther?" Lucie asked softly. "They have doctors who are expert in helping people like you. It must be worth trying at the very least?"

Uther shook his head and began to sway to and fro once again.

"Dr Hickson tells me that. He says they are especially kind at Gosforth. They don't beat the inmates there; they only bind them, plunge them in ice-water and electrify them. No, Mrs Fox, I never want to leave Sewingshields except perhaps to go to Heaven and be reunited there with my love. The wild crags and the moors will provide me with some solace in the meantime."

He was silent for several long seconds. Then he murmured: "And I do want to die, Mrs Fox, I always have. Sometimes, I imagine myself stepping off the high crags at Sewingshields and floating gently down to my death. I would have time then to properly feel the sense of relief, to know that it is all, finally, over."

He smiled bleakly.

"Don't worry though. I know I cannot take my own life. I'm denied even that. It wouldn't be fair, you see, either to Arthur or to Guinevere. But that doesn't stop me from praying for a natural death to release me from my struggles, for the one day when I might not wake up at all.

"But before that day comes, I also pray that I might see the restored kingdom of Arthur. I beg the Lord that, before the White Dragon takes me, I might see King Arthur on the throne of Britain once again with the Lady Guinevere as his queen. I pray that I might see the Red Dragon finally prevail as Merlin promised it surely would."

He looked directly at Atticus with his clear, emerald-green eyes.

"Arthur grows strong again, Mr Fox. Can you feel it? Can you, Mrs Fox?"

"What do you mean?" The sudden intensity in Uther's voice was alarming and Atticus' fingers tightened around the pommel of his cane.

"Arthur calls regularly upon me now. He tells me that although he cannot speak of it, a great event will shortly take place and our lineage will be secured. I hear the call of the bugle too, again and again, and it is getting louder.

"I heard it distinctly on Saturday. The same day, a man was found butchered with a sword. I heard it yesterday too, and now I hear that Sir Douglas, God rest his soul, has been murdered. Perhaps, and please, please God it is so, Arthur has risen again. Please God it is for good this time and he has, at last, begun to destroy his enemies."

Uther's hands began to tremor violently and he clasped them tightly against his chest. His eyes filled with angst and a great drool of saliva stretched down his beard.

"Please, leave me alone," he begged.

Atticus nodded. They took their leave and left him to his madness.

CHAPTER THIRTEEN

"So what do you make of that?" Atticus muttered after he had pulled the door shut behind them and heard the latch drop into place.

Lucie's eyes glistened in the bright sunlight as she glanced back towards the shabby cottage.

"I always did become far too involved in the troubles of the patients, Atticus. Dr Crichton-Browne at the asylum once had me write out a line, fifty times: *Close enough is proper care, but closer still would be a snare.*"

She shook her head as she struggled to compose herself. "But sometimes it is very difficult not to. The man is in a living hell, poor soul. He can't ever leave his hovel unless it is to go out alone, onto the moors, weighed down with his fake armour to chase a delusion, or to go and get his filthy, as-likely-as-not poisonous water from his draw-pump. And he can't leave the torments of his mind ever. They are always there: the anxiety; the despair; the memories of his lost sweetheart."

"And his morbid dread of a dragon."

"Yes, Atticus, that too; he has a particular fear of a white dragon. I don't understand that part at all."

"Oh, I believe I can shed some light onto it," Atticus replied, taking his wife's proffered hand as she stepped up into the style, "The battle between the White Dragon and the Red Dragon is a very famous allegory from Arthurian legend."

"Uther's sketch showed exactly that; a battle between a red dragon and a white dragon and he mentioned that his armour had been made to re-enact the battle between them at a fête."

Atticus squeezed through after her, wincing as he felt a waistcoat button scraping against the big stone at his belly.

"Quite so. In the Arthurian legends there is a tale told by Merlin, Arthur's magician, about a long running battle between a red dragon, which symbolised the Celtic Britons, and a white dragon, or the Anglo-Saxon invaders of the time. Merlin prophesied that the Red Dragon, the Britons, would prevail during King Arthur's lifetime, but that after his death the White Dragon, the Angles and the Saxons, would overcome it until Arthur is finally awakened again at 'The End of Days' to restore the Red Dragon's supremacy."

"And he thinks that Arthur has been awakened – that he has risen again?"

"It would seem so, but not only that, it appears he is also paying him house calls and bringing him his hallowed relics into the bargain."

Lucie sighed.

"It is a great pity to see Uther as he is. As Sir Hugh remarked, his life isn't much better than those of the cattle in the field over yonder – except for his art that is; he really is an exceptionally talented artist. He's obviously a very brave man too, notwithstanding his refusal to join in with the massacre at Lucknow. He saved the life of Sir Douglas, after all.

"And do you know, Atticus, under all of his dirt and his unkemptness he is actually a fine-looking man. He has a certain…vulnerability about him too, which is very appealing."

Atticus grunted.

"But why does he allow himself to remain like that? Why doesn't he simply pick himself up by his bootstraps – just as I had to do?"

Lucie grimaced.

"It's an affliction of the mind, don't forget," Atticus persisted, "I've learned to train mine as I please. I have complete mastery of my thoughts. Surely he must be able to gain control over his too?"

"You have been particularly fortunate in your circumstances, Atticus Fox and you sometimes forget that. Others, like Mr Britton, have not."

"I suppose you are right. But look here. Here is our cast of what I hope will be the murderer's footprint. With luck, the plaster-of-Paris should have hardened sufficiently by now for us to be able to lift it."

Atticus laid his bag onto a broad stone which had long ago fallen from its place in the wall and been smothered by the thick grass. Then, crouching and working his fingers under the cast, he gently eased it free from the sucking grip of the mud.

"So, Lucie," he said, carefully picking at the wet earth that still clung to its fragile surface, "Let us see exactly what manner of boot he, or she, was wearing.

"Well, upon my word, how exceedingly curious!"

Lucie dropped to her knees beside him.

"It looks like the shell of an armadillo."

Atticus Fox regarded the cast thoughtfully, turning it over and over in his hands for several minutes. It was indeed exactly as his wife had described; like the lower body of a member of the Order *Cingulata* – the armadillos – with one pointed end and a series of overlapping plates along its length.

"Upon my word," he repeated softly.

"It's the boot of a knight isn't it?" Lucie said.

Atticus nodded.

"Yes, I believe it is. It is a knight's sabaton. One of King Arthur's sabatons, do you suppose?"

Lucie threw him a sharp glance, uncertain as to whether or not Atticus Fox could really be hinting at the existence of the preternatural.

"It sounds utterly inconceivable I know," Atticus went on, "But could Michael Britton be right? Could King Arthur really have risen again?"

"Surely not; you cannot really believe that he has, can you?"

Atticus bit his lip.

"Who knows? Perhaps someone has cut the garter and blown the bugle horn after all. But it is a very good question, Lucie, and one we might well ponder as we make our way over to the Broomlee Lough."

CHAPTER FOURTEEN

The Broomlee Lough.

Could this silver veil of water draped across the fell really be the enchanted lake of Arthurian romance?

Lucie Fox sensed, perhaps with a woman's intuition for such things, some of the ancient magic of the place as she clasped her arms and shivered. Had brave Sir Bedivere of the Sinews felt it too as, centuries earlier, he had hurled Excalibur across those same glistening waters? Perhaps he too had shivered as he watched the Lady of the Lake rise to pluck it from the air and carry it once more down into the realm of the water-spirits.

"There! That must be the spot where James found Sir Douglas." Atticus' voice shattered the spell.

They stood, regarding a light wooden chair set-out at the tip of a grassy outcrop that reached out into the lake. It was a folding chair, a knock-down army campaign chair, with a leather seat hanging limp and empty from the frame. Fingers of green lichen were reaching up the legs, slowly reclaiming the sun-bleached rosewood for the moorlands.

Lucie bustled ahead to examine it and it soon became apparent that Atticus was correct; this was surely where Sir Douglas Lowther had died.

The sphagnum moss that carpeted the outcrop was spattered with what was undoubtedly dark, congealed blood. Sir Douglas, like Sir Hugh himself, had been a fighting man and clearly he had not given up this lifeblood easily. Here and there the mosses had been scuffed and kicked up into bloody tendrils and there was not one stain that had not been smeared and trodden by struggling boots.

Atticus stooped to pick up a battered silver hip flask from the very edge of the lapping waters. Its mirror polish was dulled by a thick film of dew but there was definitely something engraved into the metal beneath. Wiping away the moisture with his gloved thumb he revealed the initials D.E.L. and a familiar coat of arms with a device of six round annulets; arms that had proved so impotent in the face of whoever, or whatever, stalked these moors.

Lucie acknowledged it with a grave nod of her head.

"Do you think there could be anything else – any other vestiges from the attack that might have fallen into the lake?" she wondered aloud.

Atticus made a face. "There could be anything in there for all we know. Unfortunately, without dredging irons, there is very little we can do about it.

"James told me there is reckoned to be a treasure in the deepest part," he added after a moment, "With a magician's enchantment upon it."

"Is there really?" Lucie, her bloody turf forgotten, came to stand at his side. She stared out across the lough and watched as the wind sent shivers chasing each other about the surface.

"So the legends tell," said Atticus. "The enchantment is that the treasure can only be raised by a seventh generation blacksmith with a chain he himself forged. He must have with him two twin horses, two twin oxen and two twin lads; seven souls in all. Everything around here seems to be shrouded in mystery and magic."

He shrugged.

"I doubt if anything has been thrown in there deliberately though." Atticus glanced back towards the chair standing empty and almost forlorn. It was as if it were waiting patiently for a master who would now never return. "Whoever did this, and whoever killed Samson Elliott, wasn't interested in covering their tracks."

The big clock over the carriage house surprised them a little in that it was still so early by the time they passed beneath it to retrieve their bicycles from the adjoining stables. Atticus had left them propped against the dusty planks of an unoccupied horse stall and some wag, likely they were told Albert Bradley the puckish head groom, had hung a nosebag full of oats from the handlebars of each. But that was before James had brought Sir Douglas' mutilated corpse back from the lakeside and the humour had long since run sour.

They had somehow contrived to miss the police superintendant on the vastness of the moors. He had been and he had gone, so they took their bicycles and coasted down the steep, narrow lanes of the valley-side into the village of Bardon Mill. It was easy riding and they very soon found themselves back in the blessed normality of the bustling little railway station. There they left their bicycles with the stationmaster, deftly evading his barrage of questions, and caught the Newcastle train the few miles down the valley to the busy manufacturing and market town of Hexham.

CHAPTER FIFTEEN

When Atticus and Lucie Fox stepped down from the comfort of their railway compartment onto the broad platform at Hexham station, the very first thing that struck their senses was the pervasive and pungent stench of the town's tanneries. Hexham, Atticus suddenly recalled, was renowned for its glove and hat-making industries.

Lucie held her perfumed pocket-handkerchief to her nose as Atticus hurried off to make enquiries of one of the platform porters as to directions to the town's police station.

"It's quite straightforward," he announced when he returned, "We need to walk into town towards the Abbey and find the Hallgate. The police station is opposite the Old Gaol there."

The busy station road bordered a large and verdant orchard. It would have been a pleasant enough walk except for the steady, westerly breeze which carried the acrid fumes from the myriad mill and manufactory chimneys directly into their throats. But then the orchard gave way to rows of stinking slums and hovels and they found themselves continually switching their attention between the quaint, stone architecture and tantalising glimpses of St. Wilfred's great abbey and the piles of rotting rubbish and excrement that littered the streets.

At last, they were directed into the ancient Hallgate and found themselves in front of a neat, stone building with blue window-shutters and a large blue-glass lantern above the door marked 'Police'. Atticus pushed open the door, a bell tinkled overhead, and a harassed-looking sergeant looked up with obvious irritation from a sheaf of papers fanned across his desk like a hand of cards.

"Good morning, madam, good morning, sir," he growled.

Atticus smiled cordially and offered their calling card. Lucie had reminded him more than once on the train, and again as they had walked through the town, how important it was to keep police officers of all ranks as allies rather than enemies.

"Good day to you, Sergeant," he said. "We are Mr and Mrs Atticus Fox of Harrogate and I believe we are expected."

The sergeant's smile faltered just a little as he examined their calling card, and his warm Northumbrian accent became a degree cooler and more officious as he said: "Very good, Mr Fox, the detective superintendant has just got back. Both of you follow me please," and led them through a battered door to the rear of the station.

They clattered noisily up a cramped flight of bare wooden stairs and stopped on the landing, where the sergeant paused to straighten his tunic and button up his collar. He steeled himself and knocked smartly on a door. It carried a polished brass plaque inscribed: 'Detective Superintendant Thos. Robson'.

After a second or two, a gruff, muffled voice called: "Yes, what is it?" The sergeant twisted the brass door-knob and stepped inside. Atticus caught the words 'private', 'commissioned' and 'Fox', and stepped forward to join the sergeant in the room.

Detective Superintendant Thomas Robson hauled himself to his feet as he caught sight of Atticus and circled his broad, cluttered desk with his dinner plate of a hand outstretched. His gaze shifted onto Lucie as she followed in her husband's wake and he bowed briefly and politely to her before offering the two mismatched, wooden chairs in front of his desk.

He waited until Lucie and Atticus were seated before slumping wearily into his own chair. It creaked sharply as it caught him.

"It has already been a long day for the both of us, Mr and Mrs Fox. How might the Hexham Constabulary be of assistance to you?"

Atticus already had Lucie's agreement for him to speak directly.

"You might be aware, Superintendant Robson, that Sir Hugh Lowther has engaged us to conduct a corresponding investigation to your own into the recent death on the Shields Tower estate. That investigation will now naturally extend to include his father's unfortunate demise yesterday."

Robson was silent for a few moments as he meticulously aligned the side of a blotting pad with the edge of his desk. It was peppered with tiny pen-and-ink doodles and rather put them in mind of the walls of Michael Britton's cottage.

"I am a *Detective* Superintendant, if you please, Mr Fox, and if you will pardon me, I will be perfectly candid with you both. Yes, I am well aware of the reason you are up here in Northumberland. However, unlike Colonel Lowther, I do not believe that you will bring one atom of assistance to the case – or cases if you prefer. Indeed not! Rather, my opinion is that, at best, you can serve only to get in the way of our own professional enquiries."

The joints of his chair creaked again as he leaned forward pugnaciously across his desk.

"And frankly it does nothing to help the public's confidence in its constabulary if wealthy local landowners insist on bringing fancy privately-commissioned detectives up from the south."

He glared at them as if to reinforce his point.

"However, notwithstanding all of that," he went on, a little more reasonably, "Sir Hugh has personally requested that we cooperate to the fullest extent with you. He is an influential man here in this part of Northumberland, and generally a good friend to the police, so on this occasion that is precisely what we shall do."

Atticus couldn't help beaming. They could have asked for nothing more. He said: "Then, in return, you have our word of honour that we will do our utmost not to obstruct you, nor to compromise your own investigation in any way." He hesitated. "May I ask who the investigating officer is please?"

Robson leaned back in his chair and regarded him shrewdly.

"I am the investigating officer in both cases, Fox. This isn't Harrogate. Here at Hexham, in addition to me, we have the sergeant, whom you have already met, and just four constables. We are, as you might imagine, somewhat undermanned.

"I could have requested that a detective inspector be sent out from Newcastle, I suppose, but because of the very serious nature of the crimes, and since Sir Hugh's own father is one of the victims, I have decided to oversee the enquiry personally."

Atticus tested the waters further. "Very wise, so may we ask what your conclusions are so far?"

"You may ask of course, Fox, and I will freely admit in return that we are quite mystified at present, although our enquiries are, of course, continuing. We know for certain it isn't King Arthur's doing." Here he snorted. "And we suspect that it isn't Jack the Ripper's either, but beyond that…"

He spread his enormous hands in a gesture of bafflement. Then he said: "Sir Hugh has asked if you might speak to the coroner regarding the autopsy report, and also whether Mrs Fox could see the corpse at first hand."

"May I?" Lucie asked, "It is always preferable to reading reports."

Robson regarded them for several moments as he considered her request.

"Actually, you're in luck," he replied eventually, "A local doctor has been asked to carry out examinations on both Samson Elliott and Sir Douglas Lowther. He is to begin later today and he has agreed that you both may observe."

He grinned.

"I'll warn you though; Elliott's body in particular is in quite a poor condition. In spite of the coolness of the hospital morgue, it has already begun to…putrefy."

CHAPTER SIXTEEN

Detective Superintendant Thomas Robson obligingly delegated a constable to escort the Foxes to the basement morgue of the Hexham Infirmary, where Sir Douglas Lowther's corpse was to join that of Samson Elliott on adjacent, porcelain slabs. The Fates, after all, seldom pay heed to rank or office.

Like all morgues this place was silent and eerie, and reeked of the all-pervasive stenches of formalin and death. Atticus kept his gaze fixed firmly onto the black-and-white tiles of the floor as he followed his wife into the post-mortem examination room. Once inside, he settled himself at a small writing desk and determinedly faced the little drawers full of all manner of writing materials as he waited for the examination to begin. Robson had been entirely correct about the condition of Elliott's body and the fetor emanating from it was oppressive. In fact, this whole place was oppressive: airless, hot and intolerably close.

He breathed, deeply and slowly, and said: "I shall leave the actual observations to you, Lucie."

His wife grinned.

"Aha, Mr and Mrs Fox, I presume?"

A small, shrewd-looking man with a balding head and short goatee beard was standing in the doorway. He reminded Lucie all at once of a satyr, or an elderly pixie, and she smiled at the thought.

The man smiled pleasantly in return and introduced himself as Dr Julius Hickson, the parish doctor for Bardon Mill and the surrounding villages.

"I'm to do the necropsies on the deceased," he explained. "As always, the hospital finds itself somewhat short-handed, so you are both most welcome to assist me, should you so wish."

Atticus politely but firmly declined, and Dr Hickson and Lucie accepted heavy, black rubber aprons from a young mortuary assistant and stood like carrion crows at either side of the great white slab that cradled Elliot's bloated corpse.

"You may be the scribe in that case, Mr Fox," said Hickson. "Just note down everything I say."

Then, with a solemn nod firstly to Lucie and then to the mortuary assistant, he began.

"As we can both see...and indeed smell," Here he chuckled, "The cadaver has entered the early stages of putrefaction, with broadly to-be-expected degrees of distension and discolouration. Nevertheless, I note that the subject is a male, whom I would estimate to be between forty and fifty years of age with a naturally dark skin – almost what Professor Blumenbach might classify as Malayan – and, let me see, dark eyes and hair. His physique is not possible to determine with accuracy, since it has become somewhat distended with putrefaction, but it appears that he was neither excessively fat nor particularly thin.

"The heads sits separate from the torso upon the examination table. It appears to have been neatly, in fact almost surgically, excised with a single stroke to the neck. The wound is clean with little laceration or tearing, indicating the use of a very sharp, heavy instrument; possibly a sword or a cleaver of some sort.

"I begin with the torso. First, we must carefully remove the clothing."

He held out a hand towards the mortuary assistant, who dutifully placed a pair of large, iron shears into his palm. With almost indecent efficiency, Hickson began to snip and peel away the clothing.

"You might like to make a note, Mr Fox, that the various cuts exhibited on the subject's clothing correspond precisely with the wounds upon the underlying surface of the body. To wit: a very deep slice-wound across the whole width of the upper abdomen immediately below the *xiphosternum* and a second, similar, but more superficial, wound intersecting the first at an angle of around forty-five degrees."

"Is there also a stab-wound?" Atticus said quickly.

"Yes, I see it. The entry wound occurs slightly to the left of the sternum and directly over the heart, which must certainly have been penetrated in the process. The puncture is once again clean and I would declare it entirely consistent with having been made by an instrument such as a sword."

"Consistent with the use of a sword," Atticus repeated. "What are…what are the precise dimensions of the wound, Dr Hickson?"

"An excellent question, Mr Fox, although a quite unnecessary one, since we invariably address such matters during the course of a properly conducted necropsy. Let me see: The wound is around one and one-quarter inches in length and perhaps three-eighths of an inch wide. Please make a clear note that these are estimations only. You will bear in mind the condition of the skin on a body so far advanced in its decomposition."

Atticus took a long breath. "That is very curious. And is there a corresponding exit wound also?"

Hickson beckoned to the mortuary assistant, who stepped forward to help Lucie heave the torso over onto its front.

Lucie smiled her thanks and he blushed as red as the smears on his apron.

She stooped towards the greenish, mottled skin of the corpse and after a few seconds said: "There is, Atticus. It corresponds in size and in orientation to the entry wound, but it is a little further towards the left side of the victim's back. I would say that this indicates a sword thrust made horizontally and from the victim's right to his left."

"And I would concur with that conclusion," added Hickson.

"What are the orientations of the wounds, Lucie?"

"I would estimate that both are approximately thirty degrees to the vertical, clock-wise, as judged from the front."

Atticus grunted thoughtfully and said: "How very, very interesting."

Dr Hickson chuckled. "Necropsies invariably are, Mr Fox; they form the very highlights of my practice. How fortunate we are to have a brace of them today.

"Now, Mrs Fox, I applaud you upon your shrewd observations but if I might ask our youthful assistant to turn the cadaver onto its back once again – thank you – we will continue. There is the usual greenish discolouration around the middle of the abdomen, which has spread also to the genitals and legs."

He tugged at the edge of Lucie's apron.

"Mrs Fox, I have my own private autopsy set on the side there. If you would be so kind as to pass me the large knife and a bone-saw, we shall next examine the internal organs, beginning I would say, with the heart. If we should happen to find it contracted and empty, then we might assume that death was occasioned by the slashing-wounds. If, as I suspect, it is still full of blood, then it is more probable he was killed by *paralysis of the heart* and therefore the stabbing blow would have been the fatal one."

The steady, rasping sounds of the bone-saw beat against the tiled walls of the morgue. Atticus poured all of his attention into the notes he had made, reading and re-reading them, considering as best he could what possible events could have resulted in the stinking abomination at his back.

The sawing stopped.

"Good heavens above!" Dr Hickson exclaimed.

"What is it?" Atticus called, "Is it the heart? What does it suggest?"

"Atticus," Lucie said, and her tone was grim, "There is no heart. It's gone."

In the chill of the mortuary, time finally froze.

"What do you mean, it's gone?"

"She means that it is gone, Mr Fox, gone in the plainest sense of the word." Dr Hickson's little, pointed nose seemed to be almost snuffling at Elliott's chest as he bent over the body.

"There is nothing bar a colony of maggots in there now. It appears to me as if the subject's heart was pulled – and with no little force – down and out through the wound in the abdomen. What sort of heathen barbarian could have done this to a fellow man?"

That was a question neither Lucie nor Atticus Fox could answer.

The rest of the autopsy was conducted in a deeply troubled silence, and almost mechanically, as the full horror of the manner of Samson Elliott's death settled onto each of them. Heavy, *in articulo mortis* bruising on the right shoulder was the only other addition to their store of information, and as Sir Douglas' corpse was stretchered in and laid-out onto the adjacent slab, Dr Hickson and Lucie signed off Atticus' record and gave the instruction to the mortuary assistant to sew what remained of Elliott's cadaver back together.

"And you'll need to be quick-smart about it too, my boy," Hickson added. "I hear the deceased's brothers have been hanging around the infirmary since dawn, clamouring to undertake his funeral."

The assistant, distaste evident on his face, regarded the remains.

"Aye, I will, Doctor," he said, "Even for this place, he ain't too bonny!"

They turned then to the all-too familiar corpse of Sir Douglas Lowther. His eyelids had been slid over the reflections of Hell beneath, and his screaming, gaping mouth pushed mercifully shut. He looked a little less monstrous, a degree more human than they remembered. Indeed, he appeared almost as if he were smiling, perhaps in satisfaction at their now redoubled determination to find his killer.

"You both saw him shortly after the servant had brought him back to the Tower, I am told?" The inflection in Dr Hickson's voice turned his statement into a question.

Behind him Atticus nodded and said: "Yes."

"Rigor mortis had already set in," Lucie added. "There were signs of garrotting and obstruction of the gullet, and he has wounds identical to Elliott's across his upper abdomen."

"So I have read in Mr Robson's notes. Perhaps Sir Douglas will be missing his heart too. It was the heart of a lion by all accounts."

Hickson went straight to work with his bone-saw and knife, and it was quickly evident that his conjecture had been entirely correct: The heart had indeed been torn from the lion.

"It's damnably inconvenient," he observed. "With injuries such as his, the heart would have told us more than any other organ."

He hooked his thumbs learnedly into the straps of his rubber apron and stretched tall on his heels.

"As your wife will doubtless be aware, Mr Fox, there are essentially three modes of death. Those are known as *asphyxia*, *syncope* and *coma*. Our unfortunate friend here could, conceivably, have suffered any one of them. He may, for example, have died from asphyxia; either strangulation as a result of the silken ligature around his neck, or choking occasioned by that dried meat stuffing his gullet.

"He may alternatively have died from syncope: the failure of his circulatory system due to blood loss, or perhaps from the forcible removal of his heart.

"Or finally, and we cannot ignore the possibility in a case such as this, he may have died from coma. That may be defined as 'any cause effecting brain insensibility, which terminates in death'. He may have been poisoned by the dried meat, for example. We shall therefore need to remove the stomach, empty the contents into a dish and examine them for noxious substances."

He chuckled at the suddenly stricken expression on Atticus' face.

But Sir Douglas Lowther had not been poisoned. And although the pulmonary artery, the *venae cavae* and the thick veins in his neck were gorged with black, venous blood, Hickson, with an expression surprisingly akin to Atticus', had recorded the mode of death as being that of syncope. It was a technical, medical term, which politely served to hide the horrifying fact that Sir Douglas Lowther had died by having his very heart torn out.

As they walked slowly down the steps from the infirmary into the everyday normality of the outside world, with its stinking air that seemed now so fresh and reviving, Lucie said: "At times, Atticus, even I wonder about the capacity in man for atrocity. Samson Elliott was killed stone dead by the first thrust to his heart yet his murderer ripped that same heart out and sliced off his head. Sir Douglas…" Here, words failed even her. "Someone must be very cruel, or else must have hated them both very deeply."

She sighed despairingly as she slipped her arm into her husband's.

"And do you think that Mr Robson is being entirely honest with us in saying he is baffled as to the killer's identity? I mean he clearly resents our being here. I do wonder if he is a little more unwilling than unable to share his information with us."

Atticus considered the question as they began to walk.

"That is a very good point, Lucie and on balance, I believe the answer to it is that, yes, he is. I imagine the police are still floundering. They no doubt strongly suspect that Michael Britton is the murderer, but with no evidence against him other than his supposed lunacy and his admitted, but as yet unsubstantiated, possession of a sword, they can prove nothing that would satisfy the reasonable doubt of a jury."

"Despite what Sir Hugh believes," said Lucie.

"Quite so. One thing that does rather worry me however is the fact that Sir Hugh has now introduced an element of competition for them – that element being us.

Unwittingly, or otherwise, he has ensured that the police's investigation will inevitably degenerate into a race to find the culprit. I sincerely hope it doesn't lead them to prosecute the wrong person. Hanged men seldom appeal their innocence."

Lucie murmured her agreement and they walked on in thoughtful silence. Then she cried: "Do you see there, Atty? Those must be two of Sir Hugh's factories; 'Lowther Hat Makers' and 'Lowther Tannery', just beyond it."

Atticus looked.

Fronting the roadside a little way ahead of them was a pair of large, square manufactories. They rose, grey and austere, from behind a high, stone wall and he was reminded strongly of the Old Gaol by the police station. Beyond a common gateway, a North Eastern Railway delivery waggon was halted by the side of the road, the heavy horse that pulled it dozing in its harness, head drooping in the heat and one hind leg resting on a vast, iron-shod toe. A stocky driver, his billycock hat roosting precariously on the back of his head, was rolling the last of a dozen or so large, wooden barrels down a pair of planks at the rear to his mate below.

Nearby, a brace of 'factory workers in stained, leather aprons leaned against the wall, looking on. As Atticus and Lucie approached, they could see that each of the barrels had the letters 'AR' seared black into its wooden staves and underneath, branded in smaller letters, 'Alkali & Reagent Chemical Co., Jarrow'.

The driver pushed his hat forward, onto the top of his head, and called: "One dozen barrels of carrot juice and no kegs this time. You mad hatters have plenty to be getting on with now."

Laughing, he trotted down a plank to his mate.

One of the workers responded with an oath. The driver sniggered scornfully and nodded towards the Foxes.

"You'd better ha'd your tongues now; there's a lady a-coming."

The four men fell into silence and watched as Atticus and Lucie strolled by. As Atticus raised his hat and politely wished them a good day, one of the workers lifted a trembling hand to his mouth, a hand stained ochre to the wrist, and, leering baldly at Lucie, blew through his fingers. Instead of a wolf-whistle, a long stream of drool fell from his lips and clung in a glistening loop across his apron-front.

"There must be something in the water in this South Tyne Valley," Atticus muttered icily. "Madness seems to be everywhere."

Lucie could feel the stares of the men burning at her back and the sniggers and the whispers turning the air malevolent behind them.

"Why would they need barrels of carrot juice, Atticus?"

"Oh it isn't actual carrot juice in the barrels," he replied, "It's a chemical, an industrial chemical, used by hat makers to soften the animal fur before it is made into felt. Carrot juice is its nickname because that is what it happens to look very much like."

Lucie nodded. "I didn't like the waggon driver. He was cruel to call the workers 'mad hatters' to their faces. I think it a horrible expression."

"I remember reading about it somewhere, and I believe I made a note in my commonplace book. If I recollect correctly, it was used long before there ever was a hat-making industry. Back in Anglo-Saxon times, 'mad' meant 'angry' and an 'atter' was an adder. So to be 'as mad as an 'atter', was actually to be as vicious as a snake."

"He scarcely meant it that way though, Atty."

Lucie mused for a moment.

"But you're right when you say madness seems to be everywhere. And this place is so wild and so vast. I can easily understand why the detective superintendant refused Sir Hugh's request to search the moors for Uther's sword. With just four constables and a sergeant, they could search and search for years and still find nothing."

Atticus grunted his agreement.

"Notwithstanding that," he said, "and particularly after what we've just seen in the autopsy room, I believe that finding that sword will be the key to opening up this riddle. And make no mistake about it, Lucie, we need to do that at the very earliest opportunity."

CHAPTER SEVENTEEN

The compartment of their railway carriage was as stifling as an oven on the short return journey to Bardon Mill station, but neither Atticus nor Lucie had any thought to open a window. Instead they sat, side-by-side, in complete silence, each gripping the hand of the other, and birstled.

It seemed that it was only as they were carried away from Hexham and its infirmary, and after they had left the bustling distractions of the town far behind, that the full horror of what they had learned in the mortuary room had settled onto them. It had settled onto them as the coils of a serpent might settle around its prey.

Over the years they had read – indeed they had devoured – everything they could find about the notorious multiple-murderers: Leather-Apron, the Black Widows of Liverpool, Mary Ann Cotton and the like. But now they, A&L Fox, were part of a story as real and as diabolical as any of those. Their names and everything they were to do in the coming hours and days would be printed in black-and-white and sent to be read by millions. And as a result of Mr Stead's 'New Journalism', those newspapers would not only be reporting the 'when' and the 'how', they would also be asking the 'why' and, perhaps even more worryingly, the 'why not'. This was no *Lippincott's Magazine*, where the facts of the case were packaged and presented in convenient monthly serials, no quaint puzzle to be perused and discussed over coffee and dainty-cakes. There was a real flesh-and-blood murderer at large somewhere out there beyond the glass of the carriage windows, and they had no way of knowing where or when he might strike again.

The scream of the locomotive's whistle provided a perfect accompaniment to these thoughts as it shrieked its approach to the village. The familiar station buildings soon began to slip past their window, slower and slower, until they stopped.

Atticus and Lucie remained where they were, fingers entwined, utterly spent of emotion, staring through the window at the stationmaster, who was regarding them with eager interest.

"I suppose we had better alight," said Lucie as the whistle howled once more.

They stepped down wearily onto the platform where the stationmaster raised his hat. He looked as if he might have a hundred questions for them but, in the end, he only wished them a good afternoon before sending a porter scurrying off to retrieve their bicycles from the post office.

After picking at a luncheon at the Bowes Hotel, where Atticus insisted on paying a bemused but delighted landlord in full for their unoccupied room, they made their way back up the steep lane towards Shields Tower. Mindful of the doctor's remarks about Elliott's brothers, Atticus in particular was impatient to examine Samson's cottage for any clues it might contain.

CHAPTER EIGHTEEN

'Whosoever is delighted in solitude is either a wild beast or a god.'

There is a part of all men that is both bestial and divine, and so it is to be expected that every man will seek out a place where he might be alone.

The low, overgrown outcrop, its fissured face a mosaic of moss and lichen, is such a place. Over these many long years it has become his special place to be as alone as he ever can be.

He comes here each and every day. And each time he does, through a marshy hollow, which seems to have been scooped out of the fell with a pudding spoon, he always takes care to keep his mind busy. He busies it with thoughts of his love, sleeping peacefully in the cool, silent vault hidden deep within it; he busies it with recollections of the great dishonour she has brought upon him, and he busies it with meditations upon his sworn oath to the Fates.

He allows these thoughts to consume his mind completely, for if he allows it to wander, if he lets down his aegis for just an instant, such is the power of this place that the demons of the past will pour into his mind, horde upon terrible horde. The demons of the past will come upon him and they will drag him back to Hell.

Today, the harsh cry of a raven fills this hollow, which seems to have been scooped out of the fell with a pudding spoon, and interrupts his busy thoughts. Today, Hell is ruptured, and great shrieking hordes of demons swarm out to engulf him.

The hollow is the same; the crag is the same; even the call of the raven, jarring the calm serenity of the moors, is the same. But now, across the years, he hears again the soft voice of his mama and feels her warm, safe hand encircle his own.

In his other hand he has his sword – his first real sword. He is a warrior at last.

The raven cries again.

Across the years, there are three men ahead of them, standing by the narrow track that is the only way through the marshes they call the Fogy Moss. Even though he has seen but ten summers, he can somehow sense that they are feral and vicious. He feels his mama's hand squeezing his own and perceives that she too is afraid.

The men suddenly cease their whispering and watch them, smirking as they approach. He grips the handle of his sword.

"A good day to you," his mother says. Her voice sounds noble and commanding, but for the last ten years it has been his world and he can sense her fear.

The men stare and smirk and do not answer her. Her hand grips his, tighter and tighter, as they walk.

And then they are past. There is no danger after all. His mother's hand relaxes.

The sound of running feet; he hears the sound of heavy boots pounding on the path behind them, and then a scream. It is his mama. His own mama is screaming. The turf lurches up to him and lies cold against his cheek.

His mama screams again. Her screams pierce his very soul. He stirs and struggles up. There are the men, and they have his mama. They are carrying her, writhing and threshing, towards the rocks.

"No, Mama!"

She cannot reply. She is held fast, with a hand pressed tightly over her mouth. Bewildered, he looks around for someone – anyone – to help her, for someone who will make them stop. But the moors are empty, save for the raven perched on the rocks, his head cocked to one side, watching.

His sword!

He sees it, lying in a hagg. The sun glints on the blade as if it might somehow be magical. He is fully ten years old and he is a man, as fierce and as strong as his father.

The men are laughing now and jeering. His mama has been pushed to the floor. Her shoulder is bare and she is kicking out hysterically at the men, kicking at her skirts.

He is a man, a man from a long line of warriors, and he will save her. It is his duty.

He grasps the cold, wet steel and runs, screaming like Thunor himself, charging down the path to her rescue, to the rescue of his own dear mama.

And then he is caught in her eyes – eyes that are wide and full of fear. They are his whole world and they turn his rage to ice.

And as she writhes and kicks she screams words at him:

"No! Run! Get away! Get away from here!"

He stands, confused. She is his mama. Why does she want him to go? Go where? She loves him – doesn't she?

Yes! He roars the battle-cry of his forefathers and rushes at the men.

But they stand, and roar with laughter, and he stops. A hand clamps onto his wrist like a band of iron. It is hot, rough and calloused, more so even than his father's; it is like no hand he has known. The fine steel is ripped from his grasp as if it were nothing more than a toy and a face, full of hatred and fury that is beyond the ken of his ten short years, is against his own.

The mouth of mossy, broken teeth is moving, bellowing words he somehow cannot hear. He is dragged around and he feels the steel of his own sword lying cold against his throat.

The world goes silent, holding its breath. His mama stops kicking, stops writhing, and lies still. She is sobbing now, her slim, white legs stark and naked against the rich green of the moss.

And he stands, shivering, and feels his own warm piss seeping down his breeches as he watches each man take his turn.

"You must never, ever say anything about this to a single, living soul, and especially never to your father. Do you hear me? Promise me it. Promise me, now!"

She grabs him by his shoulders and shakes him and shakes him until, sobbing uncontrollably, he does promise. The men have gone now, his breeches are cold and the moors breathe once more.

"I'm fine. I'm really quite fine. These things can happen to a woman. It was unfortunate, that is all. It was a simple misfortune. I wish you hadn't seen it. It was just the will of the Fates."

But she is his whole world and he knows that she is not at all fine, that in some inexplicable way she has been broken.

She pats his head and stands, awkwardly and unsteadily. Her eyes search the line of the high cliffs of Sewingshields for anyone else who might have witnessed her misfortune. But there are none – none save for the Fates themselves, the raven and the restless spirits of this land.

It is many days before he ventures once more beyond the Edge of the World, to where the cliffs of Sewingshields fall sheer to the wild country beyond. Like his mother, and like the Emperor Hadrian before her, he knows now that those moors are fit only for the raven, for the barbarian and for the cruel, heathen gods.

His mother no longer takes him to sail his coracle around the loughs, or to catch frogs and newts in the boglands of the Fogy Moss, or even to play in the ruins of

Sewingshields Castle rising from the island there. She no longer goes anywhere or does anything except stay in her room, and weep and weep and weep.

And in his own private moments, when his father and the servants and the portraits of his ancestors cannot see him, he weeps too. He weeps for his lost blade of fine steel that has been cast away by his tormentors. He weeps for his mother's misfortune that has somehow taken away her spirit and left her a shivering slough. And he weeps because, even though he is from an ancient line of warriors, he is a pitiful coward who pissed himself when he should have been a man.

But then one day his mama does go out and it is again to the high moors of the Great Whin Sill. She calls him and takes him by the shoulders, and sobbing, she shakes him as she tells him how she can't be a prisoner for the rest of her life.

She can't. She can't. She can't.

She smoothes the tears from her red, puffy eyes; she stands up tall, and she tells him that they need to search for his little, lost sword. She tells him that she needs to face her demons.

So once more, he feels her hot, trembling hand encircle his own and together they march up the lanes and the paths towards the high crags. They march and they march, and she chatters and she chatters, faster and faster, until at last, she stops.

To the west, the silver-grey kidney bowl of the Broomlee Lough shines bright against the fell. Ahead, framed between the jagged edges of a breach made long ago in the long grey line of Hadrian's Wall, stands the low, ruined tower of Sewingshields Castle.

His mama stands, silent and perfectly still, staring at the ruins and staring at the Fogy Moss that surrounds it; staring and staring as her eyes grow red and her grip grows tighter.

"Mama," he pleads. He tries to tug his fingers from her hand. "Mama, please, you're hurting me."

She looks at him, and although he is only ten years old, she is his world and he senses her soul writhing in an unbearable agony.

She whispers: "I am so very sorry," and wraps her arms around him, shuddering as she sobs. He feels a tear, hot and wet, fall onto his cheek and mingle with his own.

"Why are you sorry, Mama?" He is suddenly deeply fearful.

His mama stretches to her full height, proud and determined once more. She walks forward, forward to the Edge of the World, forward to the brink of the cliffs, and steps off.

"Mama, my mama!" he screams and rushes after her.

And she is there, just out of reach, caught in the twisted branches of a rowan tree. She stares up at him, her face a deep, grey pit of pain and despair, and slowly slips away.

It is the next day when they find him, still clinging to the body of his cold, dead mama. She had been alive when he had scrambled down to her, sprawled limply across the rocks at the foot of the crag. But even though he had begged her, even though he had begged God himself for her not to die, he had watched as the yellow-grey mark of death had appeared on her cheek. He had watched it gradually spread over every part of her lovely face and he had listened as her gasping, tortured breaths finally ceased.

CHAPTER NINETEEN

The narrow lane that wound its way across the rolling hillside was stony and uneven and deeply rutted by the wheels of countless carts plying to-and-fro through the winter mud. That mud was baked as hard as iron now and Atticus and Lucie were grateful indeed for the pneumatic tyres of their bicycles as they made their way towards the short terrace of cottages Sir Hugh had pointed out the previous day.

As the cottages came, at last, into view, the faint sound of angry voices was carried to them on the afternoon breeze. They cast glances of alarm to each other and Atticus reached under the crossbar of his bicycle for the reassuring presence of his walking cane.

The voices grew steadily louder and became three, and very soon they came upon their source: two men facing one other in an obviously heated altercation across the lane in front of the cottages.

The one they recognised immediately as John Lawson, Sir Hugh Lowther's land steward, but the two others were unknown to them. A large heap of smashed furniture and other household articles lay spread across the grass by the neat, little end-cottage – the very same cottage that until so recently had been occupied by Samson Elliott.

"What is going on here, Mr Lawson?" Atticus called as they braked to a halt. The argument abruptly ceased and the two strangers rounded on the Foxes.

"Who are you? Are you this Colonel Lowther?" snarled the older and larger of the men. He pushed his thumbs behind the lapels of his jacket and swelled like a blowfish.

Atticus reached down and eased his cane free from its clips on the crossbar. He met the man's gaze steadily.

"No, sir, my name is Fox. I am a privately-commissioned detective working on the Colonel's behalf, as is my wife."

He met the man's glare before turning to Lawson. "What is going on?" he repeated.

The land steward stepped forward, still glowering at his antagonists, and tugged respectfully at the brim of his hat.

"I heard the sound of banging and crashing, just as if the very Devil himsel' were here, Mr Fox, and I hurried across to find these two fellows. They were turning ower Sam Elliott's cottage and breaking up his things like they were the Bristol rioters."

"I see," said Atticus, "You gentlemen being kinsmen of Mr Elliott, I presume?"

"Aye, we're his brothers, his flesh and blood, and we're 'ere to see to him and his things as is proper. You ain't going to stop us neither, Mister, even if you are the law."

"I am neither the law nor do I have any intention of stopping you, Mr Elliott," Atticus replied, "although Mr Lawson here may well have."

He turned back to the land steward.

"Let me explain what these men are about, Mr Lawson. Rest assured they are not rioters. You see, it is a Gypsy custom that once one of their fellows dies, all of their possessions must immediately be destroyed and burnt to ashes. Unless they do so, they believe that the deceased's spirit may return and reclaim the property as their own. Their body is usually cremated inside their caravan."

Lawson looked aghast.

"What sort of heathen, ungodly practice is that for this day and age?"

"A very ancient one," Atticus replied, "and one with some practical merit to it too. *Exempli gratia* – for example – if it happened to be a disease or an infection that had precipitated the Gypsy's death, the germs would likely be destroyed in the flames and therefore prevented from being passed on to infect others."

Lawson shook his head defiantly. "That's as may be, Mr Fox, but they were breaking the Colonel's property along with Elliott's."

"Then that is easily remedied with a simple compromise. I suggest you accompany the brothers Elliott into the cottage, explain to them how it is tied to the Lowther estate and point out exactly what is estate property and what belonged to Samson. They may then, of course, dispose of that in whatever way they see fit."

Lawson glanced around doubtfully at the strewn debris. "It still doesn't sound right to me, Mr Fox, but aye, I'm willing to do as you suggest."

Atticus turned next to the two brothers and said: "Your brother's vardo is being retained as evidence by order of the police. You must get the permission of Detective Superintendant Robson at Hexham police station before you may touch that. His body is held by the Hexham coroner but I understand it is due for release."

He then addressed all three.

"We are here at Sir Hugh Lowther's personal expense in order to ascertain exactly who is responsible for Samson Elliott's murder. Before anyone else goes in there, Mrs Fox and I must first examine his cottage for any clues which might aid us in that endeavour."

"Mind you don't take nothing of his," the elder brother warned.

"You have our word on it," Atticus assured him, and then on a sudden whim asked: "Tell me; how did you find out about your brother's death so quickly?"

"It were right easy. This Sir Hugh Lowther has kinfolk in Westmorland – gentry, the same as he. He sent word over to them and they sent one of their servants down to Appleby with the news. We were there for the Horse Fair. It was where poor Samson was bound when he was butchered to death." The brother hesitated. "They told us the one doing the butchering was a madman that lives hereabouts."

"That we don't yet know for sure." Atticus' response was guarded.

"Come on, Mister Detective or whatever y' are, it was him all right. Once we've sorted out Samson's affairs here, we'll be going to pay a little visit on this madman. You never know, with a little bit of persuasion, we might just be able to get him to admit to what he's done. It'll spare you the bother and it'll save old Lowther a lot of – ah – personal expense."

Atticus was horrified.

"No, Mr Elliott, you must not! We have a system of justice in Great Britain, which is the admiration of the world. It declares that a man must be considered wholly innocent of a crime until, and unless, he is proven guilty in a court of law before a jury of his peers. That principle is sacrosanct and you must never, ever take matters into your own hands."

The brother allowed his eyes to slowly rake Atticus up and down, lingering for an instant on the thick, pewter and ebony walking cane he gripped so tightly in his fist.

"Well ooh-la for Great Britain! So why don't you, and your toffer wife, take a note from your own lecture and go back to where you came from?"

"But my husband and I are not taking the law into our own hands, Mr Elliott." Atticus was glad of Lucie's cutting-in, and for the fact that she could remain mannerly in the face of such rank impudence. Like the drumming before a firebox explosion, a steady tick below his ear was signalling wildly that at any moment, his carefully worded arguments were liable to boil over into a vitriolic spewing of bile.

"We are properly commissioned investigators," Lucie went on, "who are scientifically examining the facts of the case. Our conclusions will then be presented, in the correct manner, firstly to the constabulary and then after that to an appointed judge and jury."

"Well our way is quicker and surer and we don't need science, nor a big, fancy bag."

The brother leered at her.

"I wouldn't mind taking you along with us though, my darling. We could do with a bit of sweet company to help us pass the time. How would you like a tasty titbit of Gypsy? They say we're much in demand amongst the fine ladies hereabouts."

He smirked at his brother.

Atticus' glare was murderous now.

"Be warned, Elliott; you go too far!"

The other snorted his contempt and allowed his gaze to creep down Lucie's figure. Atticus sidestepped to shield her and Elliott's eyes flickered up, mocking in their expression.

"Look at this, Elliott," Atticus growled, "We took a plaster-of-Paris casting of a boot print close to where the body of your brother was discovered."

Reaching inside his investigations bag, he carefully lifted out the cast and held it up for the brothers to see.

"What in God's name sort of boot is that?" Their baiting forgotten, the two brothers stared in astonishment.

"It is called a sabaton and it was the armoured footwear of a knight of the Dark Ages. Uther Pendragon, the madman to whom you refer, is not able to venture much out of his cottage at present because of the fragility of his mind, but did Samson ever tell you about the legend of King Arthur?"

The brothers nodded in unison and almost comically, their mouths falling wide like the audience at the most convincing phantasmagoria.

"I, of course, do not really believe those stories, but many do. Many folk believe that your brother's killing was the work not of the lunatic at all but of the spectre of King Arthur, awoken from the spirit realm."

He tapped the cast softly with the heavy end of his cane.

"This plaster impression would seem to support that notion. There are those who would hesitate before venturing up towards the moors of Sewingshields at present. They might well be afraid of who, or what, might find them there."

The older brother crossed himself and the other seemed to be trying to swallow. Even John Lawson looked visibly shaken.

"We will leave you to your work then," said Atticus, "I wish a good day to you all."

He put his arm around Lucie's waist and shepherded her around the still-transfixed brothers and into the doorway of the tiny cottage.

CHAPTER TWENTY

The waters of the lough, urged on by the stiff, moorland wind, reach and grasp at his feet as he stands, frozen, at its edge. Memories of the place reach and grasp at his mind, tearing it and clawing it open.

He is fourteen now, a warrior from a long line of warriors. His father is beside him and his voice is sharp and rebuking.

"Your mother is dead. She has been for nigh on four years now and no amount of blubbing or wailing will cure it or bring her back. Get a grip of yourself, boy! I don't like it any more than you do. If I could have taken her place I would, but I can't, and what's done is done.

'It was the will of the Fates. That's all, boy. *Quo Fata vocant*, it was the will of the Fates."

"No, Father, you're wrong!"

His cry carries over the lake. The myriad fowl resting on its surface hear it and take to the skies, taking his agony and proclaiming it to the four corners of the kingdom.

Like Sir Bedivere of the Sinews, he hurls his blade of fine steel out to the spirit of the water and runs and runs and runs. He flees the memories as they come to rip his mind to pieces.

And then, in the time it takes to fall from the crag-top to the rocks beneath, again and again and again, he is there. He is there, as he always is there, at Sewingshields, where yesterday, a thousand years ago, he had pissed himself whilst the demons took turns at his mama. He stops and through his agony, he prays.

At chapel they say there is but one God, and that His name is Jehovah. But his father and the old men of the estate have told him of others; of Woden, of Thunor and of Tiw – gods with fierce, Nordic names that seem somehow more real in this wild, bleak land. And his father has told him too of the Fates, who are the Norns, the Sisters of the Wyrd, who know the soul of every man.

And because, like every man, he is in thrall to the Fates, it is to them that he prays.

"Please, Norns, please bring back my mama, or else take my soul too. Please help me because I cannot bear this for another, single day. Amen."

Amen.

So be it.

And because this place is a sacred and special one, the Sisters of the Wyrd, the Norns, hear his words.

Against the outcrop, in the deep shadows of the hollow, which seems to have been scooped out of the fell with a pudding spoon, a spectre, a wisp of mist, delicate and ethereal hangs in the air. Can it be – surely it must be – the shade of his mama. He runs to it, his feet splashing and slipping in the freezing water of the haggs, staggering like a man drunk, and embraces it, trying and trying to gather it into his arms.

But wait! It is seeping from the very heart of the rock itself, through the ivy that clothes it.

He reaches out for his mama, pushing his arm through the tangled vegetation as if it is the Veil of Death. But as far as his arm can stretch, his grasping hands touch nothing. Puzzled, he delves and burrows into the ivy. It parts like a curtain to reveal a deep, black void that stretches back into infinitude.

Fingers of chilly air reach out to take hold of him and he shivers. For fourteen summers he has played here. Fourteen summers, and he never knew of this cavern hidden away behind the ivy.

There is a stone on the ground by the entrance. It is regular and square such as those the castle is built from and upon it are some objects. He stoops down to them. There is a flint strike-a-light, fashioned in bronze, a gaily-painted tinderbox and beside them, a large votive candle laced all around with a fretwork of wax.

Just a minute later and with trembling hands he has the candle lit. The flickering, yellow light dances on the walls of the cavern and stabs deeply into the black heart of the rock.

He walks forward, following the fiery ring as it draws him on, deeper and deeper. And then, in the utter stillness of the place, silent but for the thrashing of his heart, a voice screams out:

"Coward!"

He drops to the floor like a man shot, and the candle drops with him, spilling its wax and extinguishing itself and plunging him into blackness.

The voice screams again.

"*You are nothing but a coward!*"

The word is thrown back and forth, back and forth, for an age, between the pressing walls of the cave.

And then there is silence.

"Who is it? Who are you?" His whispered questions sound unnatural, high and strained, otherworldly somehow.

"*Who are you? Who are you?*" A different voice is speaking now – a mocking voice. "*Who are we, he asks us. We are the Norns, boy, the ones your father told you of. She is Urth – my sister – and I am Verthandi.*"

"*And I am Skuld.*" This third voice is younger, kinder perhaps, than the others. In fact, even through his terror, it reminds him not a little of his dear, dead mama.

"What…what do you want of me?" Even as he asks, he already knows what their answer will be.

"*We want your soul.*" The first voice, Urth's, says it. Her tone is cold and harsh and it crackles with contempt.

"*You offered it, fair and square. Don't you remember – in your prayer to us? We have accepted your terms and now the bargain has been struck.*"

"*You cannot go back on your word.*" It is Verthandi again. "*Not now. What would your father say to that? Your word is your honour, a runt's honour without question, but still your honour.*"

"*My Sister is correct*," said Urth. "*And it was us who sent the men to violate your mama. It was her misfortune, but it was your fault. You were the one who made it her wyrd – her fate. We punished her because she was the one who brought you into the world.*

"*You stood and you pissed yourself, and you did nothing. Your father gave you a sword, yet you repaid him by casting it away – just as you cast it away this day and begged us for your mama.*

"*Do you want her to come back and sing you lullabies whilst you suck on her big, white tits? Like the three men sucked on her tits?*

"*No! She knew that she had brought a craven runt into this world and she knew the only honourable path for her was to give us back her soul.*"

"Please…"

"*We will not bring back your mama.*" Skuld's words crushed him utterly. "*So, as you asked, we have taken your own soul instead.*"

"*We,*" said Verthandi simply, "*Possess you now.*"

"No!" It is too much for him to bear. For the second time that day he screams and he runs. But he knows, as the laughter shrieks in his ears, louder and louder and louder, that he did indeed ask and that now, it is too late.

There will be no escape – not ever.

CHAPTER TWENTY-ONE

When they ducked under the low, crooked lintel of the doorway and found themselves in the tiny parlour-kitchen of Samson Elliott's cottage, Atticus and Lucie Fox's first impression was one of having just walked into a child's kaleidoscope. Everything, from the pots and pails hanging from the ceiling to the trinkets on the walls, were brightly, even gaudily, painted in almost every colour imaginable. It was a larger version of the vardo in the home farm barn.

"It's so pretty." Lucie's eyes were wide as they crept assiduously around the little room and registered every detail. "Who do you suppose that lady is?" she added after a moment, "She is very beautiful."

Atticus followed the direction of her gaze. On a mantelshelf above the freshly blacked fireplace was a photograph. It was a small photograph, contained in a delicate, silver picture-frame that contrasted sharply with the rustic wood and iron of its surroundings. The subject was a tall and elegant young woman in traditional Gypsy dress.

Atticus gave a start. The dress the woman was wearing was the very same dress they had found in Elliott's caravan. He was sure of it.

"It is the dress from the vardo, isn't it?" Lucie voiced his thoughts.

Atticus picked up the frame.

"I believe it is, but as to the lady, I really have no clue as to who she might be. She is, as you say, quite striking."

He considered for a moment.

"Elliott was never married, as far as we know, so might she be his sister perhaps? She does seem somehow familiar."

He turned the frame over and twisted the tiny clips holding the plate.

"There is a date given on the back of the photograph: October, 1867."

Lucie nodded. "So she would be about the right age. That would make sense, I suppose. Why should Elliott have her dresses in his caravan though – unless she is dead?"

She watched as Atticus carefully placed the photographic plate back into the frame and then she glanced around once more at the contradiction of perfect order and partial ransack.

"Nothing else seems out of the ordinary here, with the obvious exception of the mess the brothers have caused."

Atticus bit his lip. "I kick myself over that, Lucie. I was well aware of the Gypsy traditions but I fancied we would have had more time before his brothers arrived."

He shrugged.

"But I agree with you; nothing particularly excites my suspicions here. Once we have satisfied ourselves as to the rest of the house, we can leave it all to them to do as they wish and Samson Elliott's spirit can finally go to its peace. We really don't want any more spectres returning from the Kingdom of the Dead."

CHAPTER TWENTY-TWO

The very instant Atticus and Lucie Fox slipped back between the great, carven doors of Shields Tower they were hailed by a ruddy-faced Sir Hugh Lowther thundering down the grand stairs towards the accusing finger of Urth.

"Halloa, Fox! You're back from your expeditions at last, I see. About bloody time! Collier has orders to bring tea directly you get back. You can join me in the garden room and bring me up to the present on your progress."

He steadied himself on the hand of Skuld, the nearest of the Norns, as he rounded the foot of the stairs and then strode towards a pretty, stained-glass door. Atticus and Lucie followed him gladly – the prospect of afternoon tea had never seemed so welcome.

The garden room of Shields Tower was in fact a small but exceedingly handsome orangery, whose glazed lights afforded stunning views out towards the moors. Potted lime and orange trees were set around, together with several comfortable wicker settees. Once they had taken their seats Atticus related the highlights of their long day, beginning with his discovery of the sabaton prints in the cornfield and ending with the altercation between John Lawson and the two brothers Elliott.

"I rather fear that they hold Michael Britton responsible for their brother's death," he explained, "and I have few doubts but that they will try to take revenge. They are Gypsies, so they will view it as a matter of honour. I believe I may have put them off venturing anywhere near to his cottage for the present but I suggest it would be prudent to send a constable to warn them off too, just to make certain of it."

Sir Hugh regarded him shrewdly for a while before he answered.

"Very well, Fox, I'll make that request directly. Madman or not, I certainly wouldn't want Britton to die at the hands of Gypsies."

The fleeting shadow of what might have been pain passed over his face before he rose suddenly from his chair.

"If you would both excuse me, I shall go and make the call on my telephone now."

A quarter-hour or so later, there was a gentle tap on the door, the brass knob twisted and a parlour maid entered the orangery carrying a tea service. Sir Hugh was following close behind her.

"I've done as you suggested, Fox," he boomed. "The constable from Millhouse is on his way to Elliott's cottage now to warn 'em off Britton –if he can get past the Fox and Hounds that is. The man's a habitual drunkard."

"Very good, Sir Hugh, thank you."

Atticus stood and passed him the plaster impression of the sabaton. "By-the-by, you might be interested in this; it's the cast we spoke about."

"By Jove, but this is splendid work, Fox," Lowther exclaimed in delight. He turned it over and over in his hands. "It's the very ticket; it couldn't be better. Why couldn't the police have done this, eh? That's what I should like to know. Now we have a cast of the boot. What did you call it again?"

"It's called a sabaton, Sir Hugh. It's part of a knight's armour."

"But have you been able to match it to the rest?" Lowther looked up searchingly from the cast, his eyes dancing now with excitement. "You said that you had already been to Britton's."

"We did call on him, Sir Hugh," Atticus confirmed. "And we did speak with him at some length, but that was whilst the cast was hardening and he was much too distressed for us to think of returning straight away."

"Too distressed, my arse!" Lowther retorted. "What is he, a man or a bloody little girl?"

He grunted irritably.

"You're damned fortunate you spoke to him at all, mind you. He'll usually see no one – at least no one he doesn't already know very well. He hides from 'em, by gad. Can you believe that? His doctor claims it's his illness makes him do it, but how the deuce can that be, eh? To my mind, he's either an impudent scoundrel, or a coward, or more likely yet, both!"

He glared, as if daring them to challenge him. When they chose not to, he continued: "Anyway in the second room of that mouldering pile of rubble he calls his home, Britton keeps a suit of armour. My first wife gave it to him in appreciation of that damned fresco he painted for her on the wall of your guest room."

"We saw it, Sir Hugh."

"Good! I'm pleased you've seen it, Fox because then you will also have seen the collection of oddments he keeps in there too. He believes them to be relics from King Arthur's time and he calls them the Hallows or some such nonsense."

He looked cannily between Atticus and Lucie.

"I'll wager you a guinea to a button that this cast will match perfectly the...the sabatons of that armour."

"We quite intend to compare the two at the earliest opportunity," Lucie assured him.

"Excellent! Then we are close to being able to arrest him for murder." Sir Hugh's eyes were suddenly dancing again.

Atticus could not altogether decide whether Sir Hugh's remark was a question or a statement so he said: "We are moving ever closer to being able to identify our murderer, yes. Whether that will turn out to be Michael Britton or some other person, it is yet too early to say for certain."

Lucie watched Lowther's colour rising up and flushing his cheeks and, just as he opened his mouth to bellow his protestations, she deflected the conversation.

"Sir Hugh, tell me a little more about Sewingshields Castle. Mr Britton seems to be quite obsessed by it."

He stared open-mouthed at her for several seconds before he snarled his reply.

"Sewingshields Castle – that old pile of rubble? It wasn't much of a castle when it stood. I only ever remember it as a ruin surrounded by clarts and mire. Didn't I tell you it was supposed to have been built on the site of an earlier castle which belonged to King Arthur? Camelot, some say it was.

"Britton, when he fell back into lunacy and started to believe again that he was Uther Pendragon, became, as you so rightly say, obsessed with it. Whatever the weather, he spent day and night there, clambering over the ruins and wandering about the moors and the marshes.

"I eventually prevailed on my neighbour, who happened to own the site, to let me have it demolished and the stones taken away. Fortunately he was a distant relative of mine. My ancestor, Sir Robert de Lowther, once owned a castle that was abandoned by his nephew in favour of Sewingshields, do you see? If I hadn't had it removed, Britton would surely have perished there from exposure, or else fallen to his death from the cliffs."

He closed his eyes.

"Perhaps it might have been better for him if he had."

Lucie asked: "On the morning of Elliott's murder, did you by any chance hear the sound of a bugle coming from the direction of Sewingshields?"

"A bugle, Lucie? No, I bloody-well did not."

His eyes popped open.

"Although I can guess who's prompted you to ask. Our madman's been hearing bugles calling for months."

Atticus set down his teacup with a clatter.

"Britton said that. And he told us the bugle calls had been getting louder and more frequent of late. Sir Hugh, do you know for how long he has been hearing them and, to the best of your knowledge, how frequently?"

Sir Hugh seemed momentarily taken aback by the intensity of Atticus' question. "He's certainly been hearing them since I returned from the Black Mountains expedition with the Fifth. He says he hears the bugle every week these days. As you say, it is becoming more frequent with time.

"It seems to me that his condition is deteriorating almost by the day and I've insisted that his physician, Dr Hickson of Hayden Bridge – another rank fool – calls on him regularly, as he used to do before Artie was born."

He smiled fiercely.

"I see myself as Britton's guardian, do you see, Lucie? I watch over him and ensure I am fully acquainted with the progress of his condition."

"You do seem admirably concerned, Sir Hugh," Atticus observed.

"I am, Fox, I'm very concerned, as I am for all those attached in some way to me, or mine. I'm a guardian to the whole damned lot of 'em. In fact, I'm a sort of Norn myself – a fourth Norn – in that, to a large degree, I help to decide their fate. It's the reason I commissioned your services in the first place and the reason I sit here now, asking how close you are to solving this puzzle and proving that Britton is the murderer."

Atticus sipped his tea as he considered Sir Hugh's words.

"We remain at the early stages of our investigation. So far as Britton is concerned, the evidence against him might appear damning at first sight, but a Justice of Assize might well take the view that it is entirely circumstantial. Murder investigations in particular have more twists and turns in them than the road to Paradise and it is quite possible that the murderer may turn out to be someone else entirely."

"Well I'm convinced it is all perfectly straightforward and the bloody madman needs to be hanged," Sir Hugh blustered. "He's obsessed by the legends of Arthur; both murders took place close-by his cottage and he's had a sword in there since the day he moved into it."

He held up the cast.

"Now you even have this. And make no mistake, you will find it matches exactly the armour he keeps in his own bedroom. Blast and damnation, man, it seems to me that the evidence, as you call it, circum-bloody-stantial or not, is impossible to deny."

"Yet it is still not entirely conclusive, Sir Hugh. Please do not misunderstand us; Britton may well have committed the murders and indeed, it is very likely that he has, but we cannot send a man to the gallows without proof-absolute."

Sir Hugh stared into his half-empty tea cup.

"So what would you consider to be absolute proof, Fox?"

"Well, it is a great pity that we haven't yet found the sword," Atticus replied. "Mrs Fox is something of an expert in the comparison of fingertip prints. We could have compared any prints she might have found on the sword with those of our suspects, including Michael Britton of course."

Lowther looked up and fixed an enquiring stare onto Atticus.

"Fingertip prints? I don't understand you."

"Then allow me to explain." Atticus began to purr like a cat as he warmed to his subject. "Mrs Fox uses a technique, which she first read about almost ten years ago in a scientific journal called *Nature*. It was by the learned Dr Henry Faulds, who suggested that the close examination of fingertip prints, which incidentally are entirely unique to each person, may be used to prove beyond doubt who has recently touched or handled an object."

Sir Hugh smiled in what must surely have been wonderment.

"What an age we live in these days, eh, where everything is governed by science. And how very ingenious of Lucie and Dr Faulds; it will soon be impossible to commit a crime at all."

He chortled briefly and stared again at the cast.

"Tell me: would it be useful if I were to fetch Britton's doctor over to speak to you regarding his condition? You could satisfy yourselves at first-hand about his propensity for murder."

Atticus deferred to Lucie who said: "It would be very useful indeed, Sir Hugh, but only on the strict condition that you first obtain Mr Britton's full and free permission for the doctor to do so."

Sir Hugh frowned.

"But Britton is mad. What would be the point of obtaining his permission?" He shrugged and before she could make reply said: "But very well, very well, I'll ride over to speak with Britton directly we finish this tea. I need to warn him about Elliott's brothers anyway, and suggest he be on his guard for a while. Now, Hickson is due to attend upon my daughter tomorrow morning. She's still on sick call, do you see? I'll insist he stays for luncheon and after that, we can all sit down and discuss Britton's state of mind."

It was Lucie's turn to frown.

"I'm sorry to hear that your daughter is still poorly. It seems strange because she looked well, radiant even, when we first met her yesterday afternoon, but then by dinner she had sickened. She must have declined very quickly during the course of the day."

"Thank you, Lucie. Your concern is welcomed. And you're correct too; it does seem to come and go. She won't have the sawbones examine her though. Why, I cannot imagine. It's probably the Lowther streak of stubbornness running true in her veins. But it's gone on for far too long now and I've insisted that he does."

"What are her symptoms? You know I have been a nurse."

Sir Hugh shrugged.

"Yes, well let me see now; what did Bessie tell me? She's been having frequent bouts of sickness – spewing like a bilge-pump actually – and she's been very tired too, and tearful. Not at all what one would expect from a Lowther. We're made of sterner stuff than that. It's probably from spending too much time with Artie."

"We had intended to put questions to both Master Artie and Miss Jennifer tomorrow," Atticus remarked. "I do hope she's well enough for that."

Sir Hugh flushed crimson.

"Put questions to them? Put questions to them, but what the devil for, Fox?" he snapped. "Surely to God you can't think them responsible for the murders? My father was their own grandfather, don't forget. They doted on him."

"My husband and I consider it almost unimaginable that they had anything to do with the murders, Sir Hugh." Lucie's ready smile was disarming. "But, as always, we need to apply a scientific methodology to our investigation. As well as the identification of the guilty, that means also the vindication of the innocent. It is also quite possible that they might be able to add something, even the tiniest particle of information, that could lead us more surely and swiftly to the real culprit."

"To Michael-deuced-Britton," Sir Hugh snarled but then he nodded curtly.

"Very well, then you have my permission to ask them whatever is necessary."

CHAPTER TWENTY-THREE

The next day again promised to be a hot and cloudless one. The sun had long since simmered the night mists from the face of the moors when, shortly after breakfast, Atticus and Lucie left on their bicycles to visit the site of Sewingshields Castle. Their intention was to return to Shields Tower only after the doctor had been to attend on Jennifer but in good time for luncheon. Lucie in particular had a number of questions she was anxious to put to him.

Sir Hugh had returned late the previous night triumphantly brandishing a sheet of paper footed by Uther Pendragon's neat signature. This gave his full and free permission for Dr Hickson to discuss his mental condition with Sir Hugh, with the Foxes, or indeed with the Devil, himself, should he wish to do so.

It was amongst the stones of a tumbled-down turret of Hadrian's Wall that Atticus and Lucie left their bicycles. They paused for a while at the cliff's edge to gaze out over the silver pool of the Broomlee Lough before picking their way with mounting excitement to the brooding fells below.

This setting of wild moorland, rocky crags and glistening silver-blue lakes was nothing short of breathtaking. The castle, legendary fortress of the Knights of the Round Table, must surely be even more so. They stood and scanned the broad vista before them. It would be a ruin, they knew, but, as Lucie remarked, surely there could be no more romantic ruin in all of England.

James the footman had obligingly sketched them a pencil map of the area and Atticus held it up against the landscape.

Yes, there were the Sewingshields Crags looming high at their backs. The loughs were accurately plotted, each in its allotted place. Here was the Fogy Moss and its island of firmer ground on which a vast, fairy-tale castle should be standing. But no, nothing whatever remained of Sewingshields Castle, bar a stagnant pond, an echo of the earthworks and an overgrown smattering of rubble. Sheep now grazed where once proud walls must have stood, their strength long since smashed by the Scots and Sir Hugh Lowther, and their stones parasitized by generations of farmers and villagers for cottages, laithes and dry stone walls.

Lucie confided her disappointment to Atticus.

"If you recollect, Sir Hugh did tell us that he'd demolished what were left of the ruins," he reminded her gently.

"I know, Atty, but it seems such an enormous shame that the last resting place of our greatest ever king should be so…so ordinary, and hidden under rough marshland, unmarked and anonymous."

"If it really is his last resting place."

When his wife's expression of dismay turned to puzzlement, Atticus went on: "Perhaps that is precisely what makes him such a big part of our folklore. There is no marked grave, so therefore, perhaps there is no body. If there is no body, perhaps in turn, there was no death. And if there was no death, then maybe, just maybe, we could believe that King Arthur and Lady Guinevere will indeed return at the 'End of Days' to defeat the White Dragon, just as legend promised they would."

Lucie squeezed his arm.

"Atticus Fox, I do declare you're sounding almost romantic."

She glanced around and her smile withered.

"There is something about this place though, Atty, something…eerie. It is as if we are being watched by some great malevolent force."

She shivered.

"I don't like it here. You really don't want to go searching for this vault, do you?"

Atticus smiled.

"So we can awaken King Arthur and ask him directly if he committed the murders? No, I have already seen all I need to."

"Then do you mind if we leave? Perhaps we could go back early to Shields? If we cannot talk to King Arthur, then at least we could speak with his namesake – even if his sister is still with her doctor."

Atticus scratched thoughtfully at the whiskers on his chin and said: "Even if Guinevere's namesake is still with her doctor, don't you mean?"

Seeing his wife's bemusement, he explained: "The name 'Artie', as you already know, is a pet form of 'Arthur'."

Lucie nodded.

"Well 'Jennifer,'" Atticus continued, "is the modern form of the old Celtic name 'Guinevere'."

"Is it really?" Lucie exclaimed, "How very curious."

She stared again at the loose lines of rubble littering the turf in front of them.

"Do you think there might be a link then, Atty; Artie masquerading as the returned King Arthur, and Jennifer as Lady Guinevere? After all, Jennifer did say, and she said it in deadly earnest, that the resurrected King Arthur was the killer."

Atticus bit his lip and the question was left hanging and unanswered as they picked their way back through the marsh grasses to the towering escarpment, their bicycles and the narrow road that was their route back to Shields Tower.

He watches the figures weaving their way through the Fogy Moss as he stands, silent and perfectly still, atop the high crags of Sewingshields. That is his place, his own sacred place, and they have no business defiling it with their presence.

"My Ladies?" he asks of the air around him. He speaks just loud enough to summon the spirits from their secret places, but not so much that his voice might carry down to the marshes below. And he bows his head in obeisance. It is always well to be respectful.

Fittingly it is Skuld who answers him and in her great wisdom she has anticipated his question.

"You ask what is to be done with the mortal man Atticus Fox once his wife is given to you. The answer is quite

simple: He must die. He will be the seventh and final part of your gift to us."

He is confused now.

"But the seven have been chosen already. They are—"

"No!" Urth's harsh cry scythes through his mind. *"Lancelot's death was your will, not ours. You slew him yourself for seducing your woman."*

"And we ourselves allowed him to do it." Another voice growls from the ancient stones around him. It is Verthandi's. *"To punish you for doing nothing – NOTHING – as your mother stepped from these cliffs."*

"Do I kill him now, my Lady Verthandi," he asks, swallowing the rebuke. "It would be fitting to do it here, at Sewingshields."

"Not yet: You already have your orders," Verthandi snarls and he cowers from her wrath.

"Two have fallen," Urth says, after a moment.

"Four must fall this day," Verthandi adds, calmer now.

"And one will fall in days to come." Skuld finishes the pronouncement. *"And Atticus Fox will be that seventh and final part of the wergild."*

He bows his head lower yet. They are the Sisters of the Wyrd, the Norns, who carve the fate of every man, and every god.

Quo Fata Vocant.

The Sisters know the soul of every man, living or dead, but they honour him alone by deigning to speak to him.

Sometimes when he hears their voices, so clear and so masterful, speaking from nowhere, speaking from everywhere, he marvels at how those around him cannot hear them too. It is a privilege above words to be called by the Fates, but sometimes, he is compelled to admit, it is a privilege too great for mortal man to carry.

His father once told him that he too served the Fates and that he too was bound to go wherever they called him.

Quo Fata Vocant.

But when, one day, he proudly told his father that the Fates spoke to him in voices of flesh and blood, he had laughed. He had laughed just as Urth might laugh.

His father had said that the voices were false, that perhaps he was overtired, or had fallen to opium or liquor. But he knew better and they did speak to him. They did. How could they be false when they knew so much, when they could read even his most intimate thoughts?

His father had laughed, but not for long. The very next day he had taken him to Fenham, to the regimental barracks, where a holy man discreetly sprinkled him with water and muttered strange words over him.

But Fenham is in Northumberland too and the Norns in their turn had laughed as the blessed drops splashed his skin. They had mocked the Chaplain trying to cast them forth in the name of Jesus such that they made him giggle and his father had been obliged to take him behind the barrack huts and thrash him with his cane.

And as he stands, silent and perfectly still, watching from the high crags of Sewingshields, he smiles again at what they told him the Chaplain did each night on Newcastle's Town Moor. But the memory is fleeting and he turns his mind once more to the present.

Before him, the silver ribbon of the Grindon Lough draws his gaze across to the land beyond the vallum, that vast Roman earthwork which shadows the Wall, to a road. There, in the far distance, a pony gig turns off, just as he knew it would, towards a second, more ancient road running parallel to the first. This is the Stanegate, the old 'stone road', built by Agricola. It had doubtless witnessed countless deaths over the centuries it had lain straddling this land. What would be one more?

He thinks again of his true love, beautiful in repose in her grotto over the Wall, and feels black hatred for the driver of that gig.

'Two must fall this day.'

His horse is waiting, impatiently pawing the ground. Perhaps it too can hear the call of the Norns. He gives it its head and, like *Sleipnir* itself, it carries him swiftly over the ground.

And then, in the time it takes for love to be betrayed he is there, at the cottage, with its dragon of blood on the door.

It opens before him and he beholds his enemy, he beholds Hickson, smiling the secret smile of a serpent.

Hickson holds out his hand, his treacherous mouth is speaking.

No, Pendragon is not here, he hides on the moors like the coward he is. But the doctor must not know that.

He steps through the door and smiles his own warm smile of greeting. He invites the doctor to sit, to wait, to have perhaps a goblet, a chalice, a Grail of wine.

And he smiles once more as he pours it.

Whither the Fates Call.

He smiles because this wine is poison. It is Atropos'. Atropos the Inflexible, the Inevitable, the Bringer of Death, as Skuld also is the Bringer of Death and as too is he. The grape is not grape, but poison berries.

The doctor drinks and drinks again.

At long last, it is done.

Skuld has called for the debt of his life to be repaid and it is fitting that Hickson should know it. With a snarl of triumph, he holds out the berries and says their name.

"Belladonna".

CHAPTER TWENTY-FOUR

"Mr Collier, has the doctor finished with Miss Jennifer yet, do you know?" Atticus asked the butler as they passed him in the great hall.

Collier's starched expression eased a fraction. It was rare above stairs for anyone to address him as 'Mister'.

"No, sir, I fear he has not even arrived yet, which is rather strange because he is usually very punctual, very punctual indeed."

He nodded towards a large grandfather clock standing sentinel against the wall. "I once set that clock by Dr Hickson's visit, Mr Fox, and that is God's honest truth."

Atticus hesitated.

"In that case, do you think it possible that Miss Jennifer might be well enough to answer some informal questions while she waits for him?"

"She is, Mr Fox, quite well enough," said a softer voice from behind them.

Atticus and Lucie turned to see Jennifer Lowther smiling bleakly at them from the stairs. She was clinging to the arm of a concerned-looking Artie.

"I am just a little tired, that is all," she continued, "What with poor Grandpapa and Elliott and all. Shall we go into the garden room?"

She led them wearifully through into the orangery, where, once they were all comfortably seated, Atticus said: "You must of course break off directly the doctor arrives, or if you begin to feel unwell again. We are sorry to have to ask the both of you these questions but this is a double murder enquiry and we are obliged to be as brutal as we must.

"Now, let us begin with the case of Mr Samson Elliott. Tell us: Are you both fully acquainted with the circumstances and the nature of his death?"

They both nodded and Artie said: "Of course, Mr Fox."

He reached across the arm of Jennifer's wicker chair and took her hand in his own.

Atticus glanced down at the movement. "That is convenient. Then please tell us, to the best of your recollection, where you both were on that morning of Saturday last."

It was Jennifer who answered.

"That is very easy, Mr Fox. We both rose early – around six o'clock I believe it was – breakfasted and then set off to go up to the moors. We intended to spend the whole day collecting herbs and wild plants up around Sewingshields so Bessie packed us a picnic luncheon in my wicker basket."

Lucie frowned. "But wasn't it very foggy and drizzly that day? Surely it wasn't the sort of morning to think of venturing onto the moors at all, never mind with a picnic?"

"It..." Jennifer hesitated, looking suddenly weary, and Artie took over the tale.

"We have both spent our entire lives in these parts, Mrs Fox. We know the fells and the Sill intimately and we're perfectly safe there, even in the thickest of fogs."

He grinned.

"Besides which, if you knew Northumberland, you would know that the weather can change as quickly as that that." He clicked his fingers. "As likely as not, the fog will lift before the sun rises very far. That is exactly what happened last Saturday."

Atticus asked: "Did you by any chance happen to come across the…the recluse that morning, by whom I mean Michael Britton, or Uther Pendragon as I believe he prefers to be known?"

"Uther? No, unfortunately we didn't see him."

"Why was that unfortunate?"

"Because we dearly wish we could say that we had," said Jennifer ruefully. "Then perhaps my father would stop trying to blame him for these murders."

"Amen," said Artie. He squeezed Jennifer's hand and smiled at her. "Uther might be as barmy as a fairground monkey, Mr and Mrs Fox but he is no murderer."

Atticus looked from one to the other.

"How can you be so sure of that?" he asked at last.

Jennifer seemed a little breathless when she replied.

"Because, as I said to you when we were first introduced, it was King Arthur – the awakened and returned King Arthur – who killed Mr Elliott and my grandfather, not Uther Pendragon."

Several moments of stunned silence slid past before Lucie said: "King Arthur, but surely you must be jesting with us, Miss Jennifer?"

Jennifer shook her head and held the tips of her fingers to her pursed lips.

"There is no jest, I promise you. Artie will explain it all. Please excuse me." Her voice was tight and strained and, all at once, she jumped to her feet and ran from the room.

"Will she need assistance?" Lucie asked anxiously, "If she's been taken ill, I'm a trained nurse."

Artie smiled, although, she noted, it was a deeply nervous and strained smile, which had been drained of its warmth by the deep concern in his eyes.

"No, thank you, Mrs Fox, I am certain she will be fine. I…I believe the excitement and…the heat of this garden room have made her feel a little unwell, that is all. Leave her be. I'm sure she will recover herself presently."

He forced his expression into another reassuring smile, but it was no more convincing than his first.

"But let me explain to you why we are so certain that King Arthur has risen again.

"The day Mr Elliott was killed, as Jenny explained, she and I had left Shields early intending to collect various herbs from the moors: valerian root, agrimony and ground-ivy to help ease Uther's condition and wild ginger for Jenny's. As we were following the footpath up towards Uther's cottage we heard the sound of a bugle through the fog. It was coming from the direction of Sewingshields."

"What time would that have been?" Atticus asked.

"I would estimate it as just after seven o'clock, although I cannot be absolutely certain."

"How do you know it was the sound of a bugle?"

Here Artie grinned.

"I've attended enough regimental parades with Sir Hugh to hear bugles calling in my sleep. I remember it vividly. There were seven notes: two low, two high, two low and one high, repeated thrice. Uther told us he often heard the sound of bugles up there. He said it was always connected with King Arthur's awakening. So we hurried in the direction of the sound, stopping briefly by Uther's cottage to take him with us. He has, as you will know if you have met him, a great hope that King Arthur will one day be restored to his kingdom. Unfortunately, he didn't answer our knock."

Artie smiled fondly and this time the smile did reach his eyes.

"Uther often hides even from us when we call, but his door is never locked, so we entered anyway to see if he might really be there after all. He was not, so we continued up to the Whin Sill and eventually came, just as the fog lifted, to the top of the Sewingshields Crags. Do you happen to know about the legends of Sewingshields Castle, Mr and Mrs Fox?"

"Yes, yes we do," said Atticus.

"That, in Britain's hour of greatest need, Arthur will rise again. Someone needs only to find the hidden vault wherein he lies and there draw a sword, cut a garter and blow a bugle-horn to awaken him from his enchanted sleep."

"We've already heard that story several times. Only this morning, Mrs Fox and I took an opportunity to visit the site of the castle."

Artie regarded them both intently.

"Well it's not just a story; it is God's own truth. Jenny noticed footprints in the dew on the grass. They were recent footprints – big ones of extraordinary length. We followed them over the Wall and discovered the entrance to a cave in a little rocky outcrop not far from the castle. It was on what is called the Fogy Moss, hidden behind a thick cover of ivy and brambles that had obviously just been pushed aside. We went into the cave and sure enough, just as the legend said, there was a vault, and there was King Arthur and his Lady Guinevere. The iron boots of the armour Arthur was wearing were exactly like the footprints in the grass."

Atticus was dumbfounded. He glanced to Lucie, whose expression completely mirrored his own.

"This all seems too incredible!"

"Mr Fox, I know it might seem that way but I swear on the grave of my mother that it is all true. Arthur was wearing the armour of a knight-at-arms with the Pendragon standard – a red dragon – on his helmet and breastplate. Lady Guinevere was dressed exactly as a Dark Ages queen. Oh, and by the by, Arthur was a corpse, a mummified corpse like those the farm men sometimes find in the peat haggs and Guinevere was a skeleton."

Atticus searched Artie's face for some hint of jest or invention but found none. His earnest, emerald-green eyes gazed back with the innocence of utter conviction.

"Where exactly is this vault?" Atticus asked at last.

The green eyes fell.

"I'm sorry, Mr Fox but Jenny and I have discussed this at length and we've both sworn to God, and to each other, not to reveal its whereabouts to a single, living soul – not even to Uther. We wouldn't want Arthur and Guinevere to be gawped at like…like animals in a menagerie."

"Then how do we test the truth of what you're telling us, Artie? You'll admit it's not an easy tale to believe."

"You already have my word for it, Mr Fox."

The wicker of Lucie's chair creaked sharply as she leaned forward, towards him.

"And your word is no doubt entirely honourable, but for all that, we wouldn't be doing our duty to your father if we did not seek further corroboration. Arthur, what if Mr Fox were to consent to be blindfolded whilst you took him to this cave? He could witness the truth of what you say without knowing of its precise location."

Artie bit his lip as he considered her proposal.

"I can't see any reason why that wouldn't do very well, Mrs Fox, if he gave his word of honour that he wouldn't try to remove his mask."

"Gladly," said Atticus.

At that moment, there was the sound of sharp and insistent rapping on glass. They turned to see Mr Collier standing in the open doorway, trembling like a flogged schoolboy and clearly struggling hard to control himself.

"Begging your pardons, Master Arthur and Mr and Mrs Fox, but the Colonel has asked me to summon Mr and

Mrs Fox immediately. Dr Hickson has been found dead on the road and it appears certain that he has been murdered."

Through the open door, the ticking of the grandfather clock seemed suddenly deafening as the import of the words gradually settled onto them.

Collier continued: "Sir Hugh discovered the doctor's body in his gig on the Stanegate and brought it back here. We have taken it up into one of the bedchambers. Please come directly."

Gripped tightly by the chill hand of dread, they followed him out of the orangery, where the statue of Urth pointed them up the stairway to one of the grand bedrooms adjacent to their own.

At the top of the stairs Atticus hesitated.

"I wonder if the body is in – you know – a poor state," he whispered. Lucie shrugged impatiently and pushed past him. Atticus swallowed back his trepidation, took a deep breath and followed her into the room.

It is a curious aspect of human memory that our recognition of an individual depends so much upon the context in which we find them. There can perhaps be no greater dissimilitude than that between a post-mortem examiner and his subject, so if Mr Collier had not already told them of the identity of the corpse, laid-out on the great, brass-framed bed, with its head resting on the silk pillows and its still-gloved hands folded penitently across its chest, they might well not have immediately recognised whom it was.

Dr Julius Hickson's restful attitude was in complete contrast to his face, which might have been roasted in Hell.

It was dark and red with eyes as wide and staring as dinner plates. The tiny, pixie's mouth was stretched into a scream of agony above his little goatee beard, no longer perfectly combed and waxed but matted and twisted, its grey flecks stained purple with vomit.

Despite the big casement windows having been thrown wide, the acrid stench in the room was overpowering. Vomit saturated the front of Hickson's shirt and waistcoat, where it merged with a larger and altogether more sinister stain. This second, broad and slick and red, had spilled from a by-now familiar pair of gashes that cut right across his torso; gashes which intersected below the diaphragm to form the shape of a *crux decussata*.

Sir Hugh Lowther's dark form was couched across a window seat, his head resting lightly against one of the high stone mullions. He was gazing out across the formal west gardens.

"He's stone dead, Fox," he said to the assembly of petrified grotesques there. "I found him in his pony-gig, on the Stanegate towards Hayden Bridge."

He pulled away from his window and stood to face the Foxes. Away from the light, his black silhouette took form and colour and the true horror of his drive from the Stanegate became apparent. His clothes, from his high, polished boots to the front of his fine tweed suit, were smeared and streaked in dark, glutinous blood.

He looked directly at them and his eyes, bright, staring and as wide as Hickson's, blazed out from above blood-caked whiskers, which were twisted and contorted into strange and outlandish shapes.

He seemed suddenly restless and highly agitated even for him.

"Our madman has been at it yet again." He stabbed at them accusingly with a gloved finger that was brown with gore. "Don't say I didn't warn you, Fox. Damn you!" His glare lingered on Atticus for a moment before flickering to Lucie and then back to the window.

"Death by poisoning," Lucie murmured, breaking the rapidly building tension in the room.

Atticus raised his eyebrows. "How do you know?"

Lucie stooped over the body and peered into the dead, glassy eyes.

"That would be my guess. It will take a necropsy to be certain of course, but the vomit and the way the doctor presents would be highly suggestive of it."

Atticus turned to Sir Hugh, grateful for the breath of cooler air from the window playing on his face.

"Forgive us, Sir Hugh but my wife and I will need a few moments alone to discuss the evidence this body provides. Would you be good enough to inform the police, if you haven't already done so? After that we should like to interview you in more detail about the circumstances of the doctor's discovery."

Sir Hugh's already ruddy face flushed yet darker and he muttered something about being ordered around in his own home. However, after a moment's hesitation, he strode obediently enough from the room and crashed the heavy door shut behind him.

Knowing already what her answer would be, Atticus asked: "What about Hickson's heart, Lucie? Has it been removed too?"

His wife pursed her lips so that they became a thin, troubled line.

"I believe so."

She pulled at the deeper of the two gashes to reveal the flesh beneath.

"The wounds are very deep, and do you see the way the tissue has been displaced? I'd bet our fees the heart has been taken again."

"So the murder is identical to the others – in that respect anyway. It is just the manner of the killing that is different. I hope to God he died before his heart was ripped out."

"Amen to that, Atticus."

Lucie gently touched her fingertips to the corpse's lips. Staring down at them, she recited: "Red as a beetroot, mad as a hatter, hot as a hare, blind as a bat and dry as a bone."

She made a face.

"Dr Hickson was poisoned to death. That must be our working hypothesis. If it happens not to be the case, then we will surely find out after the post-mortem."

"On to Sir Hugh, in that case," Atticus said.

"On to Sir Hugh," Lucie agreed. "I do hope he's had opportunity to calm himself a little. He was looking fit to burst earlier."

CHAPTER TWENTY-FIVE

They found Sir Hugh Lowther standing alone in his garden room, gazing out towards the wild, craggy heights of the Great Whin Sill. The large glass of brandy in his hand seemed to glow in the midday sun as it blazed down over his shoulder to project dancing, amber shadows onto the tiles at his feet.

"'When sorrows come, they come not single spies, but in battalions', Sir Hugh."

Lowther started slightly at Atticus' words. He threw back his head and drained the glass before he turned to face them, but it seemed that neither the neat spirit nor the tranquillity of the views had served to calm him.

"Sorrows be damned," he growled. "Well, what have you found? At this rate there'll be no one left here. I'll be a second William-bloody-Brydon!"

Lucie replied.

"We're quite sure Dr Hickson was poisoned to death, Sir Hugh."

"Are you by God?" Sir Hugh retorted, his eyes bulging. "And are you as sure yet who did the poisoning?"

"We aren't wholly…"

"It was Michael-deuced-Britton! I've told you a hundred times. You prove it, and I will give you a thousand guineas."

Lucie winced. "That will not be necessary, thank you all the same. Your butler told us it was you who first found the doctor's body. We need to know everything you can recollect about the discovery and the circumstances surrounding it. Neglect nothing, Sir Hugh."

Lowther snorted his derision.

"Very well, I'll play your damned games with you." He took a very deep breath and slumped onto a settee.

"Right, Mrs Fox – Lucie – here it is: I was becoming concerned about Hickson's lateness in coming to see my daughter. He's generally so punctual, do you see? Collier will tell you a story that he once set the long-cased clock in the hall by him. Anyway, eventually I decided to ride over towards Hayden Bridge, to see where he'd got to. It's just a few miles down the valley towards Hexham and it's where Hickson had his practice.

"Very soon, I spied him sitting in his gig on the Stanegate, the old Roman way that runs by the side of the road, but I could tell immediately something was queer."

"How was that, Sir Hugh?" Atticus asked.

"Well for one thing, his pony had its head down, stuffing its belly on the grass, and for another, there was something damned strange about the way Hickson was slouched in the seat.

"I galloped over and sure enough, there was Hickson, slumped over, dead as a doornail. So, I tied my horse to the back of the gig and drove it post-haste back here to Shields. Once I arrived, I shouted for Collier and between us, we lifted him out of his seat and carried him up to the bedchamber where you both saw him."

"So if he was already dead when you found him, you wouldn't know if he had been speaking incoherently, or if he had been suffering a fit," Lucie said. "Was his body hot to the touch, did you notice?"

The anger fell from Lowther's face. "Why yes, Lucie, now that you mention it, his body was still very warm."

"Did you see anyone else around the place where you found him, anyone at all?" Atticus asked.

Lowther hesitated for a heartbeat.

"Not a mortal soul, Fox."

"And where is the gig now?"

"It's been taken to the stables. His pony has been given a good wipe down and watered."

"Very good; Mrs Fox and I will examine them both presently. How far is it to this Stanegate?"

"It'll be a mile, maybe a little more, to where I found him. I'd be glad to show you if you wish."

Atticus grunted in satisfaction. "Thank you; that would be extremely helpful. We will go there directly we have finished examining the doctor's gig."

The light, two-wheeled pony-gig looked almost forlorn, standing as it was, abandoned and empty, by the doors of the carriage house. It seemed out-of-place too in that it was so very different from what one might have expected of a country parish doctor. It was a delicate, almost feminine vehicle with rubber cushioning tyres, glossy black paint and patent leather upholstery. On these rural roads, more suited to varnish and cord, it would be a stable-boy's nightmare to clean and maintain.

"It is a handsome carriage, Lucie," Atticus remarked.

Lucie did not answer him directly because, inevitably, it was she who had seen it first.

"Atticus, look at that!"

He glanced down and saw it too.

On the floor of the gig, tipping against the patent leather of the dashboard, and in full view of anyone who cared to look, was a small, bronze-coloured object. Though recently polished, it was without mark or ornamentation and most folk would have considered it much too plain and ordinary-looking to have been a priceless relic.

Lucie reached into the carriage and carefully, using only the very tips of her fingers, lifted the heavy goblet by its rim and placed it on the flat palm of her hand.

"The Holy Grail," Atticus murmured, "The proverbial poisoned chalice."

"There are no obvious finger-prints that I can see," said Lucie. "Uther polishes it every day – he has told us as much already – and Hickson was wearing driving gloves. It is rather curious that they should be so entirely absent though."

Lucie set the Grail down carefully onto the cobblestones of the yard and turned back to the gig.

"And the doctor's clothes were soaked in vomit, yet there are only a very few splashes in here. That is suggestive of him having egurgitated *before* he climbed, or was put, onto this seat.

"So if he was found on this Stanegate," Atticus mused aloud, "I wonder where precisely the poison was administered and, indeed, what type of poison it might have been. Look, there is a tiny drop of liquid at the bottom of the chalice. Might it be the vestiges of whatever killed him?"

He watched as Lucie picked up the chalice and brought it to her nose.

"I'm no expert on poisons and it could be anything, Atticus, even one of the doctor's own medicines. But there is a mnemonic we had at the hospital: 'Red as a beetroot, mad as a hatter, hot as a hare, blind as a bat and dry as a bone'. We used it to identify cases of poisoning – especially plant poisoning."

"So how might it apply here?"

"Well, we don't of course know whether Dr Hickson became mad – he was already dead when Sir Hugh found him – but we do know that his body was unusually hot. His face was very red, as you will recall yourself, and the pupils of his eyes were dilated. His lips were quite dry too – I checked them – and we know he had vomited. I am convinced he was poisoned. A lot of our wild or even garden plants are quite capable of killing a man, if you know how to use them; belladonna, thorn apple, monkshood, even common churchyard yew."

Lucie shook the remainder of the liquid – of the poison perhaps – onto her palm and inspected it.

"It is distinctly purplish in colour and it has a faint, acrid smell. It could be belladonna, Atticus." She shrugged, "Or then again, it could simply be wine."

Atticus suggested that the pony and gig be driven back to where the discovery of Dr Hickson's body had been made.

"We should be sorry if some drover has run his cattle down this Stanegate and trampled over all the evidence," he cautioned, "And the close reproduction of a murder scene can be very helpful."

Sir Hugh Lowther agreed readily to their suggestion. The pony was therefore led out of its temporary accommodation in the stable house and harnessed back into the shafts by James the footman. He had also been given the task of driving the little gig back to Hayden Bridge once the reconstruction of the murder scene had been staged. Sir Hugh was to accompany him on his own large, black stallion and Atticus and Lucie prepared to bring up the rear on their bicycles.

Grim-faced, James kept up a brisk pace along the deserted, moorland lanes and slowed only when they came to the ancient and pitted line of the Stanegate. Atticus was quite breathless in the heat of the day and even Lucie was relieved when, as they approached a small flock of sheep grazing by the lane-side, Sir Hugh finally raised his arm and shouted for him to stop.

"Here it was that I found him," he announced as he smoothly dismounted his horse and grasped the head collar of the pony. He led it around in a wide circle and onto the broad, grassy verge which bordered the way at that point.

"It was precisely…here. The pony was head-down, and Hickson was sitting in the middle of the seat, slumped to his left, rather like this."

He leaned over to illustrate Hickson's position, adopting a brutally accurate, if slightly comical impression of his death mask of staring eyes and gaping, choking mouth.

"Very good, Sir Hugh, that will do for now and we are most grateful for your assistance." Atticus wiped a thick film of sweat from his brow and felt another laid cold across his back. "James, you may return the doctor's pony and gig to its home stable now. The police will, I imagine, have informed any next of kin. Lucie and I will make our own way back to Shields Tower once we have concluded our examinations here."

Sir Hugh stared at him for a second before grunting irritably in acknowledgement of the dismissal. He remounted his horse, tipped his top hat politely towards Lucie and trotted off towards the moors.

As the hollow thudding of hooves faded in each direction, the everyday sounds of the high pastures ebbed back and Atticus and Lucie Fox found themselves alone.

"It is so tranquil here, Atticus that all these murders seem to be almost a blasphemy." Lucie watched the distant figure of Sir Hugh Lowther as he dropped out of sight into the broad concavity of the Vallum. "I wonder how he'll take the next piece of news."

"What do you mean? What next piece of news?"

"The news about Miss Jennifer," Lucie replied with a significant glance. When Atticus' quizzical expression did not change, she rolled her eyes in mock exasperation.

"Atticus, it's as plain as the nose on your face: her tearfulness; her sickness; her taking of ginger; her reluctance to see the doctor. You surely don't need to be a nurse to know that Jennifer Lowther is pregnant."

"Great Scott!" exclaimed Atticus, "Jenny Lowther is expecting? But then the identity of the child's father—"

"Doesn't even bear contemplation." Lucie finished the sentence for him. "I don't suppose for an instant that Sir Hugh would easily countenance the prospect of his daughter bearing his own son's child."

"Great Scott," repeated Atticus softly.

For several minutes, the only sounds on that part of the Stanegate were the soft cries of the sheep and the harsher calls of the waterfowl on the loughs as Lucie and Atticus each absorbed the ramifications of the bombshell.

Then Atticus remarked that it was a rather peculiar spot for a premeditated murder.

"And yet premeditated it must have been, since the killer came well equipped with both a chalice – the Holy Grail – and poison to fill it with."

Lucie stared at him thoughtfully.

"You're right. It is a very odd place for a murder, and especially for a poisoning. Poisonings aren't carried out in ambush; they're carried out by stealth. And why would the doctor be on this road anyway? It's hardly the most comfortable to travel when there's a proper lane so close."

"It isn't even the most direct road to Shields Tower either," Atticus added. "So he must have had another reason for being on the Stanegate today."

"Such as an arrangement to make a call on someone else too – someone who might live around here," Lucie suggested. "If there was, that might have been where he was given the poison."

They both gazed about themselves once again. In front of them, the stone-grey line of the Stanegate stretched forward beyond the silver blue of a tiny lake. Behind them, it crept away over the opposite horizon. In both directions it was completely devoid of humanity or habitation.

"That lake," Atticus cried suddenly. "I think on James' map it is called the Grindon Lough and I imagine it's the one that may be seen from Michael Britton's cottage."

Without another word, they broke off the lane and onto the close-cropped turf. And as that dropped away in front of them, they found themselves staring down at the bare thatch of a shabby cottage huddled in the lee of a low crag. It was the cottage they knew well to be Uther Pendragon's.

"I am rather surprised that Michael Britton's cottage is so close."

Lucie's remark was casual but the implication of her words was clear. She turned to Atticus.

"I suppose it would not have been surprising if Dr Hickson had decided to pay a visit on Britton before coming to speak with us. And remember that Sir Hugh visited Britton yesterday to seek his permission for Dr Hickson to do just that? Britton would have known about the doctor's appointment at Shields Tower today and he may well have guessed that he might call on him too. Hickson was always punctual. It would have been very easy for him to have prepared a poison and then to have administered it hidden in a drink."

Atticus stared at the cottage, his expression deeply troubled. This insistence on 'proper method' was beginning to feel like a child's silly parlour game. The game was going horribly, horribly wrong and Robson, after all, must surely have been right. This was police work.

He became aware that his wife was still speaking.

"I said that Hickson would have had an appointments diary." Lucie repeated, "He would have recorded his arrangements for today."

Atticus nodded.

"Yes, we must be sure to check that…but only after we have spoken with Britton and made a thorough search of that cottage."

Lucie's eyes drifted past Atticus and back to the lane.

"The sheep are out of their field," she remarked.

Atticus turned. "Yes, the gate has been left wide open. Are…Are you supposing that Hickson put his gig in that field whilst he called on Britton?"

Lucie nodded. "Yes, I am. And if he knew he had been poisoned, he would have left in a hurry."

"And if he had left in a hurry he would hardly have stopped to close the gate."

They started back towards the lane so abruptly that the newly-shorn sheep lining its sides galloped away as one, bleating their protests. But once they reached the open gateway, it was obvious that their eduction was correct; a distinct pair of tyre tracks showed clearly in the wet, springy turf of the field, where a vehicle, too light to be anything other than a gig, had recently been.

Atticus' fingers tightened around the handle of his walking cane.

"I think we had better make that call on Britton," he said and jabbed the cane's end into the turf.

Lucie glanced down at the movement.

"Will we be safe?"

Atticus set his jaw. "No, I'm rather afraid we might not. But this is no children's parlour game, Lucie; there have been three murders so far that we know of. We need to make certain that this thing doesn't run its course – that there aren't any more."

Lucie stared at him, aghast. "That it doesn't run its course? How many more do you think there could be?"

Atticus frowned. "Well, the number seven keeps coming into my mind."

"Seven?"

"I am not entirely sure why, but it does seem somehow significant. 'Sewingshields' means 'Seven Shields', from the shields of the seven dead kings who once came to woo the seven daughters of a local druid. The seven daughters were all slain too.

"I mentioned to you the supposed treasure in the Broomlee Lough, which can only be recovered by seven souls using a chain wrought by a seventh-generation blacksmith. We have seven relics from Arthurian legend: the sword, the garter, the bugle horn and the four Hallows. And there is something else too, something else to do with the number seven, but the devil take me if I can think what it is."

Lucie pursed her lips resolutely. "Then you're right; this is far from being a game and we must not hesitate for an instant. The lives of four more people depend on us buttoning down the identity of this murderer."

There is something in the gamut of human senses which serves to alert us to the presence of a fellow being. It was that very sense, occult and primordial, with nothing to do with sight or sound or smell, that told Atticus and Lucie, even as they approached it, that the cottage was deserted and empty, and that no one would respond to Atticus' brisk knocking at the door.

And so it was.

After several long minutes of waiting, after the flies had buzzed their indignation at being disturbed, again and again, from their vigil on the painted red dragon and had finally settled and quieted once more, Atticus lifted the latch and pushed cautiously on the door.

It creaked wide on its rusty hinges and laid bare for a second time the spartan chaos that was the everyday life of Uther Pendragon.

Feeling apprehensive and curiously guilty, Atticus and Lucie stepped across the threshold. The heavy, musty air, the strewing of pictures and drawings, the battered, broken furniture, even the used tumbler sitting on the table with a renewed film of orange dust crusting its bottom were just as they remembered them. Indeed, the only thing that was different was the presence of several small and dark-coloured berries which smeared and stained the table-top.

"Are those bilberries, Atticus?" Lucie asked, nodding towards them, "Or are they something else?"

Atticus bent forward and peered closely at them.

"No, Lucie, it is too early in the season for bilberries."

"Belladonna, then?"

He nodded.

"Yes, these are devil's cherries, botanical name *Atropa belladonna*, otherwise known as deadly nightshade."

"I thought they might be. Back when I was nursing, we had several cases of belladonna poisoning. Once, we even had a farmer who died after he ate meat from a rabbit that had been grazing on it. He looked very much as Dr Hickson did."

Atticus stood tall. "It seems that we have the poison then, Lucie. We might do well to search the rest of this cottage while the Fates are yet smiling upon us."

He glanced around at the detritus of a life broken by insanity. Uther's existence was pitiful – a body and mind remaining alive from day to tortured day. Yet his sketches and drawings were truly breathtaking. The man clearly had prodigious talent. He imagined these same pictures mounted and framed and hung in the grand houses of Harrogate. Perhaps an agent could be procured for him…if indeed it somehow transpired that he was not the murderer, of course. He even wondered for a moment if perhaps Sir

Hugh could be persuaded to become his patron, although the thought died, stillborn, in his mind.

A diligent search of the main room of the cottage revealed nothing further and so they moved on to the bedroom.

There again, everything was as before. It was the same that is, except for in two vital respects: The armour, dismantled now and tumbled across the bed, was conspicuously missing its breastplate and, just as Atticus had feared, the two remaining Hallows, the Holy Platter and the Spear of Destiny, were gone.

CHAPTER TWENTY-SIX

With his mother's milk, man learns hatred for the demons of this world.

But what is a demon but an angel that has fallen – an angel, who has looked upon the daughters of men, has seen that they are truly beautiful, and fallen.

It is easier by far for a man to hate than to love.

He stands on the brink of the world, where it ends, where once it ended, and his father's voice sounds out once again through the years.

"Don't blub, boy. It wasn't your fault. It was the will of the Fates. They wanted your mama for an angel. Accept it like a man, damn you. Accept it like a Lowther."

But again and again he sees her face falling away from him, and again and again he hears her scream as she breaks on the rocks of Sewingshields.

It was the will of the Fates.

Quo Fata Vocant.

And now they will again.

He turns. Through the field glasses, his eyes creep once more along the line of the road below. He is watching; he is waiting for the angel himself. It will be soon now. The smoke of Hayden Bridge seems so close. His sacred place is close too, and he yearns to go there.

But he is a soldier; he is an officer sworn to follow the Queen's Regulations and the *first object of his attention must ever be to watch the movements of the enemy and to give timely notice of his approach* – of the angel's approach.

So he lifts up his glasses and examines the road once more.

Then, Lo! He spies him: the enemy, the angel, the fallen angel – the Guardian Angel.

He watches his movements and, as the enemy approaches, he stands and raises his arm.

The angel that has fallen sees it, and waves back in greeting.

He stands, silent and perfectly still, watching as another seventh-part of the wergild bustles up to him, bustles up to its death.

"Good afternoon, Colonel. I'm reporting for duty, just as you ordered, sir."

James stands, smiling, to attention. He salutes, his left hand up crisp and smart, just as it was in the old days.

Sir Hugh Lowther smiles, salutes in return and points over the cliffs. He points towards Sewingshields.

James' face, the face of the angel, turns and looks. His face is glossy with sweat and it takes the glow of the sun.

The sun reflects too on the polished bronze of a platter being raised high above his head.

James looks heavenward, and sees it. His face twists in puzzlement and he watches, mesmerised, as it climbs like the very orb itself.

He hears the words that Sir Hugh screams, words that explain everything.

"Guardian Angel!"

The Holy Platter sets. It is hard and murderously heavy. The expression on the angel-face turns from puzzlement to shock and then into a bloodied mess as the footman falls, stunned, to the ground.

Sir Hugh Lowther binds the wrists tightly, but piously, together as if in prayer. It is an angel after all. He ties the ankles together too and waits.

And as he waits, he stares at the angel's face and he remembers the other times, the times long ago, before the angel fell, when they had stood shoulder to shoulder under arms.

The good times, he thinks, and then he shudders.

"*You are a traitor and a coward!*" Verthandi's voice erupts around them and Lowther springs to his feet. He glances frantically down at James, but no – thank the Lord – he hasn't moved; he hasn't heard her.

"*That was a glorious time for your Queen and country. It was a time to be a man. You served as brothers-in-arms, you and he, yet you are the one who cringes from the memory of it, like a baby.*

"*You should remember Cawnpore, Lowther; you should recall Cawnpore and Lucknow and all the other battles you have fought and you should exult!*"

'Remember Cawnpore!'

That had been their battle cry ever since they had found the butchered remains of the women and the children in the well. Remember Cawnpore? How could he ever forget it?

It had been the 16th July, 1857 when they, the first British relief force, had finally fought their way through to the city. The men of the original garrison had been massacred by the rebellious Sepoys, the native Indian troops who had risen up against the British East India Company in the Great Uprising.

That massacre was the grossest affront to the honourable rules of war. The besieged British had been granted safe passage to Allahabad in return for their surrender. But instead, they had been cut down at Satichaura Ghat on the banks of the Ganges by Sepoy bullets and by the swords of the cavalry Sowars. The British women and children had been rounded up and captured. They had been set, so they were told, to grind corn for chapattis at a villa called Bibighar, the 'House of the Ladies', in Cawnpore itself.

So he, Lieutenant Hugh Lowther, had been ordered to join a detail of other officers and men. They were to form a rescue party, to take quick possession of Bibighar, and to free those held within it.

But when they had arrived there, the House of the Ladies was silent.

"*You're too late. They are all dead*," Urth had hissed through the crackle of distant gunfire, and even as she spoke, he realised that she was right. The stench of death was once again filling his nostrils and the image of his mama once again filling his mind.

They had found them, dozens of them, piled inside a dry well. They had been butchered with cleavers; killed, stripped naked and dismembered. Some had been thrown into the well whilst yet alive.

The vengeance of the British had been as swift as it had been terrible. Those suspected of involvement were made to lick the blood of the victims from the walls of the Bibighar before they were hanged. The Muslim sepoys were made to eat pork or to smear pork fat onto their bodies – an abomination to their faith. The Hindus were forced to eat the flesh of their sacred cattle, or to rub their fat onto their own skins.

The Sisters of the Wyrd had applauded these and the other punishments set out by the commanding officer, Brigadier Neill.

"It is proper justice, Lowther, and the Brigadier is a true hero," Verthandi had told him. *"It is just and it is fitting. The rebels might bleat but they have brought it all upon themselves."*

Although it turned him sick to the marrow of his bones, he had been obliged to agree. Whenever any man baulked at the cruelty they were meting out, the cry 'Remember Cawnpore!' would go up. And whenever he, Hugh Lowther, hesitated, it was the Norns themselves who would scream those very same words into his mind.

They urged him on in rounding up the rebels and having them build a line of gallows for their own executions. It was good that these were within sight of the well so that the last thing they would see in this life would be the site of their atrocity. The Sisters cackled with laughter when the Muslims were sewn into pigskins before they were hanged, and no less when the lowliest sweepers were forced to hang those of the highest castes.

But it was Skuld, That Which Should Become, who had shocked him so profoundly by decreeing the fate of the worst of the mutineers.

"You must tell your father to have them blown from the mouths of cannon," she had whispered in her voice that reminded him so much of his dear dead mama. *"They had your women and children dismembered, so you must dismember them. It is only right. And it is a retribution they themselves have used in times past."*

And so he had. And Sir Douglas Lowther, because he was a Major in the Fifth, had listened to him – had listened to the words of the Fates. He had nodded grimly and agreed, wondering in his heart what sort of fiend his son had become.

Quo Fata Vocant.

Accordingly, those adjudged to be the ringleaders were taken to where the guns were waiting, charged and ready with blank cartridge. The soldiery and the populace had been summoned and they had stood in silence as the verdict and the sentence of the court was read out.

Screaming insults, they had been held with their backs pressed against the muzzles of the cannon and they had been lashed fast.

Hugh Lowther stood in the company of his own regiment and felt their gaze. To them, this was his idea and his alone. He had long since learned not to speak of the Norns.

The angel-faced private at his side was speaking words of support but he could not respond. It was as if, despite the blazing heat of the Indian sun, he was frozen.

Then, one by one, the guns had been fired, and one by one, the rebels had exploded in the roars of smoke and fire. The guns threw back on their wheels and veil after veil of blood doused those watching. Heads and limbs, blackened arms and legs, spun away into the air.

"They have lost all chance of entering their Paradise now," Verthandi had squealed in glee. But still he could not reply. He was transfixed – as unable to move as the poor wretches waiting for their own death yonder.

An arm, a scorched, cauterised stump of flesh arced through the air and struck Hugh Lowther full on his chest to leave a mottled print of soot and blood across the front of his dress tunic. He could only stand, staring, unable to move, and piss himself as his comrades-in-arms gagged and turned their faces in horror from the carnage.

The men of the ranks looked at him with respect bordering on awe in the days that followed. He had overheard the angel-faced fusilier telling his mess-mates as they were being laboriously ferried across the Ganges river: "He's as cool as iron, that one, just like his father, the Major. He just stood there, calm as ye like, even when their arms an' legs were stottin' off him like hailstones. I tell ye, I would follow that man to Hell and back."

"But we know the truth of it!" the Norns had taunted, and he had turned away his head to gaze across the Ganges,

towards the besieged city of Lucknow, so that none could see his shame.

And he does remember Cawnpore, and he does remember Lucknow and every other battle very often, and he does, he always does, try so hard to be exultant.

The blood has dried to a thick, dark crust when the eyes of the angel – the angel-faced ex-fusilier flutter open. It is time at last for him, for the Guardian Angel, to grow wings. He has looked upon the daughters of men, even upon the wives of men, and seen them to be truly beautiful.

And now he will fall forever. Now, he will indeed go to Hell.

CHAPTER TWENTY-SEVEN

A long, thin pall of thick, yellow smoke hung motionless in the still air over Hayden Bridge. It had spilled from the chimneys of the large brass and iron foundry that dominated this part of the valley and helped to make the village an intense bustle of industry, contrasting with the stillness of the fells around it like a bee swarm in an otherwise tranquil orchard.

A question to a ragged street urchin led Atticus and Lucie Fox over the six arches of the old stone bridge that gave the village its name to 'Asclepius House', an imposing, three-storey town house set back behind green-painted railings and a narrow, meticulously ordered garden of box and lavender.

Black enamelled letters on a brass plate fixed to the gatepost confirmed that this was the home and surgery of 'Dr J. R. Hickson, MRCS'.

With a wink and a grin Atticus pressed a sixpence into the grubby hand of the urchin and watched him tear off excitedly up the lane. He leaned their bicycles carefully against the wrought-iron railings and lifted the latch of the ornate front gate. It swung easily across the short path of quarry-tiles that beckoned them up to the house itself.

Rapping the gleaming brass knocker sharply against the tapping plate of the front door, Atticus smiled awkwardly at Lucie as they heard the sounds of movement within. A woman's broad outline formed through the leaded lights of the glazing and the shadow of a hand reached up to the latch.

"The doctor is not yet returned to his surgery," announced an elderly but formidable-looking woman, glaring at each of them in turn.

"Yes," replied Lucie gently, "I'm rather afraid that he has not. May we come inside please?"

"You will need to come back if you want treatment. Evening surgery is from six o'clock sharp. Forst come, forst seen, even if ye are gentry. Dr Hickson is very particular on that."

"And that is entirely commendable of him, I'm sure, but please, may we come inside?" Atticus tried to reproduce his wife's gentle tone. "We aren't sick; we are private-enquiry agents involved in a matter of no little gravity."

He took out his slim, silver calling-card case and pulled out a card, taking care to deliberately fold-in the bottom, right-hand corner. The woman gasped and her hand flew to her mouth. She clearly understood its meaning.

"Condolences! You have terrible news, don't you? Someone has died. Is it one of the doctor's patients? Is it old Mrs Bell?"

Atticus gently offered the card up to her.

"I fear it is not Mrs Bell. We are Mr and Mrs Atticus Fox of Harrogate. May I enquire as to your name?"

"I am Mrs Campbell; I keep house for Dr Hickson." Her voice was barely audible as she whispered through the fingers of her hand.

Still staring at the card, Mrs Campbell pulled the door wide and bobbed a brief curtsey as they passed. Atticus paused to allow her to take the card from him.

"May we?" he asked, indicating a door just beyond the vestibule. It bore a painted board marked 'Surgery'.

Mrs Campbell nodded.

The surgery-room of Asclepius House was a fairly standard affair for a country doctor; a moderately large front parlour converted into the functionality of a medical consulting room. A large, over-stuffed chaise longue stood in the centre and there was a discomforting poignancy to an empty, high-backed chair placed strategically next to it. But for the murderous intent of the as-yet unknown killer, Dr Hickson would be assuming that chair, just as he had done at countless six o'clock surgeries before now, and just as his housekeeper yet expected him to do.

There was a pair of identical chairs lined against one of the walls and Lucie gently ushered Mrs Campbell towards the nearest of them. She perched on the other and took the old housekeeper's trembling hand in her own.

"Mrs Campbell, I very much regret to tell you that we have some rather bad news," Lucie began. "Mr Fox and I have been commissioned by Sir Hugh Lowther of Shields Tower to investigate what have now become three murders committed on his estate in the space of the last week or so."

"Shields Tower estate is where Dr Hickson has been this very morning," Mrs Campbell interrupted. "He was to join Sir Hugh for luncheon, prior to seeing his daughter, Miss Jennifer."

As many folk are wont to do, Mrs Campbell had spoken between the points of hearing and comprehension. She reached the second of these, and her hands flew once more to cover her mouth.

"*Three* murders did you say, Mrs Fox?"

Lucie nodded. "Yes, I did, and as I say, I have some very distressing news for you."

She squeezed the housekeeper's hand.

"Sir Hugh had reason to summon us once again earlier today. I am afraid that Dr Hickson was given poison whilst on his way to Shields Tower, poison probably prepared from the berries of deadly nightshade. He did not survive."

Mrs Campbell stared at her.

"No, no it is not possible," she whispered, "You are both quite mistaken. You must be. The doctor has returned to the stables. I heard the sound of his pony along the back lane not one hour ago. He must still be speaking with the stable lad."

"That was Sir Hugh's footman returning the doctor's gig to your stables, Mrs Campbell," Atticus said. "We had supposed that the police would already have informed you of the doctor's death so he must have returned directly to Shields without calling. It was Sir Hugh himself who discovered the doctor's body on the Stanegate and it lies at this minute in a bedroom at Shields Tower."

Lucie gently patted her hand. "We have seen it there for ourselves. I am truly sorry for your loss, Mrs Campbell, and for the unfortunate way in which you learned of it from strangers at your door."

Whilst Lucie comforted the old housekeeper and gently brought her to terms with the news, Atticus' eyes began to rove around the room. They settled almost immediately onto a teak bureau, placed strategically to best utilise the light from the large bay window, and in particular onto a large, black, leather-bound book which lay open on its top. After a furtive glance at Mrs Campbell, who was sobbing into Lucie's handkerchief, he flitted across the room, pulled a captain's chair out from under the bureau and dropped soundlessly into it.

His stomach fluttered as he realised that the book was the very appointments diary Lucie had alluded to on the Stanegate. It lay open for that day: Saturday, 7th June 1890, where there were just three entries on the page, all of them pleasingly detailed and all of them written in a round, exuberant hand.

The first was: 'Attend – Mr M. Britton, Shields Tower Estate. Discussion of his incarceration into a lunatic asylum'. The second, just below it, read: 'Luncheon – Shields Tower, 1 o'clock sharp'. And the last: 'Attend – Miss Jennifer Lowther'.

As he pondered on these memoranda, a sudden thought struck him. He twisted in the chair and said: "I do beg pardon, Mrs Campbell, but how long had Dr Hickson been practicing medicine in this area?"

The housekeeper dabbed her eyes and considered the question for a few moments.

"A very long time now; I should say almost five-and-thirty years."

"And he would have served the parishes of Hayden and Bardon Mill all that time?"

"Why yes, Mr Fox, of course, and the parish of Simonsburn too."

"Including Shields Tower and Shields Tower Farm?"

"Yes indeed; he was hardly away from there at one time. That was before Sir Hugh's son, Master Arthur was born."

"A patient of his, Michael Britton, told us so too. Would the doctor have retained his day-books and journals from then?"

Mrs Campbell frowned.

"I expect so. He never disposes of anything, not ever. It was something that right vexed me." She made a noise somewhere between a giggle and a sob. "If he has, they will likely be in the box room over yonder."

She smiled wistfully through her red and swollen eyes.

"I know Michael Britton. It is a great pity he was overtaken by his madness, because he truly was a fine man in his day."

Atticus looked over in the direction she indicated and noticed for the first time a narrow panelled door set into the almost identical wooden panelling of the farthest wall. He glanced back to Lucie who seemed to have already read his thoughts.

"Come, Mrs Campbell, show me the scullery and I'll brew us both some tea. I'm certain it will lift our spirits no end."

The housekeeper nodded bleakly and allowed Lucie to take her arm and gently lead her out through the surgery door.

Atticus mouthed, 'thank you' and then, once the door had clicked shut behind them, stood, and with a sudden and deeply discomforting pang of guilt, hurried across the surgery.

The little box room was cramped and musty, and racked from floor to ceiling with shelves containing all manner of papers, magazines, journals and books. They were the chronicles of a lifetime spent in country medicine. As Atticus' eyes became accustomed to the gloom, his gaze was drawn to a shelf, just above head height, and a block of leather-bound journals identical to the one resting on the bureau. They were labelled neatly in chronological order: 1856 through to 1889.

"Hullo!" he murmured audibly to himself. His own voice sounded strange, awkward and slightly tremulous, as if it were some other person rifling through such obviously confidential and personal documents and not he. In that moment, it occurred to Atticus Fox what might be troubling him so much about all of this. He recalled his own medical records, and how they had once been documented and published, to be debated and discussed by anyone who cared to read them.

'This is a triple-murder enquiry,' the person with the strange voice reminded him. Again he paused at its sound and then he murmured: "Let me see, Artie is twenty-one years of age now and Lady Igraine was lost on the moors around a year after his birth. But given that we do not know precisely in which month he was born…"

Atticus reached up and carefully pulled down the doctor's journals marked 1868, 1869 and 1870.

Laying out Hickson's journals side-by-side across the gleaming teak of the bureau top, Atticus was first struck by how very similar the round, flowing handwriting of twenty years ago was to the open appointment-book of that very day. Settling once again into the captain's chair, he pulled the first, the journal for 1868, onto the blotting pad in front of him and, with the solemnity of a lector at Mass, lifted the cover.

Atticus Fox, through years of practice, was a highly accomplished speed-reader. He scanned each page both rapidly and thoroughly but he did so always with half an ear to the tiled corridor beyond the surgery door. Just as he had expected, there were frequent entries to make house-calls on a 'Mr M. Britton', whom Atticus took to mean Michael Britton, now Uther Pendragon. Uther, he recalled, had told them that Hickson used to call regularly on him whilst he was well. What did surprise him however was the frequency with which he had also to call upon Lady Lowther.

It seemed apparent from the journal that Lady Igraine, despite what they had been told from their very first day in Northumberland about her vivacity and zest for life, was prone, like Uther, to frequent bouts of melancholy. Several times Hickson had made notes of the dates when Sir Hugh had been posted abroad to fight or to help train the native troops and these were inevitably accompanied by appointments to attend upon 'Igraine' to administer the necessary comfort for loneliness and sadness. It was, Atticus supposed, the other side of the coin to having a great empire upon which the sun never set; that loved ones were often separated for long periods by trade or by war in far-away places.

It seemed too not a little bizarre to be reading at first-hand an account of events gradually unfolding decades previously which he knew of prior to this only from conversations and hearsay. A note of confirmation of Lady Igraine's pregnancy was there underlined with a thick double stroke and in the next journal, in May of 1869, an account of the birth of Sir Hugh's first-born heir, who was later to be named Arthur, was written up in terse, clinical detail.

He supposed that having a tiny baby had made life much less lonely and rather more joyous for Igraine Lowther. The journal notes following his attendances at Shields Tower became much less frequent but more medically detailed and clinically objective after Arthur's birth, and calls upon Michael Britton markedly so. That was until the 15th June, 1870, when Dr Hickson wrote just a brief, underlined footnote to the page:

'Igraine still missing upon the moors. Now forty-eight hours. Weather ghastly. Presume lost?' and Atticus could find no mention of either thereafter.

Together with a calmer but still rather shaken and tearful Mrs Campbell, the Foxes drew the blinds and closed the shutters of Asclepius House. They left a brief note of explanation pinned neatly to the front door and safely deposited Mrs Campbell with a neighbour and close friend. Then, when at last they clambered back onto their bicycles and pushed off along the cobbles of the road, Atticus related his findings in the journals to an astonished Lucie.

"I certainly had no impression that Igraine Lowther was prone to fits of melancholy," she said. "That she must have had very different private and public faces is all I can suggest. It is almost unheard of for someone to be able to completely hide such severe symptoms from those around them, but then, by all accounts, she was a quite remarkable lady."

"So we are given to understand, my dearest, but what of Dr Hickson? Did you discover anything of use from Mrs Campbell? Had he made any enemies for example?"

Lucie hesitated.

"Dr Hickson seems to have been just a regular country doctor, well-liked by everyone. I couldn't find any direct connection with Sewingshields or Shields Tower at all, other than the obvious one that he served them as a general physician.

"But, Atty, harken to this: Although Dr Hickson was a confirmed bachelor, Mrs Campbell told me that at one time she suspected he had a sweetheart. She never ever met her and Dr Hickson would never admit to it, but she was sure he was once courting."

"What gave her that notion?" Atticus asked.

"Oh, he became quite the dandy, even so far as to wear a girdle. It was then – just over twenty years ago – that he sold his old country brougham and bought the smart new gig – the one we have seen. Everyone told him it was far too fancy for a country doctor but Mrs Campbell suspected it was to take this sweetheart out across the moors. Dr Hickson would frequently ask her to prepare a special picnic for two on those days.

"But they never married?"

"No, and that's just it. It appears that this lady also vanished, quite suddenly, around twenty years ago."

Atticus was thunderstruck.

"Another one! So that makes three disappearances, all of women and all around the same time." He counted on his fingers, "Igraine Lowther of course; Michael Britton's fiancé, and now Dr Hickson's secret sweetheart. If we add those disappearances to the recent murders, that makes six. It would appear that we have fallen into a veritable hotbed of murder and mystery, Lucie, albeit twenty years apart."

"Do you remember what Uther said to us, Atticus, after we first introduced ourselves to him and told him that we had been commissioned to investigate Samson Elliott's death?"

Atticus' eyes focused onto the middle distance as he searched his memory.

"Let me see, yes, I believe I do. He flinched violently and began visibly to tremble. Then I recall that he began to drool quite horribly and needed to wipe his mouth with that grubby pocket-handkerchief of his. He seemed surprised that there had been another death and you asked if he knew about Sir Douglas. He said: 'It's started once again then'."

"Exactly so, Atticus, and he remarked that three smugglers had been mutilated and thrown from a crag, and that a soldier from Hexham had also disappeared. I wonder if they all had crosses cut into their bodies. I wonder if your six deaths and disappearances are in reality, no fewer than ten!

"Uther clearly knows much more about the murderous history of this place than he has thought fit to tell us. Perhaps we ought to be asking him a little more about that too, the very next time we see him."

Atticus could hardly have agreed more.

CHAPTER TWENTY-EIGHT

The sun streaming in through the window illuminates the hay dust, hanging and swirling and eddying in the air, and splinters into a hundred colours against the fresh-honed edge of his blade. He watches this rainbow burning against the steel, and listens to the movements of the first object of his attention – of his enemy.

The grooms have all gone now, returned to their quarters, all except Albert and he will never return.

A horse snorts. Its hoof scrapes the floor.

"Steady, lass," Albert murmurs below, "I'm not going to hurt you." His voice is muffled by the thick timber floor, but the Norns have told him that he used to murmur those very same words to his lady, here, in this hayloft. Sir Hugh Lowther's gloved fist tightens around the hilt of his sword and throttles the thought.

He has brought two swords with him this evening. One is his own; elegant, finely-wrought, invincible, and the other is Excalibur.

He stares at Excalibur lying on a bale beside him. It was forged to his instructions, but it is large and clumsy and brute. The symbols cut into the blade burn in the sun, but their meaning 'Cast Me Away' burns hotter yet in his soul.

"*It is time to engage*," Verthandi whispers but he knows it already.

"Bradley," he calls, glancing at a bale-stack, "Come up to the loft a moment. I want to speak with you."

"*Speak with him, and then carve him open like the beast-of-the-field he is. Kill him, Lowther and we will guide your swords.*"

Verthandi's orders are clear.

Quo Fata Vocant.

The dipping sun had already bathed the imposing face of Shields Tower in warm, golden light when Atticus and Lucie Fox bicycled behind their own elongated shadows down the long avenue of yew trees.

Detective Superintendant Robson was standing on the steps below the doors in apparently deep conversation with Sir Hugh Lowther. The police constable from nearby Millhouse stood uncomfortably a few feet away from them along with another constable whom they did not recognise.

Robson looked up, shielding his eyes with the flat of his hand and peering into the rays to see who it was approaching. They passed into shadow and he nodded and raised his cap in greeting. Atticus and Lucie cycled up to the steps, dismounted and offered their compliments.

"Good evening to you, I'm sure, Mr and Mrs Fox," returned the superintendant politely, if rather stiffly. "May I ask how your enquiries are progressing?"

"They are progressing…steadily, Mr Robson, thank you, and what of your own?" Atticus was equally polite and equally ill at ease.

Robson scowled. He glanced to Sir Hugh before he said: "We have almost brought it to a conclusion, thank you. The old goblet used to poison the doctor is conclusive proof of the killer's identity. These constables here are just about to leave to make the arrest of Michael Britton for all three murders."

Atticus could sense Lucie shifting uneasily next to him. She was right of course; the 'old goblet', as Robson had called it, constituted yet more evidence against Britton but it was far from being conclusive proof.

He touched her arm reassuringly and said: "*Ei incumbit probatio qui dicit, non qui negat*; Mr Robson. A man is innocent until proven guilty."

"You both have proven him guilty, Mr Fox; you were the ones to find the goblet after all."

"We shall see. Mr Robson, when your constables go to arrest Britton, and, if they find him, it is imperative that they determine whether or not he has a lance, or long spear, with him, and also a large, bronze platter. They are what remain to him of the Hallows of Arthur."

"The Hallows of Arthur? What in God's name are the Hallows of Arthur?"

"They are relics, supposedly associated with King Arthur and his Knights of the Round Table. Britton believes he is holding them on Arthur's behalf."

"I'm certain there's a connection with those relics too," Sir Hugh interrupted. He had a rare approving note in his voice but Robson snorted derisively.

"We have had three murders to date, Robson," Atticus went on, "All of them connected by Arthurian legend as well as by the methods used. We suspect strongly that if events were allowed to run their course, the Holy

Platter and the Spear of Destiny could very well become the next instruments of murder. And then there is also a bugle horn and, of course, the sword Excalibur."

Robson shook his head incredulously.

"I think the rural air must be affecting you, Fox. Excalibur indeed – the very thought of it. And who was ever killed with a bugle horn? With all due respect, Sir Hugh, this is what you get by bringing amateurs into an enquiry."

"Mr and Mrs Fox are correct, damn you," Sir Hugh snarled. "There is an Arthurian connection, only you and your county constables are too stupid to see it. And wouldn't they be better employed in going to make this arrest than in standing there like whores in a bloody souk-market?"

Robson clenched his jaws as he struggled to swallow the rebuke. He despatched the constables with an irritable jerk of his head.

"Before they go Detective Superintendant Robson," Lucie interjected, "Would you or your constables happen to know about a number of murders, or perhaps disappearances, on these fells around twenty years or so ago?"

Robson shook his head, frowning. "I wasn't aware of any, other than the three Gypsy gin smugglers who, forgive me Mrs Fox, had their private parts cut off before being thrown from the Sewingshields Crags. Gypsies feuding amongst themselves was the opinion at the time. That was, let me see, twenty-five years ago, but even twenty years ago was well before my time here in Hexhamshire."

"It was just and right to castrate them, Robson," Urth interrupted, *"And Lowther did well to do it. They dishonoured his mama and now they burn in Hell."*

"Why does Lucie Fox ask that question though? What does she know of Gibson, or of Igraine?" Skuld asked warily.

"Why do you ask that, Lucie?" Sir Hugh repeated.

Before she could reply, he said: "There was my first wife of course. She disappeared from the moors beyond the Wall around that time, but what the devil has that got to do with these murders?"

"Possibly nothing at all, but the question has been thrown up by our investigations nonetheless."

Lucie's enquiring gaze shifted to the local constable. He stepped forward and pinched the peak of his helmet.

"No murders as were proven, ma'am, apart from the smugglers the detective superintendant mentioned. But I do remember that there were two disappearances around the same time as were never properly explained."

"Tell me about them."

"Aye, well the first, as Sir Hugh has already tell'd ye, was the first Lady Lowther. She disappeared after setting off alone onto the moors one summer's morning. The second was a gentleman and an officer in the Northumberland Fusiliers by the name of – let me think on it now – Captain Gibson. That was it; Captain Lancelot Gibson. He lived over on the other side of Hexham and he vanished just a day or two before Lady Lowther. There was, and I beg ye pardon, Sir Hugh, some talk at the time that they might have run off together, but neither of them had taken any clothes or effects with them so, in the end, that seemed unlikely."

"Damned, impudent nonsense!" thundered Sir Hugh.

"But they were acquainted with one another?" Lucie asked him, ignoring his outburst.

Lowther glowered at her.

"Barely, ma'am; they had met briefly once or twice at dinner, shared a dance perhaps, but I would never admit for one minute that they were well acquainted. And Gibson was never a gentleman. His father was a common sea captain who bought his estate with prize money."

"*There!*" Verthandi spat. "*That has shut you up good and proper, Madam Nosey Parker.*"

"We searched for them for days," the constable continued, rather impertinently speaking over her. "Sir Hugh even brought a good part of the regiment over from Fenham Barracks to help us. We enlisted the help of the fox-hounds too, but even they couldn't find any trace of 'em. It was unco queer – like they had vanished from the face of the Earth."

"That man is quite correct," Sir Hugh confirmed. "I brought in the fusiliers and personally directed their search. I even provided articles of their clothing for the hounds to catch their scent but, as he says, they found nothing."

Lucie thanked him. Even for a hardened soldier, and even after so long a time, it must be painful to recall such things. She turned again to the constable.

"There were no other disappearances, Constable? Are you quite sure of that?"

"I'm absolutely certain of it, ma'am. A lot of people have perished on the moors over the years. They've fallen, or become lost and frozen to death, or mebbees drowned in the loughs. Folk have even spoken of wolves up there, taking the odd person, but no, not 'disappeared' as such, and certainly not around that time."

Robson's curiosity finally overcame him.

"Why are you asking about disappearances a generation ago, Mrs Fox?"

"We are simply acquainting ourselves with a little background to the case." Lucie smiled disarmingly. "As you will likely know better than most, Mr Robson, malice and vendetta sometimes have a habit of bridging the years and we wanted to be certain that these recent murders are not part of a series of others."

Atticus said: "Thank you for indulging our curiosity; we will no doubt speak again in due course. Good evening to you, Sir Hugh, Mr Robson, Constables."

Atticus politely lifted his bicycling cap and he and Lucie left the group staring after them as they walked their machines down the carriage road towards the stables.

"Do you really think there could be a connection between the disappearances of twenty years ago and these murders, Atty?" Lucie asked when she was sure they were out of the earshot of both the men and the ever-watchful grotesques. "Twenty years is a very long time."

"I can't help but to think that there must be," he replied. "To suffer three murders, in quick succession, in a small, rural community such as this, is highly improbable. But then to have a number of seemingly unconnected disappearances, whether that number is three or, if you include Captain Gibson, four, in that same, small area is so unlikely as to be well-nigh impossible. Lightning, as they say, does not strike in the same place twice and it most certainly doesn't strike six or seven times. That is, unless it has a very good reason for doing so – unless there is some kind of a connection."

He sighed in frustration.

"Yet equally, there seems to be no such connection at all. There are no real similarities between the recent events and those of, as Robson said, a generation ago. We have murders on the one hand, disappearances on the other. The murders left bodies in plain view with no attempt whatsoever at concealment. In fact, it seems as if our murderer almost wants the evidence to be found. Perhaps he or she is playing a game with us? But the disappearances were exactly that – disappearances, and neither the bodies nor any evidence have ever been discovered."

He all at once gasped and grabbed at his brake levers. His bicycle juddered in his hands like a newly throttled fowl and stopped dead. Lucie's heart began to swell and hammer inside her chest when she caught sight of the thunderstruck expression on her husband's face.

"What? What is it?"

Atticus did not reply for several long and almost unendurable seconds, but then he shook his head, just as if he were trying to shift some bothersome insect.

"Atticus, what is it?" Lucie repeated.

"I'm so sorry," he said. He was breathing heavily. "I have just had a profoundly awful thought. It struck me a moment ago how the Whitechapel murderer, Jack the Ripper, also left his victims' bodies in full sight with the evidence all around them. He seemed to be playing a game with the police too. I was considering whether or not our murders might really be the work either of the Ripper himself, or at least of someone aping him. I am quite reassured now that they are neither."

Lucie nodded, a little uncertainly. "If you really are sure?"

"I am. I am certain, thank you, and if you remember, the Ripper killed only women – prostitutes in the main."

Lucie nodded but the atmosphere seemed darker, altogether more menacing, as they pushed their bicycles beneath the clock tower and into the stable courtyard.

It was Lucie who eventually broke the oppressive silence, which had gathered around them.

"My bicycle is hungry, Atticus. It's had a very busy day." Her voice sounded forced and unnatural, in bitter contrast to the humour in her words. "I do hope Mr Bradley is quick with its nosebag."

Atticus' expression tightened into the narrowest of smiles as he pushed on the big stable door.

"If we aren't dealing with Jack the Ripper," Lucie continued, serious once again, "then maybe it was Michael Britton after all. Perhaps once the constables arrest him, the killings will stop."

"We can only hope so."

Atticus took Lucie's bicycle and wheeled it, together with his own, into an empty stall. The presence of the big horses around him seemed somehow reassuring.

"Let us hope they are quick about it," he added, and then after a moment: "But I cannot shake the feeling that we are missing some… Lucie, what is it?"

His wife was staring up into the roof, her face suddenly drained of its colour.

"It would seem," she whispered, "that the constables have not been quite fast enough after all. It would seem that our murderer, whoever he or she is, has already found another victim."

Atticus turned.

Above the rows of wooden stalls, at the top of a steep, narrow ladder-way, was the entrance to a hayloft. It was a big, almost perfectly square entrance, made larger in recent times to accommodate the new machine-pressed bales, and framed by timber architrave like some great old pastoral painting. But it was a picture that must have been painted not by an artist, but by the very devil, because there, picked out by the flat rays of the dipping sun streaming in through a window, was the most hellish of silhouettes.

A man's body lay on its back, sprawled flaccidly across a hay bale with its head and limbs hanging limply by its side. Standing proud and erect from its gut was the great, broad blade of a sword, its handle and crosspiece presiding over the scene like some macabre memorial cross.

Atticus retched, and grasped at the pillar of the stall for support. Pressing his eyes tightly shut against the persisting image, he forced himself to breathe, slowly and evenly, waiting for the overwhelming waves of nausea to subside.

When at last they had, he opened his eyes to see Lucie hauling herself hand over hand up the steep, timber stair-ladder into the loft entrance. Her silhouette turned black against the light and seemed to become part of the scene itself as it curled over the body.

"Is he dead?" he called up, already certain of the answer.

"As a doornail, Atticus, although I declare he still looks a good deal healthier than you do at present."

He grimaced.

"It was just the shock of seeing it there. I shall be fine presently."

Atticus set his jaw and strode to the foot of the ladder. Gripping the smooth timber sides a little more firmly than perhaps was needed, he slowly and purposefully climbed up to join her.

"So his heart has gone too," he observed.

Two great openings had been carved across the middle of the body. They gaped horribly and at the point of their intersection stood the great blade of the sword, solidly embedded into the corpse's flesh.

"The Deuce! So it is clear we are dealing with the same murderer, Lucie and I don't need to ask how he killed this poor soul. He must have ripped his heart out whilst he was still alive. He was clearly run through with the sword after these wounds were made."

Atticus stared at the great blade with something akin to awe.

"It's passed right through him – quite pinned him to the bale."

"Actually I'm not so sure, Atticus. Do you see? There is also a second wound, to his neck. That is a sword wound too, but I would say from a different, a much smaller blade."

She pointed to a neat slit, cut into the collar of the corpse's jerkin at the point of the intersection of its right shoulder and its neck. It was heavily stained with darkening blood, already thickened into glutinous ooze with time and the dust from the hay.

Atticus regarded it with revulsion.

"Two swords were used to commit the murder? So now we have two attackers. So you think that is the blow which actually killed him, Lucie?"

His wife nodded.

"I would think it the more likely. If he had already sustained his other injuries, then frankly, there would have been very little need for this. Yes, it must be; this was the first blow struck and then his body was cut open after…"

Her voice trailed away. "But we still don't know why his heart – in fact, any of the hearts – is being taken, or why he was left impaled on this big sword."

She regarded it with an expression very similar to her husband's.

"Lucie, look at those," Atticus said.

With trembling finger he pointed to the flat of the sword, to where the metal was inscribed with a series of strange and outlandish symbols.

"What are they? What do they mean?" Lucie asked.

"They are runes – ancient characters used by the Norse and the Anglo-Saxons. The first symbol is called *Tyr* and it represents the letter 'T'. The next is *Ac*, 'A'."

He stared at the symbols, silently wrestling the meaning from each.

"'Take Me Up,'" he announced at last. He craned his head to peer at the obverse of the blade. "'Cast Me Away'."

"But Uther told us—"

"Yes, Lucie, it would seem that this sword is none other than Excalibur."

Lucie did not reply and they each fell into a wake of deep contemplation as below them the horses shuffled and stirred. Then Atticus said: "I suppose we ought to summon Robson. He will most probably still be at the house with Sir Hugh."

Lucie glanced almost guiltily down into the stalls, as if Robson might already be there.

"We will, Atty – but not just yet. I think we ought to take full advantage of being the first here. I will see if there is any finger-print evidence on the sword hilt before the police disturb it and remove the opportunity from us forever."

Atticus nodded and clambered gratefully down the ladder-way into the cool, fresher air of the stables below. He lifted his investigations bag from its rack at the back of his bicycle and then, after a moment's hesitation, he turned, reached down and pulled his walking cane from its clips on the crossbar.

"How long would you estimate the poor fellow has been dead?' he asked as he climbed back into the loft entrance and gently laid the bag and the cane onto the smooth-worn floorboards by her knees.

Lucie considered the question.

"Not long; there is some sign of rigor mortis in the head and neck but the blood isn't dry, even though it is very warm up here. I would guess an hour or two at most and certainly no longer than four hours."

Atticus took out his pocket watch and angled it up to catch the light from the window.

"So death is likely to have occurred between six and seven o'clock this evening. That gives plenty of time for our murderer, or murderers, to have made good their escape."

He picked up his cane.

"Notwithstanding that…Lucie, if you check for fingertip prints, I'll make certain they really have gone. It seems curious that they should have left that sword and I wonder if we might have disturbed them and caused them to flee. I will also see what other evidence they may unwittingly, or otherwise, have left for us."

Lucie smiled but anxiously and without conviction as she pushed open the bag.

"You will take care, won't you?"

He grinned back, equally unconvincingly, and tapped the ebony side of his cane with his knuckle.

Then he turned and applied his full attention to the hayloft.

It struck Atticus Fox immediately how neat and ordered everything was – something he could appreciate even in something as mundane as a loft of hay. The only caveat to this was a single stack of bales which had evidently been pushed from its place to tumble chaotically across the floor. Indeed it was on one of these bales that the body now lay impaled.

Atticus had the immediate impression of an ambush; that the dead man had been suddenly and overwhelmingly assailed by an attacker, or attackers, most probably concealed behind the stack. But had he, or they, been surprised by the victim, been forced to seek cover behind the stack, or had they lurked there, armed with their swords, with deadly malice aforethought?

Could anyone, he reflected, go about armed with swords without malicious forethoughts?

As her husband stood and pondered these questions, Lucie Fox worked her ostrich-feather brush carefully and deftly around the hilt of the sword. It wouldn't do to let the fine, grey finger-print powder drop onto the victim's wounds. She was rather helped by the fact that the sword was embedded so firmly into the hay bale beneath the corpse, and she reflected as she worked that whoever, or perhaps whatever, had wielded that great, two-handed sword, must have used immense force to do so.

Made suddenly anxious by her thoughts, she glanced around into the deep shadows that surrounded her. There was only Atticus, preoccupied in thought, gently pulling at the whiskers of his chin. Of the killers there was no sign, either in the loft itself or in the stables below. The horses were pulling at their hay nets or dozing in their stalls seemingly oblivious to the deadly drama that had unfolded so recently just a few feet above their heads.

She turned to the sound of Atticus' boots clattering across the bare boards towards her.

"There is absolutely no sign of anyone here, Lucie," he said, crouching by the bale, "And very little else in the way of evidence to help us pin down this brute."

"I have been a little more successful. Do you see here? I have been able to discern three distinct sets of finger-prints on the handle and this top part of the blade. Two of the sets are remarkably similar, although one of those shows heavy wear and some scarring. By their size, they must be the prints of fully grown men.

"The third set is quite different; it is much smaller, such as might have been made by an older child or a woman. If it was left by a woman, it is most likely to have been a gentlewoman because there is very little evidence of wear to the pads."

"Three sets!" Atticus was both delighted that she had found the prints and somewhat surprised at the number. "This is excellent, Lucie. I'll set about gluing-up some paper to lift the prints if you would get some of your glass plates on which we might preserve them. Then we can begin to compare the fingertips of those close to the murders and thus eliminate them from our suspicions or otherwise. This is good, hard evidence and we can move forward with this blessed investigation at last, before anyone else gets killed. Upon my word, Lucie, this is becoming more like the East End of London than a rural village in sleepy Northumberland."

CHAPTER TWENTY-NINE

When Atticus and Lucie Fox returned to the solid and reassuring presence of Shields Tower, they found the constables gone and presumably already on their way to arrest Michael Britton.

Sir Hugh Lowther and Detective Superintendant Robson had moved indoors. They were relaxing in a pair of low armchairs in the great drawing room, each with a generous measure of brandy in one hand and a large cigar in the other.

Sir Hugh stood abruptly as the Foxes entered. His ruddy face might have been from the effects of the brandy or from the heat of the crackling ash-log fire.

"Aha, Fox, you're back. You took a devil of a time to stow your bicycles and no mistake, but no matter, no matter. May I offer you a glass of something to restore you? Robson and I are working our way through a very agreeable bottle of cognac and I can order-up tea or coffee for Lucie."

Atticus stood tall.

"Sir Hugh, Detective Superintendent Robson, I regret to inform you of our discovery of yet another murder victim."

One heartbeat became two. Sir Hugh cast a glance at Robson who was staring open-mouthed at Atticus, utterly stunned.

"Another murder," the superintendant spluttered at last.

"*Another gift to the Fates and another blow for justice,*" Urth corrected him.

Atticus nodded.

"Quite so. Another murder, in the hayloft above Sir Hugh's stables, not more than four, and more likely less than two hours ago. A man was stabbed, and impaled on a sword. He has the usual wounds across his abdomen and if you would both care to set down your brandies and cigars, we will tell you more about it as we take you there."

Several minutes and a hastened walk later, Atticus stood back to make way for Sir Hugh and the detective superintendant to enter the stables.

"We took the opportunity to take fingertip print evidence from the sword," Atticus called as he followed Lucie through the broad carriage door in their wake.

There was only the clatter of boots on ladder rungs followed by a single gasp from Robson. Then Sir Hugh reappeared, leaning out from the loft. He was smiling.

"Damned good show, the both of you," he cried. "Then it's almost over? You have your conclusive evidence, so now you'll be able to prove who the murderer is."

His black stallion in its stall below whinnied at the sound of his voice.

"We're not quite there yet, Sir Hugh. Up to the present time, we have only got so far as to identify prints from three persons on the grip and forte, which is the top part of the blade. We need now to—"

"I'm a soldier; I know what a damned forte is, Fox. But you say there were three sets. How in deuce can there be *three* sets?" Sir Hugh's expression had switched from delight to bewilderment.

"There are definitely three sets of fingertip prints: two left by men and one by a woman, likely a gentlewoman, or perhaps a grown child. We need next to take impressions from anyone who may have come into contact with the sword and compare them to the ones we've preserved from the scene on our little, glass plates."

Robson's disembodied voice carried through the hatch.

"Does this technique of finger-print comparison really work, Fox?" It sounded keen with interest. "The constabularies are under some pressure to adopt it."

"Indeed it does work – excellently well. What are called the friction ridges of the fingertips form patterns that are quite unique to each person. I believe it to be nothing less than the greatest breakthrough in the entire history of crime detection."

"Indeed?" Robson replied. "That is some claim! I can see the finger-prints clearly in this grey powder that seems to be everywhere. You say there are three parties to the murder?"

"We say that we have identified three different sets of finger-prints on the sword, nothing more," Lucie corrected him. "It has been handled by at least three people, any one or more of whom could be the murderer. Equally, it remains possible that those prints may have been left quite innocently, although that, I should say, is rather unlikely."

She peered up at Sir Hugh, who was staring distastefully at the transfixed corpse.

"Do you recognise the poor fellow, Sir Hugh?"

"*Yes, tell them who it is*," Verthandi urged him.

Lowther dragged his gaze away from the body and fixed it onto the Foxes.

"Very well; yes, I do recognise him. He has worked here, in these stables, for nigh on thirty years now. It is my head groom, an oaf by the name of Albert Bradley."

An image of their bicycles, standing in a horse stall with nosebags full of oats hanging from their handlebars, formed instantly in Lucie's mind. She thought of the impish sense of humour behind the practical joke, and the contrast with the bloody, lifeless corpse lying sprawled above them was stark.

Robson reached forward and tugged at the thick crosspiece of the sword. It was solid and unyielding.

"The heart's been removed again," he observed, "and this blade is in devilish deep. It looks as if this fellow – Bradley you say his name was – has fallen back onto the hay bale and then been run through with this sword? Ye gods, but it must have been some blow; it has quite nailed him to it!"

"We do not necessarily think so, Mr Robson."

Lucie climbed nimbly up the ladder.

"It appears that someone, an accomplice armed with a lighter sword perhaps, struck the first blow. That caused the smaller wound to the base of the neck. The larger sword was thrust through the body and into the bale very soon afterwards."

"But why would anyone want to do that?" Robson said, bending to examine the neck wound. He sighed in exasperation. "And it's another sword killing, Sir Hugh. No doubt we shall be having yet more preposterous rumours of King Arthur's resurrection flying around the parish. I declare, your ancestor would have done better to have chosen a different site for the building of Shields Tower."

Lowther snorted irritably.

"King Arthur's resurrection be damned. I recognise that sword."

"Yes, we noticed the blade has been engraved with runes. It would appear to be Excalibur." said Atticus.

"Excalibur!" cried Robson.

Sir Hugh looked across to Atticus, his sapphire-blue eyes burning with sudden intensity.

"Exactly so, Fox and what is more, I am certain I know its present owner."

"Who – who is it?" Robson snapped.

"Michael Britton. It's Michael Britton's sword and I know that because I was the one who gave it to him. I recognise it from those marks on the blade. They are runes, just as Fox has said."

He turned to Robson. "When your two constables get back with the madman, Robson, Mr and Mrs Fox can examine his fingertip prints. They will then be able to prove what I have been saying all along: that he is your murderer, your now five-time murderer!"

"Four-time," Atticus corrected him.

"Four-time then! Damned insolent pedantry; isn't four times bad enough? Four, five, or whatever the blasted number is, Britton will finally go to the gallows where he belongs, with everyone knowing what he is. As for the rest of us, we will all, at long last, be able to put this whole sorry business behind us and get on with the rest of our lives. Good evening to you all."

With that he turned, and with a deadly look on his flushed face, pushed roughly past Lucie and thundered down the ladder-way.

Several uneasy minutes after Sir Hugh had stormed from the stables, there came the sound of more heavy, hobnailed boots clattering on the blue bricks of the stable floor. The faces of the two police constables peered out sheepishly from the shadows.

"Good evening, sir," said the one they did not recognise, lifting off his helmet, "I was told at the house that the detective superintendant would be here."

His expression betrayed an earnest wish that the detective superintendant would be nowhere near and it was really quite disconcerting to see a county police officer seeming to be so nervous.

Atticus was about to respond when Robson's voice boomed irritably from above.

"I'm up here in the hayloft. Well? Have you arrested him?"

There was a long, strained silence, which the local constable broke first.

"I regret very much to report that we have not been able to, sir. When we arrived at his cottage, he was already gone. It looks like he's been away from there for some time. We could find no trace of him anywhere nearby."

There was a whispered oath.

"Well then, you had both better begin to search further away," he raged as he half-climbed, half-leaped down the ladder-way. "There's still a bit of daylight left and even then it'll be more than half-moon. Go back; find him; arrest him. Do not, under any circumstances, even consider coming back without him. If you do, then if I don't have your miserable guts for it, Sir Hugh Lowther most certainly will."

"Did you find the lance and the platter?" Atticus asked.

The constables looked down shamefacedly. Plainly they hadn't.

Robson boiled over again. "I have another dead man up there, damn you, Constables. Albert Bradley, Sir Hugh Lowther's groom of thirty years, has been at the receiving end of a murderous attack. That makes four murders altogether and no fewer than two – two, hark you – today! We still have a lunatic murderer abroad somewhere on the moors and to top it all, it appears that he is now armed with a bloody great lance."

There was a pause.

"Well, Constables, what are you still standing there for?"

There was another beat of silence followed by an almost comically frantic mêlée as the two constables realised they had been dismissed and quite fell over themselves in their haste to escape.

Robson watched them as they scrambled out through the stable door. Then he turned, calmer now, and addressed the Foxes.

"Forgive me the outburst and the oaths, but the imperative here is that we capture this madman before he kills again. I will send for you both once we have him safely in our custody so you can lift his finger-prints as Sir Hugh ordered. If we can persuade a judge of the efficacy of the technique, then he can be hung or incarcerated as His Lordship feels inclined. Either way, the chief constable, Sir Hugh Lowther and the gentlemen of the press will all be appeased, and the folk of the South Tyne valley will all be able to sleep a little more soundly in their beds."

"Mr Robson," said Atticus softly, "You forget that Mrs Fox discovered *three* sets of fingertip prints upon that sword. I am afraid there will be, without doubt, a great deal more to this case than the arrest and fingertip printing of Michael Britton."

Robson coloured. "I am well aware of that, Mr Fox." He laid heavy emphasis on the word 'Mister', but the uncomfortable, perhaps even guilty, look in his eyes drew the force of his bluster.

"And please be mindful that this is a serious business – police business – and that folk are dying. I don't doubt but that in your hearts you both know Britton is guilty. I know Britton is guilty, and, to his credit, Sir Hugh Lowther has always known it. So the sooner he is locked safely away in Hexham gaol, the sooner he will be prevented from killing anyone else."

Atticus shrugged.

"Then you will be very pleased to hear that we don't actually require Britton in person in order to be able to lift his prints. We can do that from any smooth, hard object he has recently handled. If we have your permission to enter his cottage, we might even be able to do so tonight. Our intention was always to return there."

Robson's expression lightened.

"Well that's one scrap of good news at least. I've no more constables to spare but if you think you'll be safe up there on your own, then yes, I'd be delighted."

The last red glow of the sun seems to turn the western horizon to fire – the fires of Hell. It bathes him in its light and turns the steel of his breastplate and the tip of the great spear he holds aloft as red as the smouldering hatred in his heart. There is an abomination upon this moor and his hatred can, at last, burst into the raging conflagration that will send it to the Inferno. It will be the sixth part of the wergild to be paid to the Norns.

"*SHE COMES*," Verthandi screams in triumph and the soldier in him cringes.

"Hush, my Lady," he whispers, "lest she hears you."

"*She will not hear me*," Verthandi retorts and he knows it is so. He has long since learned that few have the honour to hear the words of the Sisters. But then he too hears the footsteps of the abomination. He sees her broad, black silhouette rising in the moonlight.

Engage the enemy. Steady now.

He lowers the spear, the Spear of Destiny, until its fiery tip points to his quarry.

"*Use it well,*" Verthandi exhorts him, "*and we will guide your arm.*"

"My Lady, I will."

He stands, silent and perfectly still, his body almost a part of the shadowy moorland that surrounds him, and he waits and watches as she draws near.

Unfortunately there were neither lamps nor lights of any kind in Michael Britton's deserted cottage, and the combination of dirt-encrusted windows and darkling sky meant that Atticus and Lucie reluctantly elected to return there at first light the following day.

It was as they were squeezing back through the narrow style, by the very place where Samson Elliott had met his death, that they heard it. The pure, strident note shattered the brittle tranquillity of the gloaming.

It was the note of a bugle.

The call was exactly as Artie Lowther had described it to them and Atticus could picture him, could almost hear him, as he had told them: 'There were seven notes: two low, two high, two low, one high; repeated thrice'.

At first the sound seemed to come from everywhere; from the moors, from the rocks, from the very air itself. But then, as they listened, they realised that it had both source and direction. It was coming from directly behind them, from beyond Britton's cottage, from the great black crags of the high Whin Sill and the fells of Sewingshields beyond. And it was exultant.

And, as they looked, they were both convinced that they glimpsed the silhouette of a tall, solitary figure striding among those rocks, sure that the moonlight had glinted off what might have been steel plate on his breast as he turned and disappeared back into the shadows of the crags.

Lucie hugged herself as she stood, cased between the big stones of the style.

"I don't like it, Atty," she said. "Whatever it is, leave it be. Let us get back to the Tower."

Atticus looked at his wife and saw his own fear reflected there. For a moment he thought of giving chase. But night was closing in and whoever, or whatever, the figure was, it clearly knew the country well. So it was with only the very tiniest of regrets that he agreed.

CHAPTER THIRTY

When Atticus and Lucie toppled gratefully past the corner of Shields Tower into the blessed sanctuary of its moon-shadow they could plainly see a figure, taller, softer and more benign than the watching grotesques, standing in the pale light of the gibbous moon. It was standing at the entrance to the avenue and from the way it was peering anxiously into the shadows it was plain that something was terribly wrong.

Atticus hailed it. "Hullo there. Is something amiss?"

The figure started and whirled around to face them and the moonlight revealed the face of Mr Collier the butler.

"Oh, Mr and Mrs Fox, thank the Lord you're back!" Relief washed away all trace of his usual manner. "You haven't seen anything of Miss Armstrong by any chance?"

Atticus and Lucie exchanged a dread-filled glance and Atticus said: "We have not. Why do you ask? Is she missing?"

Collier nodded. "I fear so. Twice a week, Miss Armstrong visits a lady-friend who lives alone up on the moors but she is always returned by ten o'clock sharp. She is very particular on that score. Tonight she's still not back, and what with two more murders today – Dr Hickson's and poor Albert Bradley's – I truly fear for her safety, especially as she always stops by the madman's cottage to deliver him his food parcel."

"We have just come from Britton's cottage ourselves," returned Atticus. "We saw nothing of her there, nor of him come to that. Perhaps she is still at the house of her friend?"

"I presume you know where that is?" Lucie asked.

Collier nodded. "Yes, ma'am, it's not that far – no more than a mile and a half from here."

"Then get a lamp and make sure the Tower's doors are securely locked. We'll go with you to try to seek her."

As Collier hurried off to do as he was bidden, Atticus turned to his wife. In the moonlight, his expression seemed especially grave.

"There are still two of Arthur's Hallows left, Lucie: the Spear of Destiny and the Holy Platter, and I can only pray that I am wrong about them. I declare, why any person would want to venture out alone onto the moors after today's awful events is quite beyond me, and particularly just to pay a regular house-call."

"I don't think Miss Armstrong would easily be intimidated," Lucie said quietly.

Atticus could not disagree. "She's a strapping, well-built lady to be sure," he said. "I for one wouldn't want to take her on, but nonetheless—"

"And it was surely more than just a house-call," Lucie added.

She seemed amused by his sudden puzzlement. "You really haven't guessed have you?"

"Guessed what, my dearest?"

"Atticus, Bessie Armstrong is quite obviously a sapphist."

"She's a what?"

"A sapphist – a uranist, a lesbian woman. Can't you tell?"

Atticus was aghast.

"A woman who prefers…who prefers intimacy with other women?"

Lucie nodded.

"No, I really didn't have an inkling. Good lord! Are you sure? I've read of such women, of course, but I never dreamed I would ever actually meet one. Perhaps I might have in Paris, or in London even, but surely never here in Northumberland."

"Well I should say there are two in the county at least. It's a lady-friend that Miss Armstrong visits on the moors after all."

Collier's sudden reappearance killed the conversation. He had a pistol in one hand and a large, copper bulls-eye lantern in the other.

"I've locked the doors, just as you ordered, Mr Fox," he said. "All except the scullery door but Grey, the coachman, is guarding that with a fowling piece. James isn't back yet from Hayden Bridge."

Ominous foreboding lent wings to the trio as they hied through the deep shadows of the avenue and up the steep lane beyond. The air chilled perceptibly as they climbed to the higher ground of the fells and then, just as they reached the crown of the hill, the dark verges on either side of them gave way to the broad junction of the Hayden Bridge road.

"Not far now," Collier panted. But instead of the right-hand route to Hayden that they had followed earlier in the day, he shone the lantern beam to their left, which the shadowed letters of the wooden signpost opposite announced was the road to the strangely named village of Twice Brewed.

It was as they looked along the sweep of that road, uncannily white in the moonlight and stark against the black moors around it, that Lucie screamed.

It was a brief scream but shrill, a scream truncated by her natural courage and by her long familiarity with the human form at its most grisly. Perhaps it was this scream that somehow fortified Atticus; that prevented his usual, visceral reaction, as he stopped short and could only stare across the lane at what lay in front of them.

Standing proud and erect from the tangled shadows of the roadside vegetation was what he recognised immediately and with crushing certainty as a lance. His eye was drawn down the long length of the slender shaft, through the bleached stalks of the grass, quivering and swarming in the trembling light from Collier's lantern, to the unmistakeable shape of a human body.

As if to a silent cue, they ran to the macabre scene. It was the murder Atticus had dreaded was inevitable. Not inevitable in the fact that the body spread on the grass before them in its man's shirt and breeches was instantly recognisable as that of Sir Hugh's housekeeper; indeed, in the very moment he had seen her there, the theories that had begun to form in his mind during the three days they had been in Northumberland had, all at once, been shattered. It was inevitable only in the fact that the instrument used to murder her was one of the remaining Hallows. It was the Holy Lance, the Spear of Destiny.

He gazed down at the dead woman, her face frozen in pain and terror. What was it Lucie had called her, a sapphist? He had heard her kind called the 'third sex'; a woman who, despite opportunities to be married and settle down to a 'proper, practical life' had continued to choose intimacies only with other women.

"Her sapphism has killed her," he murmured.

"What on earth are you talking about, Atticus Fox? Being a sapphist didn't kill her; some monster killed her!" Lucie's rebuke was furious as she kneeled to examine the wound.

The lance had penetrated deep into Bessie's lower abdomen and the prolonged agony of her death was evident in the hideous contortions of her face, and by her hands, which still clutched the shaft, as if even in death she was yet trying to pluck it away.

"No, no, Lucie!" Atticus protested, "I didn't mean it in that way. Please don't misunderstand me; I only meant that—"

"Halloa!"

The shout came from the swarming blackness behind them. They whirled round. In the long, swaying beam of the lantern, the pounding of heavy boots became two constables hurtling towards them, their capes billowing behind like the wings of avenging angels.

They clattered to a halt.

"Mr Collier! What in God's holy name has happened here? We heard a scream." The Millhouse village constable caught sight of what lay in the grass at their feet. "Bloody hellfire!"

"The scream was me," Lucie admitted, "when I saw Miss Armstrong's body lying there."

The constables continued to stare. They seemed to have been struck dumb.

"Bessie Armstrong – the housekeeper at Shields Tower," Collier added.

"Why is she dressed as a man?" the second constable asked after a moment.

There was another long, awkward silence, filled only by the distant purr of a nightjar, which Lucie eventually broke.

"I believe she felt more comfortable dressed in that way."

"I see. Well thank you, ma'am; we'll take charge of this now."

He stepped forward and grasped the shaft of the lance.

"Don't do that!" Atticus snapped, sending something unseen scuttling away through the grass. "You'll compromise the evidence."

The constable glanced sideways at him. "We're police constables, as you can clearly see, sir. We carry the Queen's warrant on our truncheons, and we know very well what we are about."

With a brief but appalling sucking noise, he eased the lance free from Bessie Armstrong's corpse and, smeared in lumpy, congealing blood as it was, held up the tip in front of his face, regarding it with detached interest as a farrier might inspect a new-forged shoe.

"Is this the lance you asked us to get for you?"

Atticus nodded.

"Well we have it now and you'll be welcome to collect it from the station in Hexham – once the superintendant has finished with it, that is."

Lucie had bent low over the corpse and gently pulled aside its hands. The silver moonlight illuminated two long and bloody gashes drawn across the shirt beneath in the form of a *crux decussata*.

"Britton's ripped her heart out an' all," the constable growled.

Lucie spent some time carefully probing the intersection of the gashes with her fingertips.

"No, I don't believe so. Not this time."

"What's that?" Atticus forced his gaze back down to the body.

Lucie pressed on the wounds.

"Do you see? These cuts are only superficial. No-one has removed the heart, or anything else, from this body."

"How extraordinary," Atticus exclaimed.

"Do you suppose that this might be an imitating-murder?" Lucie suggested, "Committed by someone trying to copy the broad manner of the others but without knowing the full details of them?"

"That is quite possible, Lucie," Atticus agreed, "Other than in the rather inescapable fact that it was committed using another of the Hallows."

"The superintendant will have a better idea," the constable said firmly. "We need to get the deceased back to Shields Tower. We can take a better look at her there."

CHAPTER THIRTY-ONE

Atticus Fox decided not to sleep that night. Instead, after they had informed a fulminating Sir Hugh Lowther of his housekeeper's death, calmed a still profoundly distressed Mr Collier, and after Lucie had settled sufficiently to kiss him goodnight and curl up snugly under the counterpane, Atticus picked up one of the oil lamps. He gathered up his travelling chess set, poured a large glass of chalybeate water from a freshly filled jug and slipped out of the door.

His mind was a maelstrom of unconnected facts, suspicions and conjectures. In truth, he felt a little like a music hall turn, juggling balls or spinning plates and trying with every ounce of his concentration not to allow any single one of them to drop.

What he desperately needed to do now was to think. He needed to ponder each and every one of his thoughts, relate them somehow to each of the others and then piece them all together to form that elusive picture that was the identity of the murderer – the murderer who had struck five times now in the space of a single week and three times that very day.

The house was deserted, save for the phantoms and spirits conjured onto the walls by the lamplight. Atticus flitted down the stairway by the ever-watchful Urth, past the great long-cased clock with its deep, metronomic tick and reached, at last, the blessed quietude of the orangery. There he set down the oil lamp, his chess set and his water onto a side table and allowed his tension to vent in one long sigh. Here, he would be able to focus his mind absolutely onto the facts of the case and the strange but undeniable links between these murders and the legends of King Arthur.

There was a very particular link to the supposed Arthurian relics and he listed these in his mind: The sword, the garter, the bugle horn and the four Hallows proper. There were seven.

There had been five murders and there were seven relics. Should they expect therefore, two killings more? Or were they already too late? Had the killer, or killers, already committed the murders and, like Bessie Armstrong, did they await only their grisly discovery.

He quailed at the thought.

Seven relics.

There was something else about the number seven too, something maddeningly elusive that niggled at his mind.

Instinctively he reached for the glass of chalybeate water and the movement, reflected in the black panes of the orangery wall, caught his eye.

There was the horrific butchering of the victims too, and the tearing out of their hearts through the curious X-shaped gashes cut across their torsos. All except Bessie Armstrong that is; the wounds on her body were little more than skin deep.

He took a sip and thought suddenly of Lucie, quite lovely and absolutely at peace somewhere above him and he felt a momentary urge to join her in the warm, safe bed. But his mind was racing and he knew that on this night he could have no such tranquillity.

Was Lucie right though? Perhaps Bessie Armstrong's killer was merely aping the *modus operandus* of the real murderer after all. In his mind, Atticus retrieved the still-vivid memory of the bloody gashes in her shirt. No, they were in precisely the same position as those on the other victims' bodies and in the same style of cross – the *crux decussata* – the form of the Cross of St Andrew and of the Saltire.

He reached across the table and moved a white pawn forward across two squares of his chessboard.

St Andrew's Cross – the symbol of the Scots. For centuries the Scots, and before them the Picts, had ravaged this very land. Was there a connection there perhaps? Atticus slid his chessboard round and moved an ebony pawn to meet the threat from its carved-ivory opponent. No, he was quite sure there was not. It was merely a coincidence. The link was Arthurian.

The *crux decussata* was also the Roman numeral for 'ten' from *decus* meaning honour, glory and, yes he remembered with a start, completeness. Where they to expect ten murders in total therefore, and not seven at all? Again, he thought not. The link to the number seven was too strong, too powerfully suggestive.

The keys to unlocking this puzzle were the number seven and Arthurian legend. Atticus stared through his shadowy reflection on the orangery glass into the blackness of the night beyond it and thought of Michael Britton, out there alone somewhere. Could he really be the murderer?

Atticus sighed ruefully as he thought of the statue at the foot of the stairs. If only he could read men's hearts as the Sisters of the Wyrd could read them, and write their destiny in runes.

In runes!

There was a rune that was formed as a cross – a *crux decussata*. It was the rune – Atticus frantically sifted his memory – it was the rune *Giefu*, the runic character for the modern letter 'G' and the symbol for gift. Giefu was the seventh rune of the *futhorc* and the reason the number seven was considered to be lucky by the ancients.

Dear lord, could that be it? The seven relics were for seven deaths; perhaps they could also be for seven gifts. But gifts from, and to, whom? Gifts of death would almost certainly be ritualised in some way and the hearts been removed from all of them – all of them barring Bessie Armstrong.

But why?

A dark shadow falls across Lucie Fox as she lies in slumber and a phantom with piercing blue eyes stands, silent and perfectly still, and watches her.

"*Do you see her beauty?*" Skuld whispers, taking care not to wake her.

He nods. "Yes."

"*And do you remember our promise to you?*"

He nods once more, suddenly breathless.

"There is but a single part of the wergild remaining; that which is Atticus Fox, and then we will cause Igraine's spirit to fill her and become yours once again."

"Thank you." His voice is husky, barely louder than the pounding of his heart.

"Look at her," Verthandi commands him.

Obedient to her call, he reaches down to the bedcovers. His hands tremble and his breath catches in his chest. She is quite beautiful.

"LOOK AT HER! You want to, don't you?"

Yes, he does want to. He wants to so very much. Gently he lifts the bedcovers and draws them back. Fingers of moonlight from the annulets cut into the window shutters lie across Lucie's – no not Lucie's – across Igraine's cotton nightdress, pure, white, and virginal once again. They lie across her breasts, the slender line of her shoulder, her—

"Touch her now!" Verthandi's voice is urgent and masterful. It cannot be resisted.

He nods.

His fingertips slip across her cheek and the sculpted line of her jaw. Her skin is warm and soft, so very soft, and so feminine. She gently nuzzles her cheek into the pillow and bares her slender neck to his ravenous gaze.

Without waiting for Verthandi's prompt, Sir Hugh Lowther slips his trembling fingers behind the nape of her neck and gently traces the line of her throat with the tip of his thumb. At his touch, her breathing begins to quicken and to deepen, and he watches, transfixed, as her breasts rise and fall in the moonlight and press against the thin cotton bodice of her nightdress.

"Do you see how she already responds to your touch?" Skuld whispers.

Sir Hugh cannot reply. His hand stretches wide and envelops the mound of her breast. He gently squeezes and feels it swelling into his palm.

Lucie sighs softly in her sleep and he feels her nipple rise and harden.

"NOT NOW, LOWTHER!"

Urth's sharp cry shatters the tension into a hundred pieces and he starts and draws back his hand.

"Not now. She is not Igraine yet. She is still Lucie Fox and will be until the madman is shamed and her husband slain. But remember well the feel of her tit. It is a sign of our promise to you."

When Lucie Fox stirred from her sleep early the following morning, she shivered. Her mama would have told her that someone must have walked on her grave. For some reason both her blankets and her counterpane had slid from her bed and she had awoken feeling disturbed and discomforted, just as if she had escaped from a nightmare she could no longer recall.

On the floor below her, Atticus, by contrast, was feeling calmer than he had in days, relaxed and strangely energised by his new thought and purpose. Truly, he was utterly exhausted, and truly, he could still not quite fit the piece of jigsaw that was the murder of Bessie Armstrong into the puzzle, nor fully comprehend why the hearts of the victims might have been torn out. But at least he had now, if not a theory, then at least the workable basis for one.

Unfortunately that theory also pointed to the fact that the cycle of murders was far from complete and the knowledge of that remained to trouble his mind.

He poured the last of the now tepid water into his glass and thought once more about his principal suspect, the one who was most likely to hang, with a deep mix of emotions. He was angry of course; angry that the lives of five people had been so brutally cut short; angry that the lives of two more were in mortal peril and furious at how that of an eighth might be destroyed. But he felt also a great sadness for the agony of the tortured soul who could see no other option in the destiny of his life but that of murder and revenge.

CHAPTER THIRTY-TWO

"Isn't a red sky in the morning supposed to be some kind of warning?" Lucie remarked as they rounded the corner of Shields Tower to a dramatic sunrise of crimson and blue. She tucked her arm into her husband's and frowned. It felt strangely odd, as if she had been in some way disloyal or.... She shook off the feeling as ridiculous and said: "If it is, then that is the great-grandfather of all warnings."

Then she asked: "Anyway, Atticus, have you finally determined who our murderer might be and, by-and-by, did you win your game of chess?"

Atticus shook his head.

"The games were all stalemates," he said, "Which is good. It means that my mind remains perfectly objective. As for the murderer's identity, I find myself again in something of a stalemate and that is not quite so auspicious. I have a reasonable suspicion but I would put it no higher than that.

"Lucie, you discovered three sets of fingertip prints on the sword we can call Excalibur. At least two more people are in great danger for their lives so it is vital that we identify the owners of those prints as swiftly as we are able. Also, James must have returned from Hayden Bridge by now. He told us he served with the Northumberland Fusiliers and I need to find out a little more about bugle calls."

The whitewashed walls of Uther's cottage seemed to glow crimson as they reflected the dying embers of the early morning sky. But, just as before, they knew the instant they spied it that it remained eerily deserted.

Atticus rapped on the peeling paint of the door above the great red emblem of the dragon.

"Uther," he called, "Uther Pendragon, it is only us; Atticus and Mrs Fox."

There was no sound. Lucie touched his arm and pointed to a small parcel lying on the trodden ground to the side of the door. It was wrapped in brown paper that had been shredded and torn.

Atticus stooped to pick it up.

"Bread and cheese," he noted, pulling aside the wrapping, "Although the birds or the rats have clearly been at it. We must have overlooked it last night."

He knocked again, more briskly this time, and then lifted the latch and pushed open the door.

Atticus and Lucie stepped across the threshold and glanced about. Even in the short time since their previous visit the sense of desolation and abandonment had heightened palpably.

"This will serve us excellently well, Atty," Lucie said, picking up Uther's glass tumbler with its crusting of orange sediment. "There is a full set of prints here."

Atticus laid the ragged food parcel onto the table and swept aside a pile of mould-peppered sketches to allow space for his wife to work. Lucie took her ostrich-feather brush from the enamelled tube in which it was kept and twisted the cork from a flask of dusting powder. As she settled to her task, Atticus took the opportunity to examine once again Uther Pendragon's cottage.

"It still bothers me that Sir Hugh continues to allow Britton to stay here," he remarked as he gazed around the squalor.

"He has the debt of honour," Lucie replied without looking up from her tumbler. "And I suppose that underneath all of his bluster, he must still hold a man innocent until it is proven otherwise."

Atticus grunted.

"Quite possibly, but it still rings out of key. The man is convinced Britton is a five-time murderer yet he keeps him here, a mere stone's throw from his own son and daughter and the rest of his household. Indeed, he allows his son and daughter to visit him, and even required his housekeeper to deliver a food parcel to him twice each week."

He nodded to the ragged remains of the parcel on the table.

"Murderer or not however, there can be little doubt that Britton should be taken into a lunatic asylum, for his own safety as much as anyone else's."

"I agree, Atty, but don't forget that Sir Hugh made a promise to his father. He may be many things, but word and honour are everything to him."

Lucie held a small glass plate, onto which she had fixed several dark blue paper strips, up to the light. There were three other identical plates laid side-by-side on the tabletop.

"Here you are, Atticus," she said grimly, "Michael Britton's prints match exactly with one of the sets we took from the sword hilt. It is the set that exhibits the extensive scarring."

She shrugged.

Atticus stared at the incriminating prints through their thin glass mount.

"Then that will certainly be enough for Robson and, as likely as not, for a jury too, given the force of the other evidence."

Lucie shrugged again.

"It's damning to be sure but, as you said yourself, not entirely conclusive given that there were two other sets on the sword too. We need to find the owners of those prints today. Northumberland is a large county. Where do you propose we begin?"

"Well," Atticus replied, "Northumberland is a vast county but all of this appears to be centred on Shields Tower and the home farm, so I suggest we begin there. But before we do, I'm going to take a look at Britton's drawpump. This orange water still intrigues me greatly and I need to look at a fresh sample."

There was no back door to Michael Britton's cottage so Atticus followed an obviously well-trodden path around the crumbling walls to the windowless rear. For a man obsessed by the moors and crags of Sewingshields, Atticus mused, the pump momentarily forgotten, there could scarcely be a better place to live. In front of him the ground rose steadily, punctuated here and there by long, shallow crags and yellow mounds of gorse, to finally break open against the rocks of the high Whin Sill. The panorama was as beautiful as it was dramatic.

Atticus' attention returned to Britton's cottage. There were rocks here too. In fact, the cottage had been built in the lee of one of the wide, low outcrops of rock that were repeated up the hillside beyond. The draw-pump was nestled tightly against this, encased in a tall, wooden housing, with an iron handle on one side and a lead spout on the other gaping over a mossy, stone trough.

Atticus grasped the handle and heaved down on it. The pump primed immediately and spilled its load of water through the mouth of the spout. He scooped the tumbler under the flow and held it up to the light. There was indeed a faint but unmistakeably orange hue to the water. Stepping up astride the slippery sides of the trough, he shuffled off the rotting lid of the pump's housing and peered down inside.

It was still early and the low angle of the sun could illuminate only the top few inches of the naked and ochre-stained wood. Beyond that, the wet lead of the pump mechanism glistened back at him from the gloom. But it was enough. Atticus grunted in grim satisfaction and set the lid back into place.

CHAPTER THIRTY-THREE

By the time Atticus and Lucie Fox returned to Shields Tower, the household was only just beginning to stir into life. Sir Hugh had taken an early train to some regimental business in Newcastle, so their only company that morning in the breakfast room was that of Master Arthur and Miss Jennifer. They were both bursting to know more first-hand of the Foxes' grisly discovery in the hayloft.

"I heard that Albert Bradley's body was almost cloven in two, Mr Fox," Arthur recounted breathlessly. "And that the steps of the loft were literally running with blood. Is it true it was done with Excalibur itself?"

Atticus seemed to be engrossed in salting his breakfast porridge so Lucie replied.

"It was not quite so gory or dramatic as you describe, Arthur although yes, the body of Mr Bradley had been impaled on a very large, two-handed sword. As for it being Excalibur – the real Excalibur – well, we can't be so sure about that. It might have been an excellent copy perhaps."

She smiled indulgently at them.

"I recollect that you are both convinced that King Arthur and Lady Guinevere have risen from their grave?"

They both nodded and Jennifer said: "They are risen, Mrs Fox, but from an enchanted sleep, not from a grave. That is what the legends say."

Lucie acknowledged the correction with another gracious smile.

"You also agreed that Mr Fox might be taken blindfolded to this vault where you say you discovered them."

Artie cast a glance to his sister and shifted nervously in his seat.

"We have discussed it again since and Jenny agrees that we may show you the vault, but only on the strict condition that you both come, that you are both blindfolded and that you both swear that you won't breathe a word of it to a single, living soul."

Neither Atticus nor Lucie answered immediately, but Artie seemed to read their expressions.

"Forgive us but we must be certain that the location of the vault remains a secret."

"Of course you must, and thank you." Atticus glanced up at last from his porridge. "Mrs Fox and I will discuss your kind offer after breakfast. For now, we have examined the sword we found in the groom's body – be it Excalibur or not – and discovered three different fingertip impressions upon the hilt. I must explain that the patterns on one's fingertips, what we in the profession of criminal detection call their *minutiae*, are quite unique to each and every person. If we find the owners of the fingertip prints therefore, we have almost certainly found the murderer, or murderers.

Lucie said: "We can also eliminate innocent persons from our investigation in exactly the same way. You will understand that it is almost as important for us to discover who does *not* own the finger-prints as it is to find who *does*. Before you go off to church, Master Arthur, Miss Jennifer, would you consent to be the first to be eliminated by having your finger-prints taken?"

"Will it hurt?" Jennifer asked.

Lucie chuckled.

"Not in the least; all we do is simply spread printers' ink across a glass plate and then gently press each of your fingertips in turn onto it. We press them again onto some moist, clean paper and thus produce an exact likeness of your minutiae."

"Just exactly as a printer might set about reproducing a woodcut," added Atticus.

"In that case we should love to be the first. How very exciting," Jennifer leaned across and kissed Arthur on his cheek. "I can hardly wait. Old Reverend Kerr won't like it, though, if we go to church with inky fingers and leave finger-marks all over his clean hymnbooks."

Lucie laughed.

"I imagine he would not, so it might be prudent to have some hot water and soap fetched."

"I'd better arrange that myself," said Jennifer, "Bessie, or *Miss Elizabeth* as I am supposed to call her now that she's the housekeeper, visited her lady-friend last night and she hasn't returned yet."

She giggled suddenly and Artie grinned.

Atticus cast an eye to Lucie who shook her head by just the tiniest degree. It was not their place to break such dreadful news to them and, which was more, they still urgently needed their finger-prints.

Immediately after the breakfast had been cleared, Lucie set up her finger-printing paraphernalia on a side-table in the orangery. By coincidence, it was the very same table that her husband had used the previous night in his solitary deliberations. She had just finished smearing a film of black printing ink across the surface of a plate when Jennifer arrived carrying an enamel basin full of steaming hot water and a square of hand soap. She insisted on being the first of the pair to have her prints lifted.

"May I have a second copy of my own and Artie's finger-prints as a keepsake?" she asked as Lucie took her hand and extended her slim forefinger towards the plate.

"Of course," said Lucie.

"May I…may I have them on the same sheet of paper?" A faint red flush bloomed on Jennifer's cheeks.

"I do not see why not."

The clock in the great hall had not struck another quarter before Atticus and Lucie had obtained an excellent facsimile of the Lowther siblings' minutiae and, as promised, had made a second, identical impression for them to keep as a souvenir. Artie and Jennifer huddled together on a settee, poring excitedly over the paper and comparing it with their own, freshly scrubbed fingertips.

"I'll have it mounted and framed with locks of our hair and put next to my bed," Jenny announced. "Oh, Papa, look here! We have had our fingertip prints lifted. Isn't it a marvellous curiosity?"

Sir Hugh had returned from Newcastle and chosen that precise moment to enter the room. With rising fury, he glowered at the proffered square of paper, tore it from his daughter's hand, ripped it venomously into a hundred pieces and hurled them savagely against the glass panes of the orangery walls.

Jennifer gaped at him, her expression stricken, then gathered up her skirts and ran from the room as the fragments of paper began to fall softly onto the tiled floor.

"Jenny!" Artie called and rushed after her.

Sir Hugh turned his wrath onto Atticus Fox.

"How dare you?" he bellowed. "How dare you abuse my hospitality and my hand of friendship in this manner?"

"Sir Hugh, I must—"

"I am your employer. I pay your fees. I commissioned you in the first place, by god. Yet you take the finger-prints of my own family, under my own roof, as if they were no more than common criminals."

He pointed a trembling finger towards the scattered pieces of paper that littered the floor.

"That is what I think to your evidence, Fox. You will leave this house forthwith. You are dismissed."

"*Not the woman, you fool!*" Verthandi reminded him.

"Very well; Lucie will stay, but you will submit your own account forthwith, sir. There is a money order office at the railway station and I will settle it directly. Then, by my oath, I will see to it that you never work in Northumberland again."

"Very good, Sir Hugh," Atticus replied with a dignity he did not feel. "So be it. We will pack our belongings and we will leave your house just as you wish. *Quo Fata Vocant.*"

"And don't you ever take that motto in vain, Fox. Strike it from your calling cards or I'll have you horsewhipped, damn your impudent hide! But Lucie stays here with me. I need…I need this murderer caught."

CHAPTER THIRTY-FOUR

"But surely you don't intend us to simply abandon the case, Atticus?" Lucie pushed one of the divided skirts she used for bicycling savagely into their trunk. "People's lives are at stake. Perhaps if I tried to reason with Sir Hugh when he's calmed a little?

Atticus pulled his expression into a smile, hoping to mask both the inexplicable emptiness and the rising indignation he was feeling after being bawled out of the morning room.

He said: "Of course I don't want to abandon the case, Lucie. This all needs bringing to a conclusion, and quickly too. Besides, how often are we presented not just with one murder but with a whole string of them and the culprit still at large? No, fee or no fee, he, or they, need to be brought to justice and we are the ones to do it."

"Ought I to stay here then, as Sir Hugh insists I should?"

Atticus considered Lucie's suggestion.

"No, it is too dangerous. Let us take up our room at the Bowes Hotel and bring this sorry saga to its finish from there."

Lucie pressed her lips tightly together.

"But as you said yourself, Atty, the whole of this case seems to centre on Shields Tower, so dangerous or not, surely we cannot miss the opportunity of me remaining here? Sir Hugh will keep me safe, I'm sure; he seems to like me and there's James and Mr Collier too. And you'll only be a mile or two away in the village."

Atticus made a face.

"I declare I really don't like it, but if you are sure."

"I am. I'm quite sure. I'll meet you down at the Bowes once you've settled in."

CHAPTER THIRTY-FIVE

The Bowes Hotel, a small village inn set on the main street of Bardon Mill just above the railway station and adjacent to Messrs Errington and Reay's busy pottery works, was a far cry from the grand hotels of Harrogate, but it was clean and respectable enough. Atticus' decision to pay for their room there, despite their being lodged at the Tower, had proved a fortuitous one. As Mr MacLellan, the fussy, bearded innkeeper, had explained over the tiny reception desk, "I could have let that room thrice-over to various gentlemen of the press. We're expecting a canny few tomorrow on the early trains from Newcastle and Carlisle. They believe all this might be Jack the Ripper carrying on from where he left off in London."

Atticus stared at him. He was glad enough to have his room but the very last thing he needed was a swarm of newsmen at his door, plaguing him to death with mindless questions and childish speculation, or worse – whipping the entire countryside up into a vengeful mob.

"No, Mr MacLellan, you must tell them that it is very unlikely to be the work of Jack the Ripper,'" he said firmly, "or Leather Apron or the Whitechapel Murderer, or whatever other name they might care to conjure up.

"Yes, I do realise that his last murder – poor Mary Kelly in Dorset Street – was not so long ago and that he has never been brought to justice. I will admit too that I did, briefly, consider the possibility that he might be responsible for our own deaths. Much of the local opinion in Whitechapel at the time was that the perpetrator was a Gateshead man, and Gateshead, of course, is not so very far away from here. But Jack the Ripper's methods were very different from those used by our own murderer and his victims were all women, drunken prostitutes in the main.

"There is one striking similarity however: Jack the Ripper left his victims' bodies in full view, almost as if he wanted the police to find them, and our murderer seems very much inclined towards playing the same game."

Mr MacLellan drank-in the words greedily. They would make him a minor celebrity in the public bar that evening.

"Take as long as you like for me, Mr Fox," he muttered conspiratorially. "I wouldn't want to see anyone else killed – of course I wouldn't – but for all that, this affair is...well...I'll admit, it's very good for business."

He hesitated for a moment, scratching at a long-dried ink spot on the blotting pad in front of him, before asking the inevitable question.

"I was just wondering, Mr Fox but can you tell me: Are you close to finding the real murderer? Is it Michael Britton? The whole parish is buzzing for news."

"Mrs Fox and I have our suspicions as to the murderer's identity based on certain evidence we have found, but we do not yet have definite proof of guilt."

The innkeeper darted him a quick, nervous smile.

"If it isn't to be Jack the Ripper, it would be even better for business if it might be King Arthur himself who had…risen from his vault." He giggled suddenly. "Many folk in the village truly believe he has."

"And on the face of it, much of what we have found points to that as actually being the case. At the site of each murder, we have found relics and items relating to the Arthurian legends. It is a most curious case, a most curious case indeed!"

Mr MacLellan seemed to take heart from Atticus' words.

"They do say that Shields Tower is built on the site of a fortress which belonged to one of King Arthur's mortal enemies. They say that when Arthur rose again, he would surely take his revenge upon its inhabitants." He eyed Atticus' suddenly amused expression and quickly added: "Utter tommyrot, of course; I wouldn't believe it for a second, but…there are plenty of them that do."

Atticus could barely suppress a smile as he followed Mr MacLellan up to his lodging.

"There's a plate of cold badger in the saloon, Mr Fox, or pork if you prefer. I'd better put your bicycle in my back parlour if you ever want to see it again and then I'll arrange for your trunks and luggage to be collected from Shields Tower."

"Thank you," said Atticus, "Mrs Fox will be arriving here presently. Perhaps you could show her up directly she does?"

It is a particular gift of lovers that each may sense somehow the presence of the other. So it was with Atticus Fox. He glanced up expectantly several moments before there came an insistent knocking on his door, and an ashen-faced Lucie stepped inside.

They embraced and Lucie said: "I almost didn't make it here. The door of the bedroom was locked by mistake and it was nearly five-and-forty minutes before Mr Collier came past and heard my cries."

"How alarming!" exclaimed Atticus, "And how very odd, too. Should I send down for a brandy?"

"No, thank you, Atticus; I would much rather get on with examining the finger-prints we took this morning. Goodness knows how we are going to procure any more of them though; Sir Hugh isn't going to be the least co-operative."

Lucie laid out the little glass plates onto the dressing table top. Each had a strip of blue paper glued to its underside, which in turn carried the precious facsimiles of the finger-prints she had taken from Excalibur.

Atticus, for his part, took out his pocket notebook into which he had pressed their copies of the prints from Artie and Jennifer. He laid them next to the plates and reached into his bag for his examining glass.

"There is no need for your lens, Atty," Lucie said. "We have both of the other matches right here."

She was entirely correct. The whorls and loops of the finger-prints they had lifted from Artie and Jennifer Lowther were identical in every respect to those under the glass plates.

"It shouldn't come as too great of a surprise to us," Lucie went on, "I said there was something about those two that didn't sit quite right with me. Do you remember my impression on first meeting them, that they seemed more like lovers than brother and sister?"

"Half-brother and sister," Atticus corrected her.

"Well I'm perfectly convinced that Jennifer is pregnant and that the most likely father to her baby is her own half-brother. What a scandal that would cause and what damage to the honour of the Lowther family name were it to become known. Sir Hugh would be quite beside himself."

"An example of which we have recently seen at first hand," agreed Atticus.

"Exactly, and it can easily be imagined how that might become a cause for murder. I'm speaking of the elusive 'why' in all of this, Atticus. What if Jennifer and Arthur are the murderers and not Michael Britton at all?

"Consider that the doctor, Julius Hickson, is called to examine Jennifer Lowther, but is found dead before he is able to do so. He would almost certainly have recognised her condition for what it is and then felt compelled to inform Sir Hugh. Jennifer, of course, could not have allowed that to happen. She already knew that the doctor would be on his way to Shields Tower and, presumably, which road he would be most likely to take. It would have been quite straightforward for her as his patient, and a very beautiful and charming one at that, to have lured him into the cottage and then into drinking from a poisoned cup."

Atticus considered her hypothesis.

"And she would have left the belladonna in Britton's cottage in order to point our suspicions towards him?"

Lucy nodded. "Yes."

"I suppose that would explain Hickson's death very well, but what about Sir Douglas, and what about Elliott and Bradley and Bessie Armstrong, Lucie? How would their murders fit into your theory?"

Lucie frowned as she stared down at the little file of glass plates.

"I suppose it is quite conceivable that the other victims may have known, or at least suspected, what was going on too. I saw it straight away, after all. If that were the case then they too would have needed to be silenced – before they could run and tell tales about it."

Atticus rubbed his chin.

"Yes, yes, I do see the possibility."

"Or alternatively, what about this: What if Jennifer had been having an affaire with Elliott, or with Bradley, or conceivably, with both of them? After all is said and done, many women would find something romantic, titillating even, about both a Gypsy and a stable groom."

Something resonated deep within Atticus' mind and he said: "Yes, I had a similar thought. But then that supposition falls apart immediately with the murders of Sir Douglas and Bessie Armstrong."

Lucie shook her head.

"Maybe with Bessie too, and if with her half-brother, then why not with her own grandfather? What if Jennifer had wished to end the relationships, but they were unwilling? Perhaps she saw their deaths as the only way to ensure their complete and permanent silence."

Lucie's train of thought raced on.

"Uther told us that his sword – a sword he believed was Excalibur – was stolen the day Elliott was killed. Artie and Jennifer have admitted to being inside his cottage that very same morning, and then a sword – Excalibur again – was used in the murder of Albert Bradley. The sabaton prints in the earth, the sound of the bugle, the Grail, the garter, the Spear of Destiny and Excalibur were all used because they would have the whole world believe King Arthur had risen from his vault. And don't forget; they have stated they believe that to be the case on more than one occasion."

"But that would be madness," Atticus protested, and Lucie pursed her lips.

"Yes, it would."

The atmosphere in the tiny lodging room settled into a brittle and brooding silence as each was absorbed in their thoughts.

"Artie and Jennifer seem convinced that they have discovered this lost vault of King Arthur," Atticus remarked after a time.

"Yes, that's what they claim, anyway."

"Do you recollect that Artie said it wasn't far from the site of Sewingshields Castle?"

"Yes I do; he said it was at the end of a cave, hidden behind brambles and undergrowth. Are you suggesting that we search for it?"

Atticus nodded.

"Yes, I rather believe we should. Artie has offered to blindfold us and take us there. That would, of course, be a ludicrously foolhardy thing to do if he and Jennifer were in fact the murderers. But if we were to search the area ourselves, even if we don't actually find the cave entrance itself, we should quite likely meet with one or the other of them. Artie and Jennifer clearly spend much of their time there, and Uther Pendragon is obsessed with the place. It would be inviting trouble for me to roam the Lowther estates so soon after my altercation with Sir Hugh but Sewingshields is on a neighbour's land. It would be a first-rate opportunity to question them further."

CHAPTER THIRTY-SIX

As Atticus and Lucie Fox gazed across the fields and moors of Sir Hugh's estate from the steep road that snaked its way up the valley side, Lucie remarked how strange and different it felt to be looking in on them as unwelcome outsiders rather than as honoured guests.

Atticus shrugged as he pushed his bicycle up the steepening slope and reminded her that in their capacity as investigators, it was important that they should always consider themselves to be outsiders in any manner of enquiry.

"I know it brought the wrath of Sir Hugh down onto me, but it really is the only way to maintain proper objectivity," he explained.

"I suppose you are right, Atticus," Lucie conceded, "but it is nice to stay at the Tower. It makes one feel so very *grand*... Hullo, what's that up on the skyline?"

Atticus glanced up, shielding his eyes from the fierce rays of the midday sun. There, on what must be the Hayden Bridge road, which stretched away across the horizon, was a little block of red. Now and again there were flashes of light as the sun glinted off bare, polished steel, and a distant, rhythmic crunching carried in the hot, still air.

"Soldiers!" cried Atticus, "And on a Sunday too. That is curious. Come on, Lucie, they're heading along the road towards us. If we're very quick, we might catch a word with them as they pass."

Despite the punishing gradient and the burdensome weight of their bicycles, Atticus and Lucie made the junction at the top of the lane in double-quick time. The company of soldiers was still a good hundred yards away and, as they waited, their eyes were drawn continually to the little patch of flattened grass that marked the place of Bessie Armstrong's final few brutal moments of life. It felt almost as if her shade had lingered to haunt it.

A sudden and perplexing thought occurred to Atticus. He said: "Lucie, do you remember your suggestion that one or more of the murder victims might have been having an affaire with Jennifer Lowther?"

Lucie nodded.

"And I said that the idea falls apart if one includes Bessie Armstrong?"

"Yes, I remember. I speculated that Jennifer might be having an affaire with her too."

Atticus' face twisted into a moue of puzzlement.

"I meant to ask you at the time: how could that be? How could she be involved…in that way, with both men and a woman at the same time? I mean, it was a man – most probably Arthur – who caused her to be pregnant, surely?"

Lucie giggled.

"Oh, Atticus, we shall make a medical man of you yet. Yes, it would have certainly been a man who caused that. But let me explain it to you: Unless Jenny is firmly of the 'third sex', as Bessie Armstrong was for example, it is quite possible, indeed not uncommon these days I'm told, for a lady, or indeed for a man, to be intimate with both men and women. It is called bisexuality and it used to be treated in the asylums with cold baths and electrifying apparatus, but not so much these days."

Atticus felt at that moment as if he too had just been subjected to one or other of those very same pieces of apparatus. His racing thoughts galloped ahead of the tramp of the approaching troops.

"Good morning, Sergeant," Atticus called to a soldier marching to one side of the main body of men. He did not reply immediately. Instead he brought the troop smartly to a halt before striding briskly to where the Foxes stood watching.

"Good morning, sir, madam. I must warn you both to take the very greatest care. There is a dangerous lunatic at large on these fells. My men and I have been detailed to search for him."

Atticus feigned surprise.

"A dangerous lunatic?"

"Aye, sir, a lunatic murderer who's killed at least six people that we know of. We're to capture or kill him on sight. If I were you, I'd stay away from this area until we have dealt with him, lest you and the lady become his next victims."

Atticus had a suspicion that the young fusilier was rather enjoying the drama of his Sunday morning diversion.

"It is a big moor to search."

"Indeed it is, sir, but we're just one part of a whole battalion that's been called in. Every man is a Northumberland Fusilier so you wouldn't find better. Each squadron is beginning at a different point of the compass and converging in towards the most likely place he'll be. There's no escape for him this time."

"Converging on Sewingshields Castle perhaps?" Atticus ventured

The sergeant's eyes narrowed.

"Aye," he replied, "How did you know that?"

Atticus ignored the question.

"At Sir Hugh Lowther's own request I should imagine?"

"You're right again, sir. The colonel offered the regiment's assistance to the Hexham police this morning. He's called the foxhounds out too, I hear."

The sergeant glanced at Lucie. "If you and the lady wish, I could spare one of my men to escort you safely down to the village."

"Thank you, Sergeant, but we won't be needing an escort. We are actually privately-commissioned agents trying to apprehend the murderer ourselves. We were the ones to discover the body of the latest victim, over yonder."

The sergeant' gaze followed the sweep of Atticus' arm to the trampled square of verge and an expression of shock flitted across his tanned, battle-hardened face. He and his men traded death daily on the battlefields of the world but it was a very different thing to stumble across it on the grassy verge of an English country lane.

Atticus said: "But thank you for your warning. We will of course take every care for our safety."

"Very well, sir. Good luck."

They watched as the detail, still in perfect formation, marched away.

Once it was out of earshot Atticus said: "The sergeant said six people had been killed. *Six* people, mark you. It would appear that we have no time to lose if summary justice is to be avoided.

"Lucie, the focus of the search is to be Sewingshields Castle. Let us make God's own speed there and pray that we're not too late."

CHAPTER THIRTY-SEVEN

The Foxes saw no trace either of Uther Pendragon or of Artie or Jennifer Lowther as they hurried to negotiate the winding, boulder-strewn paths across the Vallum, the Wall and the Great Whin Sill. Nor had they when they finally abandoned their bicycles and turned east along the base of the steep escarpment, towards Sewingshields itself. Lucie said as much to Atticus, adding that they must be thankful that there was no sign of the searching troops either.

Atticus halted where their path cut across the foot of a brutally high crag.

"These are the Sewingshields Crags, Lucie. By all the gods, this is where we should find them."

They glanced around and around, and it was Lucie who had the misfortune to see it first.

"Atticus!" she cried and pointed to the base of the crag.

Amongst the scree and the fallen rocks there, lay the corpse of a man. It was lying on its back, perfectly and unnaturally straight, with its hands bound, palms together, over its chest and its blood-caked head resting on a large, bronze platter. A number of short white sticks radiated from its back and were spread against the turf – turf that was almost black with blood.

"The blood eagle," Atticus blurted, and vomited.

"What is a blood eagle?" Lucy whispered. There was indeed something akin to an eagle's wings in the way the white sticks were fanned out.

"That is." Atticus replied, jerking his head towards the body.

"It's diabolical," he added after a moment. "It was a punishment execution used by the Anglo-Saxons and the Vikings, whereby the victim's back was cut open and his ribs pulled out and twisted to form the shape of an eagle's wings. If he was lucky, they would pull his lungs out too, so he could suffocate to death. If he was not, they would fill the wounds with salt."

Lucie stared at the corpse. Her eyes widened. "Atticus, that's Sir Hugh's footman; that's James!"

Atticus stared at the face, bloodless and waxen white against the dew-dulled bronze of the platter. It was tortured and twisted in death and one eye was a trailing, bloody mess, ravaged by a scavenging bird or some other creature. But his wife was right – it was James, James with the angel's face.

Lucie reached down and tugged aside his heavy coat. Cut into the flesh just beneath the tightly bound wrists was a cross – a *crux decussata*, or perhaps the rune *Giefu* – horribly enlarged at its centre, where someone might have pushed in a fist and drawn out something vital.

"His heart's been taken, Atticus," Lucie said, "Just like the others. But why has his murderer put a platter under his head?"

"It's not just *a* platter, Lucie; it is *the* platter, the Holy Platter – Uther's platter. Don't you recognise it? I don't recall a platter being any part of the ritual of the blood eagle though."

"The angel-faced fart-catcher," Lucie mused bitterly. She squinted up the menacing loom of the crag, as if the killer might yet be there, leering down at them from its summit, and a sudden thought struck her.

"Angel-faced!"

Atticus was regarding her with curiosity.

"Atticus, he's an angel. Don't you see? There are his wings, and the platter is his halo. And look at his hands; he's praying!"

It had to be true.

Atticus said: "So the fusilier sergeant was right, and James was the sixth. I'm wondering how he knew that, and, which is more; which poor soul is destined to be the seventh and last?"

Lucie gnawed at her lip.

"The Spear of Destiny, Excalibur, the Holy Platter, the Holy Grail, the garter and the sword from the vault; they've all been used. There is only the bugle horn remaining. Atticus, how could you possibly kill someone with a bugle horn?"

The sound of a bugle rent the air.

It came from behind them, from the wild bog-lands to the north – from Sewingshields Castle.

"Come on, Lucie," Atticus cried, "There's nothing we can do for James now save to find his murderer."

Lucie nodded grimly and took his arm. Atticus heaved their bag onto his shoulder and gripped his heavy cane. He would surely need it this day. They glanced at the hellish figure for one final time before cutting away from the short turf of the footpath into the deep cotton grass and sedge of the moor.

There were heathlands too at Harrogate, acres and acres of them on the rolling hills by the town. They had sanded paths and tea gardens, and they were nothing like this place with its tangles of heather and hidden drops and deep, freezing haggs.

"Thank goodness for this rational dress," Lucie said, stepping over the dense mound of a bilberry bush, "I would have got nowhere in a proper length skirt. Maybe that was what happened to Lady Igraine and—"

"Hist!"

Atticus stopped and put a warning hand on her arm.

"I thought I heard voices," he whispered.

"Yes, you're right. I hear them too. They're coming from directly ahead."

Atticus squeezed Lucie's arm and then beckoned for her to follow. Slowly and with infinite caution, they crept forward up a low rise, their nerves stretched taut as bowstrings.

Gradually the voices grew louder and more distinct. They seemed to be those of a man and of a young woman.

"Artie and Jennifer," Lucie mouthed.

Atticus stilled for a moment. She was right and the voices, indeed those of Sir Hugh's daughter and her half-brother, were low and urgent.

Atticus and Lucie inched forward once more. The ground dropped before them to reveal a broad and shallow depression containing a stell – a roughly-built sheep shelter of a form so common in these parts.

Standing within the circle of this stell were Artie and Jennifer Lowther.

"But you must, you must." Jennifer was saying, her voice desperate and imploring. "My father has the Hayden foxhounds and half the regiment out." She bent forwards, toward the wall. "He hates the very sight of you. He'll have you shot or torn to pieces by dogs. Do you want that? Don't you understand?"

"She must be talking to Michael Britton," Lucie whispered and Atticus nodded. They had found them all, it seemed, all three of the persons whose finger-prints matched those they had found on the fatal sword grip.

Jennifer was still talking.

"Uther, if you won't do it for me, do it for Arthur. Do it for Arthur and the Lady Guinevere. You must, must hide yourself." She leaned across to Artie and whispered something into his ear. He nodded eagerly.

As if addressing an infant child, Jennifer sank to her knees.

"Uther, we know for certain that King Arthur has risen. We know he killed those people."

A faint, mumbling whisper carried to them, audible, but so muffled that neither Atticus nor Lucie could make out the words.

"No we are not!" Jennifer retorted. "We do know it was King Arthur, and we know because we've found him. Artie and I have found his vault. Honour bright we have. It is less than fifty yards away from where we are now, at the end of a hidden cave. We followed King Arthur's tracks through the grass on the day Sammy Elliott was killed and they led us straight to it. He had fallen back into his enchantment by the time we arrived, but we saw the brass bugle and the garter—"

"And Lady Guinevere," Artie broke in, "And some little barrels marked with his initials: AR – Artorius Rex. If you will just stand up and walk, we'll show you for yourself. Uther please, come with us!"

Atticus steeled himself. His thoughts and conjectures of the previous night, which had so stubbornly refused to harden with the seeming paradox of Bessie Armstrong's murder, had, all at once, crystallised in his mind and now it was time to act.

Transferring the shaft of his cane into his left fist, he stood and marched over the brow of the depression towards the scene unfolding in front of them.

A twig cracked like a pistol shot beneath his boot. Artie whirled round to face them and Jennifer rose swiftly to her feet.

"Mr Fox," Artie cried, spreading out his arms to shield Uther like a mantling hawk, "Mrs Fox too. Good day to you both. We imagined you must have left Northumberland by now."

"Atticus politely bowed his head.

"To have left Northumberland would have been to have turned back on the path to justice. How could we, in all good conscience, have done that?"

The seconds began to stretch out into a silent stand-off that was quickly broken by Jennifer.

"Uther did not kill those people."

"So we have just heard. However, with the very greatest respect to you both, the weight of the evidence against him is such that it is going to take a little more to convince a judge and jury of that than the word of a single lady and gentlemen, even ones who express their beliefs so ardently as you."

Jennifer and Artie exchanged unspoken words and Jennifer shrugged resignedly.

"Very well," said Artie, "We have offered it already and now there seems to be little alternative – for any of us. We will show you the vault where Arthur and Guinevere lie and then you must believe us. Mr Fox, would you please be kind enough to assist me with Uther? Sir Hugh's fusiliers will be upon us ere long, and we don't want an innocent man shot out of hand."

"We certainly do not," agreed Atticus. "Quickly then, show us this place."

He grasped Lucie's hand and together they hurry-scurried down the slope and into the little stell. Artie appeared to be unarmed, so Atticus passed Lucie his cane and then their bag. He reached down towards Uther, recoiling momentarily at the stench of his greasy, unwashed body.

Artie grimaced.

"Forgive him, Mr Fox, but when he is overwhelmed like this, he struggles to find the inclination even to wash as he should, especially when his circumstances are as spartan as they have been of late, sheltering in this sheep pen."

Atticus waved away the apology. He looked down at the man who believed he was a king and thought that, in spite of the steel breastplate he wore under his ragged jacket with its motif of a noble red dragon, he had probably never seen anything less regal. Even after such a short time of living rough, Uther's clothes were damp and mouldering and crusted in mud; his hair and beard matted and unkempt, and he stank like a wet animal. But by far the most wretched thing about him, and to Atticus' mind quite the most troubling, was his mien. His expression was of complete hopelessness and utter despair.

Atticus slipped his fingers under Uther's chin and gently lifted up his face. It was swollen and slack from lack of sleep and from the countless tears that had left their tracks in the grime on his cheeks. Uther's eyes gazed out exhaustedly, focussing on nothing through half-closed lids.

"Michael," Atticus called softly.

At the mention of his birth name Uther's eyes crept up to meet Atticus'. The effort of the movement seemed to have cost him every last particle of his strength.

"It's time to go."

At a nod from Artie, they reached under Uther's arms and hauled him to his feet.

"Thank God," breathed Jenny. "This way, quickly now." She beckoned them out from the stell and up onto the exposed moor, striding out in the direction of the broad and treacherous marshes that ringed the site of the old castle at Sewingshields.

"It is just as it was at the Alambagh." Urth's acid tone – which, now that he thought about it, rather put him in mind of old Mrs Ryan, his father's bombastic housekeeper – voiced his own sudden thought.

As he surveyed the movements of the enemy, the acres of marshland laid out far below reminded him very much of the approach to the walled palace that commanded the road to Lucknow, then made fortress by the Sepoy rebels.

He recalled that it had been Urth then too, who had called out to him through the crackle of the skirmish-fire and the roar of the artillery pieces.

"Look, is not he the one who tried to cast us out in the name of his god?"

Lieutenant Lowther had known instantly whom she meant. Ahead of him, the regimental chaplain was crouching in a bombshell crater, ministering to a young fusilier, who sat shaking his head in bewilderment and terror as his lifeblood seeped across his tunic.

"Yes it was," Lowther had confirmed, knowing already that it would be Verthandi who would speak next – and what she would call upon him to do.

"Kill him for us."

"But, Verthandi, he is a fusil—."

"Those are your orders. Obey them! Are you a mutineer now too? Shoot him, we say!"

And he realised once again the depth of the Sisters' wisdom. Because here, in the heat and the chaos of battle, one conical bullet dug out of the flesh of a corpse would look much the same as any other and many on both sides carried the very same Lee-Enfield rifles.

Quo Fata Vocant.

A glance across the marshes of Sewingshields, across the broad Fogy Moss, might have reminded one of a vast, country meadow, perhaps like the Stray of Harrogate, dotted here and there with reeds, and with patches of sedge grass and gorse. However, as Atticus now knew, the sedges hid deep, icy haggs and the gorse was impenetrable. It was difficult enough going for a strong, fit man. Encumbered as they were by the dead weight of Uther Pendragon, it had become ten times so.

Eventually, they stumbled over the stony crest of a rise and Jenny whispered: "It's not far now; we're almost there. The cavern entrance is just over yonder."

She pointed towards a low, overgrown crag, patched green and brown with moss and lichen. It formed one side of a deep, marshy hollow, which seemed to have been scooped out of the fell with a pudding spoon.

"I see nothing," said Lucie.

"It's very well hidden, Mrs Fox, behind that big drift of ivy and brambles. If we can shake off the hounds, he should be safe enough in there for now."

"Horseman!" hissed Artie, "Over there, on the crag-top."

All of them, except Uther, turned and looked up – up to the very tops of the great cliffs of Sewingshields. Sure enough, standing quite still in the ruins of the Roman Wall that snaked along the top was the black silhouette of a solitary horseman. It was impossible to tell at that range and with the light at his back who the rider was, much less whether or not he had spotted them. But then, like a phantom, he was gone and the long line of the cliff edge stretched empty and unbroken.

Atticus said: "Quickly, let us get into this cave. It wouldn't do at all if that was one of the fusiliers, heading directly for the castle". At that moment, heavy raindrops began to strafe the ground around them. He looked up into the angry clouds which had gathered unnoticed over their heads and added: "The Fates, for once, seem to be on our side. This will surely slow them down".

They scrambled down the steep side of the hollow, the leather soles of their boots slithering and slipping on the long, coarse grasses. Jennifer, unencumbered by man or baggage, hurried ahead, splashing through the sodden ground.

"Be sure to come through the haggs," she called as she began to cast around in the grass around her, "Your feet will get a soaking, but the hounds won't be far away and it might just break the scent."

She sprang to the ground and tugged a short but stout tree branch free from the clinging grasses. Then, like a rondel dagger, she drove it through the thick mantle of vegetation that cloaked the crag at that point. It parted to reveal a deep, black void. A wisp of mist began to form and hang in suspension like a ghost, as cool air spilled out into the heat and humidity of the day.

"Quickly, get inside," she urged them, her arms beginning to tremble under the great weight of the ivy.

"Is this the vault?" Uther raised his head from his chest and spoke now for the first time.

"It is the entrance to the cave passage that leads to the vault." Artie's breathing was laboured under Uther's weight and his face glossy with sweat. "That is where we will find King Arthur and Queen Guinevere – if they aren't already awake, that is."

He cast a glance at Atticus.

All at once, Uther rose and lifted his arms and his weight from the shoulders of Artie and Atticus. He stood upright, swaying slightly like a man drunk. As he did so, Lucie stepped forward and pressed close behind Atticus. She slipped the thick shaft of the cane into his hand.

"Then I will enter by my own strength." Uther's voice was suddenly strong and vital.

Atticus ran forward and took the weight of the branch from Jennifer and she, in her turn, took Uther's hand in her own, and drew him gently into the blackness.

Atticus, with a flinty glance to Lucie, dropped his branch and ducked after Artie beneath the tangle of herbage. There was a sudden damp and musty smell and he felt a snag on his shoulder as a briar thorn hooked and then broke off into the fabric of his jacket. Then there was just a chill, and utter, utter blackness.

A match flared in front of him. It illuminated the statuesque form of Jennifer as she held it delicately between her fingers and reflected in the wide, bright eyes of Uther and Artie on either side of her, looking on. She dabbed the match head onto the broad wick of a coal miner's lamp and the stronger, steady light grew and filled the cave.

For a cave it was.

Atticus looked around. Behind him, the entrance was gradually being sealed off by the veil of ivy, weirdly white in the lantern light, sinking slowly back into place. In front of him, beyond Artie, Jennifer and Uther, the fissured walls of the cave passage disappeared away into a deep, black nothingness.

Something moved.

He flinched, startled, and looked down. It was a toad, just a big toad, creeping awkwardly through the dust of the cave floor and away from the glare of the unfamiliar light.

"Perhaps we are a little nervy, Mr Fox?"

Atticus glanced up to see Artie regarding him with an expression of amusement, or was it mockery, on his face.

Instinctively, Atticus transferred his cane to his left hand and gripped it firmly by its shaft. He felt emboldened. For all his height, Artie was little more than a child, after all.

He said: "A little wary, I should rather say, Artie. Now please, after you; I'm impatient to finally see this vault".

Smirking, Artie took the hook of the lamp from Jennifer. He lifted it high, and led the way into the black depths of the cave.

After no more than perhaps fifteen or twenty paces they came to a shallow, left-hand bend in the passage. The lantern shadows jumped from wall to wall and as Atticus followed them round, he stopped, frozen in his tracks, his mouth falling agape into a rictus of horror.

In front of them was a large, almost perfectly circular cavern, or perhaps it was, after all, a vault, hewn from the rock by man or dwarf. The lowest parts of the walls were lined all round with small, crudely-dressed stones onto which broad, flat coping stones had been laid to form a continuous shelf or bench. It struck Atticus later that they had almost certainly been stripped from the ruins of Hadrian's Wall. On one side of this shelf a brace of small, wooden kegs had been placed, side-by-side, each branded with the letters 'A' and 'R' in burnt, black characters. Next to these, the light of the miner's lamp reflected off the polished brass of a military bugle and on what a second glance revealed to be a neat stack of the plate and mail that made up a harness of armour. A great, empty helm sat by this stack, the polished, white dragon of the crest seemingly about to leap, snarling from its place, directly at their breasts.

None of these, however, were what had caused Atticus to gasp, nor to cause Uther Pendragon to drop suddenly to his knees and cry out in anguish. The reason for that lay instead in the terrible sight which lay directly ahead of them.

On the great slabs of the bench at the farthest point of the vault, two figures were perched beside one another. One was a skeleton, the ghastly white of its skull seeming to flicker and dance in the lantern light so that it became almost alive. It was a woman, or at least it was dressed as a woman, with a long, slender, blood-red gown hanging limply from the bare bones of its collar. Rising from her skull was a hennin – a tall, conical hat with a long, sheer veil trailing behind, its rich red hue causing the white of her bones to stand out yet more starkly. From the vertebrae of the neck, a large, gold locket, bright and untarnished, hung on its chain against the bones of the hollow breast.

The second of the figures was neither flesh nor bone, but something in between – a grotesque caricature of a human being. It was clad in a full suit of medieval armour, so that only the face was visible beneath the visor of the great helm and its own crest of a fiery, red dragon.

But God forgive the face.

The desiccated, yellow skin was stretched thinly over the bones of the skull, its teeth protruding through the open slash of the mouth below a nose that had all but shrivelled away. The worst by far, however, were the eyes; flat, dark and sightless, and yet staring back at them in an earnest and everlasting agony.

As Artie had told them – though had not truly warned them – it was a corpse. It was a human corpse, mummified by the dry air of the cavern, and perhaps by something else.

"Behold Artorius Rex, King Arthur Pendragon of the Britons and his Queen, the Lady Guinevere." Artie sounded like the caller at a thrupenny freak show.

"Now do you believe us, Mr Fox?" Jennifer added triumphantly.

"No!" Uther's shriek was magnified and thrown back and forth a thousand times by the obsidian walls of the vault. Then, as no more than a croak: "It's not her, Jenny; it is not Guinevere."

There was a long and uncertain silence.

"But it must be," Jennifer insisted. "It all fits perfectly, don't you see? Here is a vault close to Sewingshields Castle. There is a bugle horn and a—"

"Jenny, that isn't Lady Guinevere there."

Uther grasped great clumps of matted hair in his fists.

"It's Igraine!"

Jennifer Lowther smiled fondly and shook her head.

"But it must be Guinevere, Uther. King Arthur's mother died in a monastery. I thought you would have known that."

Uther staggered to his feet. He turned to Artie and his eyes were stricken, like the eyes of the mummified corpse itself.

"Arthur, I'm so very sorry, but that is your mother who sits there; Lady Igraine Lowther. The White Dragon took her as I said it had, as I always said it would."

Artie stared at him, trying to make sense of his words.

"Come now, Uther." Jennifer took his arm. "It is just your delusions, your illness, telling you such nonsense. This lady is clearly hundreds of years old. Just look at her dress! Artie is but one-and-twenty."

Uther tugged at his hair in frustration.

"What I'm saying isn't my illness. It is the truth!"

He snatched Jennifer's hand from his arm and pushed it away. "That lady died just twenty years ago, on these moors. I recognise the dress and I recognise her locket. It is Lady Igraine Lowther, Arthur's mother and my true love, who was soon to be plain Igraine Pendragon."

Inside the cavern, the world finally stopped.

Artie whirled around. His eyes were aflame with passion and the dancing lights of the miner's lamp.

"But it can't be. It can't. You must truly be mad to say such a thing!"

"On the contrary, Artie; Mr Pendragon is entirely correct." Atticus' voice sounded unnaturally loud in the reverberant space of the vault, but calm and reasonable nonetheless. "Regrettably, it is almost certainly your mother sitting there. The man who killed her also killed six and very possibly seven others—"

"It is not entirely the truth!" The new voice, loud and stentorian as Verthandi's boomed and rolled around the cavern like a volley of cannon.

Sir Hugh Lowther was standing at the vault entrance, cutlass in hand, his face thrown into eerie relief and twisted into an expression of the utmost loathing and contempt.

"Yes, it is the truth that Igraine Lowther sits there. Arthur, you make the acquaintance of your mother at last. Be joyful! Isn't that what you always wanted? It is the truth also that she died a little more than twenty years ago, but not on the moors, Britton. Indeed not. Igraine died here, in this very vault. As for whether or not she loved you, who can say for sure?"

He smiled ruefully.

"Half the scoundrels in Northumberland would perhaps wish to lay claim to that particular honour. One of them sits there, next to her, in the armour."

"Would I be correct in my eduction if I were to identify that particular scoundrel as the late Mr Lancelot Gibson?" Atticus asked.

"*How does he know that?*" Urth cried in amazement.

Lowther shrugged in response and turned his penetrating gaze onto him.

"Very good, Fox. Yes, those are indeed the mortal remains of Lancelot Edward Gibson, my one-time comrade and companion-in-arms in the Fighting Fifth."

"With whom your wife was having a romantic entanglement?"

"*Having a romantic entanglement?*" Urth spat. "*There was no romance about it. He knew she was an actress, little more than a whore, and he simply wanted to fuck her.*"

"*More like she wanted to fuck him,*" Verthandi quipped and her sisters sniggered.

Sir Hugh seemed to wrestle with himself for a moment before he addressed himself to Atticus' question. When he did speak, his voice was cold and hard.

"I suppose it depends very much upon your view of romance. You see, Igraine was an actress. She was a creative, imaginative person, who had created a fancy for herself of being ravished by a knight in shining armour. I suppose the fact that Gibson's Christian name was Lancelot pushed her towards him, or perhaps him towards her. Either way, he betrayed me by obliging her, using the armour from my own house to do it, by God!"

"*She fucked him, and all his brother starlings,*" Urth taunted.

"I know that!" Lowther roared and Jenny sobbed. He closed his eyes for a time, waiting until the discipline of the soldier in him took hold once more.

"Igraine was meticulous in keeping a diary, Fox. She recorded everything she did, no matter how…carnal that might have been. Then one day, the Norns – the Sisters of the Wyrd – spoke to me. They told me to read it. And so I did. I read a fine, old tale of treachery and lust. For example, in the case of Gibson there, take the 17th of May, 1868."

Lowther reached into the pocket of his tunic and pulled out a crumpled and, even by the imperfect light, much soiled sheet of paper, which might have been torn from a book. He glanced to it and read:

"*Today, I went over to Hexham on the invitation of Mr Lancelot Gibson. He had his own carriage fetch me so he might borrow a suit of armour from the stairs. What a pretty surprise it was to discover that he had sent a present ahead for me – my own medieval gown and hat. They suit me perfectly. It is his wife Victoria's birthday next week and to celebrate, we are going to perform a one-act play he has written for her called* Lancelot and Guinevere. *Mr Gibson was quite as dishonourable as the character he is to play! He was as keen as mustard, and no sooner had he got me into the dress than he got me out of it again too. Ooh la! How could I refuse a gallant knight in shining armour?*"

Sir Hugh stuffed the paper back into his pocket and the hurt and bitterness in his expression gave way to raw anger.

"Gibson can play that character now for the rest of eternity." Lowther glowered into the sightless eyes of the mummy and the Norns cackled with laughter. "He was a fellow officer in the Fighting Fifth, and what he did was unforgivable."

"So Gibson died here, in this cavern too?" Atticus asked. "I suspect it was before Lady Igraine though, rather than afterwards. There were two screams of a woman reported the morning she disappeared, one after another."

Sir Hugh nodded.

"Once I knew for certain of her adultery, and more importantly, I knew with whom, then our destinies were written for us. *Quo Fata Vocant*, Fox; 'Whither the Fates call.' We both appreciate the significance of those words, do we not?"

He smiled wistfully.

"I invited Gibson to ride with me. I told him I had private concerns in my marriage about which I desired his most discrete and confidential advice."

He smiled again and this time it was chilling.

"The ruse worked like a charm. He could not contain himself with curiosity about whether or not I suspected him. Very foolishly, he agreed to meet in secret, by the Roman Wall.

"I told him I fancied that Igraine might be spreading her favours outside of our marriage vows and that even my son, who was a little over twelve months of age at the time, was likely to have been fathered by another. Under a pretext of showing him my evidence, I brought him here, to this old gin smugglers' cave, which I had the misfortune to become acquainted with as a boy. I had previously fetched the armour, the armour he had used to seduce my wife, and set it up just where you're standing now, Fox.

"When he saw it here, he knew finally the game was up, that I knew everything.

"And so it was, Fox; his game was well and truly up. I have travelled the furthest outposts of our Queen's great empire, teaching the natives and the savages to mind their manners. But I never dreamed I should ever need to do the same in Northumberland, to a fellow officer and a gentleman.

"He paid the price. Yes, sir, he paid it in full. I killed him as honour demanded. I cut out his treacherous heart and embalmed the rest of him – the carroting juice from the 'factory worked admirably for that – so I have been able to keep him here ever since, dressed in the armour as you see him now."

He chuckled.

"That night I posted a type-written envelope to Igraine. Inside was an invitation to a tryst in this vault. I had shown it to her when we were first courting so she knew it well. She used to call it her fairy grotto. Then I initialled it 'LEG' – 'Lancelot Edward Gibson' – so she could be sure whom it was from.

"Again, my strategy worked. She set off alone the following morning on some lame pretext of visiting a sick cottager on the moors. But instead, she came here. I followed her."

He chuckled again, more harshly this time.

"Forgive me but it was so very amusing, do you see? Igraine could, on occasion, be somewhat, shall we say, excitable. When she entered the vault, she began to roundly scold the suit of armour, armour you will recall that contained only a corpse. She told him that he was wasting his time; that their love-affaire was over and that he should go back to Victoria. She also said that she dearly loved another. Naturally there was no reply from him, so she stepped forward to lift the visor and…"

He grinned maniacally, leaving the sentence hanging horribly in their imaginations.

"That was the cause of the first scream I presume, Sir Hugh?"

"Precisely so, Atticus; you don't object to me calling you Atticus do you? We are becoming so very well acquainted with one another after all, telling our life stories as we are."

"I do not object at all, Sir Hugh, but tell us about the second scream."

"The second scream? The second scream came when she turned to see me behind her, standing just here, where I am now, although I cannot suppose I looked quite as ghastly as the corpse. Nevertheless, I did have a sword in my hand, this one as it happens." He tapped the pommel of a second sword hanging in a scabbard at his side. "I was forced to use it, both to satisfy my honour and to wipe out her sins. It was to my sorrow because, in spite of everything, I still dearly loved the woman. I still do, Atticus – now more than ever.

"I come here every day, to this vault, to tell her of my day and to remind her that soon she will live again. But on that particular day, I killed her, and I sat her body on the bench there, next to her adulterous companion.

"I needed to possess her, Atticus. I needed to be the one who'd had her in the end. So I removed her flesh and I ate it – starting with her heart. I ate what I could manage and then, when I could eat no more, I sliced up the rest and cured it to make biltong."

"You ate her flesh – human flesh?" Atticus asked, appalled.

Lowther nodded, grinning at Atticus' scandalised expression.

"Her heart tasted a damn site better than Gibson's did, I can tell you. But the Norns commanded me to save some of her to share. They reminded me that she did love one other and that he too should be allowed to feast on her."

He stood, straight-backed and proud.

"*Quo Fata Vocant*. Whatever they command, I must do it, no matter how painful it might be.

"When Igraine's bones had dried out, I dressed her in that gown that Gibson gave to her. But I suffer no dust to lie upon it, Atticus; no sir, I do not. I keep her bones white and the gown clean. She and Lancelot have kept each other company ever since and he must watch as I kiss and embrace her each day, knowing that never more can he come between us."

CHAPTER THIRTY-EIGHT

Atticus Fox regarded Sir Hugh Lowther with horror.

"So then you plotted your revenge on your wife's other lovers?" he said, "And took it upon yourself to commission the statue of the Norns?"

"Atticus, you are very good, very good indeed. It is a great pity that this will be your final commission. But yes, once Igraine was dead, the Norns commanded me to read her other diaries too. When I did so, I discovered in detail how I had been made to look a fool, not once, as I had already discovered, or even twice, but many times.

"The Fates, the Sisters of the Wyrd, saw my anguish and they were merciful. They told me how I might both exact my revenge, and right forever the wrongs that had been committed. The Norns are the Fates of the Teutonics, of the Angles and the Saxons, past, present and future. It seemed appropriate to commission that particular statue of them in gratitude for their great kindnesses to me."

Atticus said: "It was the statue that first aroused my suspicions towards you, Sir Hugh – that and the sword you used to kill Elliott. The Norns seemed to be more totems than *objets d'art* to you, and the figures were positioned so symbolically: Urth, the Norn of the past, with her hand posed as if to point an accusing finger directly towards Igraine's bed chamber; Verthandi, the Norn of the present, watching over you now, and Skuld, the 'future', and as you told us, your particular favourite, looking out across the empty moors. Unless I am very much mistaken, she faces directly towards Sewingshields and this very vault."

Sir Hugh smiled his gelid smile once more.

"My destiny is bound up with Igraine in her death just as much as ever it was during her life.

"It occurred to me that Arthur could not possibly be my son, because at the time he must have been conceived I had been in India training the Sepoys. When Igraine begged forgiveness for her affaire with Gibson, she admitted also that he was the father."

Artie, who had been standing with his back towards them, staring at the mortal remains of his mother, turned suddenly with a bewildered expression on his face.

Sir Hugh fixed him with a cold glare as he continued.

"She blamed *me* for her actions, did you know, Atticus? She blamed me, by God! She said that I, in leaving her alone so often and for so long, had driven her into the arms of another.

"Bah, stuff and nonsense! I was simply doing my duty. I was serving my Queen and my empire, and as a knight too, by Jove – as a real knight, a fighting knight, dubbed by Her Majesty Queen Victoria herself. Why did she need to fantasise about a make-believe?

"There was also the Gypsy Elliott. She found the idea of a tryst with a 'hot-blooded Gypsy', as she described him, as irresistible. She would steal off to his vardo whenever the inclination took her. As often as not, he would move the damn thing to some secluded spot up on the moors so they wouldn't be seen. It was my pleasure to finally ram a sword through his treacherous heart; the same heart he said she had stolen from him. But, do you know, he was quite wrong? She hadn't stolen it at all. It was still there when I reached inside of him and dragged it out of his miserable body."

"Was the heart the gift, Sir Hugh, or was that the death itself?" Atticus asked.

"What the dickens!" Sir Hugh stared, open-mouthed. "You know about the gifts? So the Sisters do speak to you, after all. But no matter, no matter; our destinies are carved already. The lives are the gifts. There are to be seven in total. But the heart was mine. All of the hearts were mine; mine to take and mine to eat, so that never again could they come between me and my love."

"God forgive you, Lowther; you're nothing more than a savage!" It was Atticus' turn to stand aghast.

Sir Hugh scowled.

"I am nothing of the sort! I brought the hearts back to this cave and ate them in front of Igraine with chutney and fine Beaujolais wine. Does that offend your Harrogate sensitivities? And, by-the-by, it was the Norns who suggested I eat 'em so God has precious little to do with it. Igraine's love and devotion will come to me next time – all of it – just as it should. After all is said and done, I am her husband."

"And you stabbed Samson Elliott through the heart, because he had given it, through his love for her, to Igraine?"

Sir Hugh nodded.

"I see that we are like-minded, Atticus, so you will see the appropriateness in it all. Then I sliced through his miserable neck. He'd lost his head to her too, do you see?"

"And the wounds across his belly; they were the sign of the gift – of *Giefu*?"

"They were. Each sealed a slaying as one seventh part of my gift to my Ladies the Norns."

Atticus glanced uneasily at Uther, who was standing with his head bowed, trembling. He said: "We have discovered only six bodies so far. There is a seventh?"

"There is to be a seventh," Sir Hugh corrected him.

"In addition to your first wife and Mr Gibson?"

Sir Hugh nodded.

"And in addition to the three Gypsy smugglers and the old regimental padre, and all the rest of them. You see, in her diary, Igraine confessed her...her love for Michael Britton. Gibson, Elliott and the others were apparently 'mere diversions to add a little excitement to an otherwise dull and lonely existence in a rain-sodden wasteland'. She certainly had a way of expressing herself, don't you think? But she also had the temerity to actually fall in love with Britton.

"I regretted killing her at first – for a time anyway. I kept asking myself if I couldn't simply have overlooked her adultery. Maybe I had neglected her after all. Perhaps I could have had her flogged and said nothing more about it.

"But when I read that she had fallen in love with Britton I was glad then that I had killed her, because then I could begin to forgive."

He saw the puzzlement on Atticus' face and snorted.

"'Only by the shedding of blood can there be remission from sins.' Isn't that what St. Paul wrote in the good book? Once there is death, then all sin is forgiven, or so our old padre said in his final service, just before I shot him."

His face darkened once more as he added: "In any event the Norns decreed it. It was our fate – all of our fates – carved indelibly in runes."

"So you intend to kill Michael Britton now, I take it, Sir Hugh? Is he your seventh victim?" Atticus knew he needed to keep Lowther talking. The searching fusiliers must find them soon.

"Michael Britton, the one who, more than all the others, has so profoundly humiliated me? No, he is not one of the seven. But his life has been given into my hands all the same and I am determined to shame him before he dies, just as he has shamed me. The dishonour will be purged; make no mistake about that."

"His life has been given to you? Given to you by whom?"

The blue of Sir Hugh's gaze grew steely, became yet more piercing.

"By the Fates themselves, of course. By the Norns. They spoke to me many years ago to tell me that his life was mine to do with as I wished."

"But how could they have spoken to you?"

Now it was Lowther's brow that wrinkled in puzzlement.

"What the deuce do you mean? They speak to me in the same way that you, or Collier, or anyone else speaks to me – in the same way they speak to you."

Atticus Fox stared at him in disbelief.

"*He doesn't believe you.*" Verthandi whispered. "*He chooses to deny us, just as all the rest have chosen to deny us. Now you know why we have ordered he be killed.*"

"So…you needed to keep Michael Britton here, dependent on the alms you provided until you could move against him," Atticus pressed, "You needed him to be insane."

"Quite so, Fox. When Igraine disappeared, Britton's insanity returned…with a vengeance." He smiled briefly as he reflected on his choice of words. "Because he had fallen in love with Igraine and yes, fathered a boy called Arthur, and, according to Hickson, because of the association of this whole area with King Arthur, Britton began increasingly to have delusions that he was actually Uther Pendragon."

"You said the boy's father was Gibson?"

"That is what Igraine told me at first. I learned later from her diaries that the boy was Britton's. Apparently, she pretended it was Gibson's because she believed that I would never act publically against a fellow officer, especially an officer of the Fifth.

"Publically I would not of course, but she hadn't counted on the possibility that I might act against him in private.

"She never believed me, Atticus, when I told her that the Norns spoke to me, so she never realised that she could never truly hide her secrets."

"*Foolish girl,*" Urth agreed.

"And so you began to plan your revenge on Britton?" Atticus prompted.

"Yes I did, and with the splendid luxury of having time, plenty of time, to do it. Britton's delusions were a heaven-sent opportunity for me to ensure that he was crushed utterly."

"And of course you knew that the real King Uther Pendragon died after having his water supply poisoned by his enemies. That is presumably what gave you the idea of the carroting liquid."

"A stroke of genius, don't you think? I needed Britton to be completely mad, so yes, for these many past years, I have been tampering with his water supply."

"What, Mr Fox? What is he saying?" Jennifer spoke for the first time, her voice barely louder than the hissing of the lamp.

Atticus turned to her.

"I'm very sorry, Jennifer, but you will be aware that your father owns a hat manufactory in Hexham?"

She nodded. Her eyes, stricken, wide and unblinking carried two tiny lantern flames reflected at their centre.

"There is a material used in such factories to soften the animal fur before it is made into the felt used to fashion hats. It is called nitrate of mercury and it has a distinctive orange hue, hence its common name of 'carroting liquid' or 'carrot juice'."

He lifted his cane towards the little barrels stacked on the stone-topped bench.

"The letters 'AR' burned onto those kegs do not stand for *Artorius Rex* at all. They are simply the initials of the Alkali and Reagent Company of Jarrow-on-Tyne, makers of, amongst other things, nitrate of mercury, and suppliers of that particular material to your father's factory. Your father had a quantity specially packed in those little kegs and delivered along with the usual full-sized barrels. Being small and light, he could easily transport them to this cavern, ready to be used in his plot.

"Nitrate of mercury has been shown over time to cause profound symptoms of madness in the workers who use it, characterised by tremors, drooling and, yes, delusions. That is one origin of the popular saying 'as mad as a hatter'. I recognised symptoms similar to Mr Britton's in a pair of your father's workers, who were taking a rest break as we happened to pass."

"*Igraine was a hat. She was often felt,*" Skuld quipped and her sisters laughed raucously.

"Please don't say that," Sir Hugh begged.

"She needs to know what has been happening, Sir Hugh," Atticus retorted. "Jennifer, your father has been adding nitrate of mercury to the pump behind Mr Britton's cottage for years."

Jennifer Lowther looked directly at her father.

"But why, Papa?" she asked simply.

"Because he took my wife and my honour from me, Jenny, and because he broke my heart."

"And because he wanted Michael Britton to be blamed for the murders of Samson Elliott, your own grandfather, Dr Hickson, Albert Bradley, James the footman and Bessie Armstrong." Atticus spat out the name of each victim in turn.

"James? Bessie Armstrong?" Jennifer cried. "James and Bessie are dead? But when – and how?"

"We found Miss Armstrong's body late last night on the road from Twice Brewed," Atticus recounted. "She had been impaled on the lance Mr Britton believed was the Spear of Destiny. James' corpse lies even now at the foot of the Sewingshields Crags with his head resting on the Holy Platter."

Atticus bit his tongue. He had hurt Jennifer and Artie already by thoughtlessly blurting out the news of Bessie's murder. He did not now want to add to that hurt by describing the horrific way in which James had met his death. His tone hardened. "Your father wanted Britton to be disgraced as a lunatic murderer and so he left a series of clues for the police, and for Mrs Fox and me, to find."

Sir Hugh smirked, glaring triumphantly from one shocked and bewildered face to the next. Then all at once, his expression faltered.

"Where is she?" he roared, "Where is Lucie Fox?"

He looked around, wildly now, his eyes frantically searching the vault.

Now it was Atticus' turn to smile, even though it was formed from the most brittle of veneers.

"She isn't here. She remained outside the vault when the rest of us entered. Be warned, Sir Hugh, Lucie will have watched you come in; she will have listened to every word you have said, and she is doubtless, even at this very moment, summoning the forces of justice."

"*He lies*," Verthandi sneered.

Sir Hugh regarded Atticus with something akin to delight.

"Damnation, Fox but on occasion you impress me. I commend your extraordinary coolness under fire. You really would have made a very good fusilier officer.

"However, I know very well that you're playing a game of bluff with me. If your wife really had gone to summon help, she could not have heard my, shall we call it, confession. If she has lingered to hear it, then she is still here, around Sewingshields. No one gets out of the Fogy Moss quickly.

"Notwithstanding that, my men are fast closing the net on this place, so I must make quick work of my business here and then ride her down before she has opportunity to make mischief. Her fate has already been carved. It is futile for her to resist it."

He grinned.

"But yes, Atticus, to answer your question, I wanted you all to believe that Britton had masqueraded as the risen King Arthur in committing the murders. Not only could I settle the long overdue debts of honour and make my gifts to the Norns but I could also have Britton take the blame for it all. He would suffer the complete ignominy and shame he so richly deserves. A quite brilliant strategy, don't you think?"

"In certain respects, yes," Atticus conceded. "Except that your clues were not only rather too obvious, they were also fatally flawed."

The grin on Lowther's face stiffened.

"Allow me to explain, Sir Hugh: In the case of Samson Elliott, the first of your latter-day victims, the thing that struck me immediately was that although you invariably left the running of your estate to a manager – a 'peasant-in-chief', as you called him – this year you took a keen personal interest in one field in particular. It was the field adjacent to Mr Britton's cottage. You insisted, against all proper advice, that it be ploughed and sown with wheat. The consequence was that in order to avoid running over the growing crop on his way to Appleby, Samson was forced to take the headland path around the outside of the field, and therefore directly past Britton's cottage.

"You thereby ensured that not only could your ambush be carried out with much more certainty, but the finger of blame would also begin to point to Mr Britton.

"Elliott, superstitious as he was, believed he had seen the ghost of a knight-at-arms on the moors. You, Sir Hugh, were that ghost! You were wearing the armour that bore the Lowther emblem, the *dragon argent, passant*; the white dragon, whose sabatons left the prints in the earth. You knew that Elliott would confide his fears to someone and you hoped that after his death, that person would come forward to tell the police, or us, about them. We would naturally link the knight to Mr Britton, who kept an identical suit by his bed and who would not venture out of his cottage without wearing at least the breastplate, and as often as not the entire harness.

"Then we come to the sword stroke that killed Elliott. The necropsy on his body indicated that the blade of the sword used to kill him was long and slender and not a bit like the great two-handed sword Elliott thought was Excalibur. It was more like a modern-day regimental sword in fact. It also had a full hand guard rather than a simple crosspiece."

"How in God's holy name do you know that?" thundered Sir Hugh.

"I quite easily educed it," Atticus replied evenly. "The angle of the wound in Elliott's chest was approximately thirty degrees off the vertical. I tried your own sword, you will recall, before our first dinner at Shields Tower, and when I made a lunge with it, the guard had the effect of turning my hand by that same amount. A sword with a simple crosspiece like Elliott's would not; it almost certainly would have resulted in a wound that was vertical.

"And next we come to the bugle call that was heard over the moors on the morning of Elliott's murder. You yourself blew it in order to lure Britton away from his cottage so that you could lay the trail of footprints and spring your ambush. Artie was also out on the moors that morning with Jennifer. He also heard the bugle call and, in his deposition, was able to describe its note exactly to me. It sounded very similar to the one we heard ourselves last night, and then again earlier today, the one I confirmed with your butler as being the modern parade ground call to 'Rise to Arms'."

He looked pointedly at Lowther who simply shrugged.

"Then we come to the second murder; that of your own father. Sir Douglas was killed by choking, by strangulation and by having his heart torn out."

Sir Hugh smiled the gaping smile of the dragon of his crest.

"Yes, he choked on her."

"He choked on whom, Sir Hugh."

"He choked on Igraine, of course; who else?"

"What? That biltong, it surely wasn't…"

Sir Hugh gaped again.

"Yes, Atticus, that biltong was the last of what remained of Igraine's body. Properly made, it lasts almost forever."

"But why murder Grandpapa? Mr Fox, I don't understand." Artie appealed to Atticus.

Urth answered for him. *"What is there not to understand? It's quite simple; your grandpapa was dabbing up your mama. She needed a proper man in her bed don't you see – a real warrior?"*

Sir Hugh stamped a glossy, black boot and the rowel of his spur jangled.

"It is very simple, Artie," he growled, "Even for one of your limited intellect. I fed your mama to your grandpapa, as well as to the madman."

"You are an abomination! You are a…a monster!"

Sir Hugh bristled, and on the vault wall behind him, his black shadow swelled menacingly.

"*Quo Fata Vocant*," he hissed. "My father seduced the wife of his only son. He paid his dues. The will of the Sisters be done. Amen."

"James told us your father thought Igraine the most beautiful woman in Christendom; that she was so lovely she was good enough to eat." Atticus was appalled by the revelations of his own recollection.

"That is exactly so, and don't they say: 'Be careful what you wish for, lest it comes to pass'?"

Atticus said: "And it was you who killed Dr Hickson." Infuriated by Lowther's mute and lingering smirk he went on without waiting for a reply. "You claimed to have discovered his body on the Stanegate after he failed to keep an appointment. Actually, his first appointment that day was not with Jennifer at all; it was with Britton, at his cottage, and with you, Sir Hugh.

"I took the opportunity of reading Hickson's journals of twenty years ago. There I discovered how he used to call on Lady Igraine to administer 'comfort' for her frequent bouts of melancholy – melancholy, mark you, which struck her only during your own times abroad.

"Mrs Fox was told by his housekeeper how the doctor once had a secret sweetheart, who went missing on the moors around the same time as your own wife. Michael Britton told us how his own fiancé also disappeared on those same moors, again around the very same time. The disappearances of three women so close to each other should have caused an almighty brouhaha, yet the long-serving constable had no recollection of any of them, other than that of Lady Igraine Lowther."

He jabbed the tip of his cane towards Sir Hugh.

"That is because they were one and the same, were they not? Dr Hickson's sweetheart and Mr Britton's fiancé were both, in fact, your own wife."

"Yes, Atticus, yet again you are quite correct." All traces of triumph had drained from Lowther now to leave only weariness.

"Whilst I was in India, she asked her doctor – as ladies are wont to do, I believe – to provide her with physical, what is politely called 'comfort' in my absence. Igraine found it irresistible, and she soon persuaded Hickson to cross over the boundaries of proper medical practice and engage upon a full-blown affaire. She wrote in her diary how excited she would feel to be offering herself up to him; how she would yearn for her next appointment. Forgive me, Jenny, but it is the truth.

"Of course he obliged her with no-end of appointments, flying up and down the Haydon Road in that fancy damned cart of his. Few men would resist her, I suppose.

"When Igraine fell pregnant, Hickson was mortified. He presumed it must be his own child since I had been away in India for some considerable time. But when Igraine told him that the bastard was actually Michael Britton's he was disconsolate, especially since Igraine also confided in him that she loved Britton and intended to divorce me in order to marry him. It was then that Hickson stopped calling on Britton and only began again years later at my own insistence, when I needed to monitor the progress of his insanity."

Atticus stabbed at the air with his cane again and the polished horn at the tip darted in the lantern-light.

"You did meet him at Britton's cottage, Sir Hugh, but alone, since you had already frightened Britton off with warnings of the Elliott brothers coming to take revenge. You offered him a drink, a drink from Mr Britton-cum-Pendragon's supposed Holy Grail, to which you had added poison prepared from the fruit of *Atropa belladonna*."

"Yes I did. He took the drink readily enough. It was a gloriously hot day after all and belladonna is sweet, if a little insipid. After he had drunk it, I told him what it was: witch's nostrum, a preparation made from belladonna and monkshood. I prepared it myself, to a recipe I found in the book I bought for my daughter on her seventeenth birthday. Do you recollect that your wife had it open on her lap the very day you arrived at Shields? I don't mind admittin' it gave me quite a turn! I thought that you'd found me out even as I'd only just begun.

"Belladonna has a most curious effect. Did you know, Atticus that it paralyses the vocal chords and renders the victim mute? You did? So you'll understand that Hickson could neither call for help nor raise the alarm. All he could do was run. So he ran. And as he ran, my poison was driven deeper and deeper into his body.

"It was a beautiful irony that a doctor should have died as a result of a drug and a greater one yet that that drug was prepared from a plant called belladonna, which in Italian means 'beautiful woman'. It was a beautiful woman who first marked him out for death and a beautiful woman that accomplished it.

"He was very weak by the time he reached the Stanegate and I finally put an end to him. I ate his heart too. I don't know what was wrong with him, but I felt damned peculiar afterwards. He must have been bad."

"He wasn't bad, Sir Hugh," Atticus replied, "You simply took in some of your own poison when you ate his flesh."

"Oh, but his heart was bad; his heart was as bad as a doctor's could be. He swore the Hippocratic Oath to do no harm. Yet he betrayed that oath, he betrayed Igraine's trust and he betrayed me. He could not live. Skuld called for his life and he duly rendered it, through a poisoned chalice."

"Ah yes," returned Atticus, "the chalice; the first of Arthur's Hallows. It was cunning of you, Sir Hugh, to place them with Britton so that you could use them to implicate him in your campaign of murder. The sword you gave to him when his doctor confiscated his old naval cutlass. The others he believed were given to him by King Arthur himself."

"The sword I gave to him," repeated Sir Hugh. "Britton, or as he had become in his own mind, Uther Pendragon, began to believe that Artie and Jenny were actually King Arthur and Queen Guinevere, come to visit him. I presume it was because he already knew that Arthur was his son and Jenny happened to be with him.

"I encouraged them to accommodate his madness. I told them it might help him. I even told them to take him an old goblet and platter I'd brought back from India under the pretence that they were the Grail and Platter of the Hallows."

He laughed suddenly and harshly.

"The Spear of Destiny was a British Army, standard-issue lance and the sword a Dervish one I took from a desert tribesman in the Sudan. Did you know that most of the Dervish swords are copies of the weapons the crusaders used to carry, Atticus? No? Well they are. Pass-made, naturally, but good enough for my purposes once I'd had a smith add the runes to the blade. First-rate job of it he made too, for an illiterate Fuzzy-Wuzzy. It was good enough to fool even King Uther Pendragon, himself."

"And you used it in the killing of Albert Bradley?" Atticus cued.

"I did indeed."

At the recollection, Lowther's expression became suddenly as hard as the whinstone of the walls around him.

"Albert Bradley, my head groom. Every day for these past twenty years I have had to endure his loathsome face, smiling and being polite and wishing me a good day. All the time he carried in his heart the knowledge that he too had betrayed me. I hope he is rotting in Hell!"

"*He is,*" Verthandi confirmed gleefully, "*But he comforts himself by remembering your wife and every cry, every moan she made. He was hung like one of his horses.*"

"So you ambushed him, Sir Hugh, in his hay loft?"

"Eh? What did you say? No! It is my hay loft, Fox – not his. And no, I did not ambush him; I stood and faced him like a man. But like the Gypsy, my father and the doctor before him, he became a victim of the very instrument of his betrayal. You see, he used to lie with my wife in my hayloft. She described it in her diaries as her 'roll in the hay'.

"Yesterday evening, I waited until there were only the two of us left in the stables. Then I pushed a stack of bales over and cried out for him to come up. When he did, I challenged him about what he had done. He admitted to everything there and then, and begged my forgiveness."

Lowther wrinkled his nose.

"I told him what I have told you: that there can be forgiveness only with death. He wept like a puppy, begging me to spare him, saying that it was all my wife's doing and that she had led him on so. Miserable bastard! But the Sisters had decreed that he must die. I rushed him and finally put an end to his pathetic, treacherous life."

"With your regimental sword to his neck? The wound was identical in size to that found on Elliott."

Lowther nodded painfully.

"His hurt was over in an instant. Mine has lasted these twenty years. Revenge has dulled it a degree, but God knows, it continues still. But not for much longer."

"*God knows?*" Skuld screamed and he winced. "*God knows? What does Jehovah know against the wisdom of the Sisters, Lowther? We carve the fates of gods as well as of men.*"

Atticus cut short her tirade.

"You pinned him to a hay bale with your Dervish sword, knowing that Britton's fingertip prints would likely be upon it?"

"I remembered what you told me about the infallibility of fingerprint evidence, do you see, Fox? One day, I had come here to sit with Igraine and could scarcely believe it when there, lying on the bench behind the kegs, was the sword. I supposed Britton must finally have found the cave entrance and hidden it here. I knew he'd stashed it somewhere away from the police, but until then I hadn't had a notion where – unless he'd tossed it into the

Broomlee Lough of course, just as Sir Bedivere threw the real Excalibur to the Lady of the Lake. What a stroke of luck! It was certain to have his finger-prints on the hilt. So I put on my gloves and took it with me when I went to deal with Bradley.

"After I had killed him with my own sword – I am much more comfortable with good, Sheffield steel – I took Britton's Excalibur and drove it through Bradley's wretched body into the hay bale below. The same hay, mark you, he had lain upon with my Igraine."

Artie's voice trembled as he said: "It wasn't Uther who left the sword here that day, Sir Hugh; it was us – Jenny and me. We found the cave on the day you murdered Sam Elliott and believed that we had discovered King Arthur's vault. We thought it would be a perfect place to hide the sword, which we had taken from Uther to prevent him cutting himself. We even believed it might have been the real Excalibur."

Atticus found himself puzzled.

"I don't understand, Artie. Why would Uther – why would Mr Britton – cut himself with his own sword?"

Jennifer answered. "Because sometimes he hates himself so much because of what he has become, that he wishes only to injure himself, to cause himself hurt. At other times, the only escape he has from the awful memories whirling around and around inside his mind is the pain of self-mutilation. His arms have no skin left on them that isn't striped and lined with cicatrices."

Atticus cast a glance at Britton, a broken giant of a man, standing with his head bowed, and he paused for a moment to swallow the lump that suddenly held back his words.

"The cycle of murders continued with the killings of James and Bessie Armstrong, Sir Hugh?" he managed to say at last.

Lowther nodded.

"You talk of Elizabeth Armstrong; lady's maid, nursemaid, governess, housekeeper and intimate companion of my wife. Do you happen to know what she was?"

Atticus nodded.

"You have just told us. She was your housekeeper, and before that she was your children's governess and—"

"Yes, yes, and before that she was Igraine's lady's maid, but I repeat, Fox: Do you know what she was?"

Atticus all at once realised what he was driving at.

"She was a sapphist – a uranist, a lesbian woman." He repeated Lucie's description of her. "But she was still your children's nanny. Perhaps you would care to explain to them what it was that warranted your murderous wrath falling upon her?"

"If I must," Lowther replied. "The answer is simple enough, because it was for precisely the same reason it fell upon the rest of them."

Atticus made a leap of faith onto Lucie's worldly wisdom.

"What – she was having a love-affair with your wife too?"

Sir Hugh nodded wearily as Artie and Jenny looked on, utterly stunned.

"I had no idea that women could…love men and other women at the same time," Jenny spluttered at last.

"Then now you have proof positive that they can, Jenny. Bessie Armstrong was a theatre acquaintance of Igraine's, whom she engaged as her lady's maid soon after our marriage. She was quite an attractive woman in those days, I suppose, if a little manly in her deportment. Now I believe that they were intimate even before we were married and that their intimacy simply continued. Once Igraine went missing, I kept Bessie on as a nursemaid to Arthur, and then in turn to Jenny after I married Gibson's widow Victoria. Once they had grown up and left the nursery, I appointed her as their governess."

"He must think you let her use Jenny!" Verthandi warned him.

Sir Hugh's eyes suddenly burned intensely blue against the shadows of his face.

"You see, Fox; I'll always know what you're thinking."

"What am I thinking, Sir Hugh?"

"That there was a risk to my daughter given Bessie Armstrong's perverted attraction to women. You're thinking she might have tried to turn Jenny into a sapphist like herself."

Atticus frowned.

"I was thinking nothing of the sort."

"She never once touched me, Father!" Jennifer exclaimed indignantly. "Artie and I have known for years what she was, but that didn't make her some kind of predatory beast-of-the-field. She was quite content with her own lady-friend. It was almost…well almost as if they might have been married. I have suffered a hundred more vile propositions from your precious fusiliers than ever I have from Bessie Armstrong."

Sir Hugh scowled.

"Then there is your answer, Fox. But in any event I would have taken the risk. Yes, sir, I certainly would have. I needed to keep Bessie bound to Shields Tower, until I could take my revenge on her too."

"Which you finally did last night, as Lucie and I and Mr Collier discovered."

"Yes, which I finally did. After I left you at the stables, I came here and fetched the Lance. I knew that Bessie would be alone on the road from Twice Brewed so I went to ground and lay in wait for her.

"Just as night was falling, I saw her bustling along the lane." His eyes flashed. "Arthur has called me an abomination, but let me tell you now; what she did with Igraine was the true abomination. But I'll grant Bessie Armstrong this: She faced her death like a Briton. There was no weeping or swooning or begging for her life. No, sir! She once boasted to Igraine that she would never feel the prick of a man, begging your pardon, Jennifer. Now you could say that she finally has, but she took it – the spear, the Spear of Destiny, the spear of her own destiny you might say – with courage and with dignity. I for one, salute her for it.

"James on the other hand, served with me for years in the Fifth, in the 'Old and the Bold', and he screamed like a baby. Bold – pah! I knew he was too damned pretty to be a soldier."

"Anyone would have screamed in suffering what you did to him. It was diabolical."

Sir Hugh's cold, blue eyes seemed to cut through Atticus like honed steel.

"Yes it was diabolical, Fox; I agree with you, and I shall tell you why. James was Igraine's fart-catcher in her time, did you know?"

Atticus nodded. "He was her footman."

"Yes, her footman, attending to her every whim and standing behind her at the dinner table. He served no useful purpose there except in catching her farts. They say that ladies compete with each other as to who might employ the most handsome footman. Igraine always said that James had the face of an angel and it took her no time at all to seduce him into her bed. And so the angel fell, Atticus. He fell, and became a demon. So you're right; 'diabolical' expresses it admirably."

He squinted inquiringly.

"Did you find Britton's finger-prints on the lance I left in Bessie, by and by?"

"We didn't get the chance to look for any. Robson's constables commandeered both the body and the lance shortly after we made its discovery. The only fingertip prints we have found are the ones we took from Excalibur."

Lowther grunted.

"Once I had killed Bessie, I blew the bugle horn as close as I dared to Britton's cottage. I was trying to lure him back there so that those fool constables could take him prisoner. So they were with you and her corpse all the time!"

"They were."

"Well prints there were, Fox; I checked for them myself. If they're still there, perhaps I'll be able to persuade Robson to lift them. But if not, as you say, we still have the prints you found on the sword hilt."

Atticus said: "You might remember that we found three sets of fingertip prints on that sword. We've since identified whose were the other two; they were Arthur's and Jennifer's, I presume from when they brought it from Britton's cottage and hid it here. The presence of their prints on the murder weapon would be quite as damning as his."

Lowther regarded Atticus with amusement.

"I hear very well what you say, Fox, although, of course, it makes not one jot of difference now."

In Atticus' mind, a single, great knell of dread sounded. He began to babble.

"No, no, you are correct, Sir Hugh. As you say, it makes little difference. You have made a frank confession, a full admission before us all. I applaud you. *Fiat justitia ruat caelum* – Let justice be done though the heavens fall. This has been a veritable bloodbath; eight people murdered and six in a single week. Even Jack the Ripper did not manage that."

"It needed to be over quickly, Fox." Sir Hugh's tone had ceased to be cordial; it had a steel of menace to it now. "I needed to complete those killings before either Britton was arrested, or any of the other parts to my gift realised what was happening and escaped me."

"Of course, Sir Hugh, I understand, but it is finished now. You have taken your revenge and your honour has been satisfied. Come; let us go to Mr Robson. Let the villagers go about their business once more without fear or hindrance. It is time for you to follow whatever destiny Skuld has written. I truly believe she will be merciful."

CHAPTER THIRTY-NINE

Atticus Fox made as if to move towards the vault entrance but Lowther stood his ground, minacious and unmoving, blocking his path.

"No vengeance should ever be taken without first offering a full and proper explanation," he said.

"Let us get out of this accursed vault, Sir Hugh." Atticus' dread effervesced into raw, visceral fear. Where was Lucie with those damned soldiers? "I thought you said—"

"You misunderstand me, Fox. I am not making a confession; I am merely giving my reasons for what is to come. You see, it makes not one jot of difference whose fingerprints are on that sword because the only persons who will leave this vault alive today will be my daughter, and of course, me. The rest of you will become, very regrettably, the final victims of a deranged madman."

He grinned and lifted up the sword he was carrying, tapping the flat of the blade with his knuckle.

"Britton, do you happen to remember this?"

Michael Britton's gaze crept along the floor of the vault towards Sir Hugh. He nodded.

Lowther went on: "Yes, it is your naval cutlass, which Hickson took from you all those years ago. Firstly I must tell you that it is a very poor weapon – all second-rate cast-iron and shoddy steel. We would never accept swords of this quality in the fusilier regiments. Nevertheless, it will suffice.

"Once I have killed your son and Mr Fox and finally, you yourself, Michael Britton, I will return it to your own hand for the police or my fusiliers to find. We must make certain there is plenty of good finger-print evidence on it, eh, Fox?"

He chuckled and from the flickering shadows the Norns screamed in laughter.

"I will tell them that I found you standing over your fresh-dead victims. I had to kill you of course, to save my own daughter. Your memory will be held forever in the contempt it has for so long richly deserved."

He turned to Artie and his face hardened further, into an expression of the most complete loathing.

"Arthur, the bastard son of my whore of a wife, the cuckoo in my nest; I have brought you up as my own. But only, mark you, because it would have been too much of a slur on the family name to have admitted to what you really are. But now you know the truth: You are the illegitimate offspring of a madman and a harlot. Now you will understand completely why I always forbade you from joining the Fifth. You have weak blood, Arthur, and a lack of moral fibre. Like your father before you, you would have turned coward in the face of the enemy. You would have destroyed the fine reputation that generations of fighting Lowthers have built up."

Arthur met his gaze steadily.

"I have known and been proud of my real father for years, Sir Hugh."

For the very first time, the mask of composure slipped completely from Lowther's face.

"What? You knew? How the devil could you have known about that? I haven't told a soul. Did Britton tell you?"

"He didn't need to. I knew because my mother understood that one day you would try to kill her. She wrote me a letter before you eventually did and left it with Bessie to pass on. She wrote how much she loved me and how much she loved my father too, my real father, Michael Britton, a gentle, intelligent and sensitive man, and a brave man, who was cursed only by circumstance."

Sir Hugh stared at him, open-mouthed, for what seemed to be an age.

"I see. Then your mother had more brains than I gave her credit for, but it matters not. You will soon be joining your father for all eternity – in Hell."

"Papa, no!"

It was Jennifer, her cry almost a scream, magnified and mocked a thousand times by the flinty walls of the vault.

"It is a matter of honour, Jenny. Let it be. You will understand when you are older."

"Papa, are you truly a monster? Would you…would you even murder the father of your own grandchild?"

Lowther stared at her, speechless, as his mind worked to comprehend her words.

"What? What did you say? What grandchild?"

"I am going to have a baby, Papa. That is why I have been ill. Artie is the father – the father of your grandchild."

Sir Hugh closed his eyes and swayed a little on his feet. When he opened them again, they burned with the twin fires of hurt and anger.

"Then you too have dishonoured me, Jennifer. You have brought shame onto the House of Lowther and you have sullied yourself. But there will be no scandal. I will not have another Igraine. You have sealed your own fate."

He turned to Atticus.

"*Quo Fata Vocant*, Atticus. You are in the enviable position of having been called by the Fates, but then you know that already. Our destinies, and those of our respective wives, are woven inextricably together, it seems. When I engaged your services, I was simply looking to commission an enquiry agent. You were supposed to follow my markers to Britton's door and denounce him as the murderer. For that, I needed someone with wit; someone who already knew, or could be told, about the Arthurian legends and be capable of piecing together my clues.

"But who can fathom the will of the Norns? They brought me you, Atticus Fox, and they brought me Lucie. When I lost my temper and bawled you out of my house, I risked losing everything. You see, it is *your* life that is the seventh and final part of my gift. It is you I must kill, and you I must mark with the seventh rune."

"But you've killed seven times already."

"I've killed many, many more times than that, Fox, both on and off the battlefield. But those deaths were never part of my gift. You, however, are. I need Igraine, my only true love, to return to me whole and unsullied. The temptations she so unfortunately succumbed to in her last life have been removed now. I, myself, have devoured their hearts, all except Bessie Armstrong's that is; I would never risk weakening myself with a woman's heart. Britton will be shamed, Igraine will rise, and you, Atticus Fox, are now the only thing that stands between the will of the Norns and its final accomplishment.

"Of course, I know you will submit willingly to your fate. Whither they call, Atticus, just like me, you will follow."

"But how do I stand in their way, Sir Hugh? I never even knew Lady Igraine, much less carried anything on with her."

"Haven't they told you? Don't you listen to their words? You see, Atticus, I have been offered the most precious thing. All I must do is offer seven lives as gifts to the Norns and, in return, they will give me back Igraine with her honour restored, whole and unblemished."

"How could they possibly do that?"

"It will be miraculous. They told me that once the gift is complete, and once Britton has been humbled, they will take her spirit and they will put it into the mortal body of another. That woman is to be your wife Lucie Fox, and that is why you must be the final part of the wergild."

He raised the cutlass.

"This will be a famous opportunity for you to serve the Fates, Atticus. Your journey here to Hexhamshire has become truly serendipitous for us all."

Atticus leapt back, pulling sharply on the thick, pewter handle of his cane. From its shaft he drew a long, slender, steel blade and brandished it defiantly at Lowther. The light from the miner's lamp quivered back and forth along the thin steel ribbon, as it trembled in Atticus' hand.

Sir Hugh hesitated and ran his tongue over his lips as he eyed it with relish.

"Upon my soul, Fox, a sword-stick – a toy sword. So you want to make a fight of it eh? Bully for you!"

On this last syllable, Lowther lunged forward and brushed away Atticus' flimsy weapon in a great, sweeping, back-handed stroke of his cutlass. It struck a single, orange spark on the wall of the vault and clattered away into the shadows.

"Oh, what terrible luck, Mr Fox," he mocked.

Pressing forward, Sir Hugh Lowther shadowed the four as they drew back, like some demented sheepdog with its flock, grinning madly as he lifted the cutlass again to begin the slaughter.

"Drop your sword, Lowther."

Sir Hugh twisted, arm aloft and poised already to meet this new threat.

"Lucie Fox, there you are, my dear. I was becoming rather concerned as to where you might have got to."

"I told you to drop your sword. Do it, Sir Hugh. Do it directly." Lucie stood, feet apart, gripping a length of broken tree branch like an oversized cudgel. Her expression was ferocious.

Lowther dropped back against the side wall of the cavern, his eyes flitting continually between Lucie, her branch and the others as he rapidly and coolly appraised the situation. He was an experienced, first-line soldier in the British Army and to him this was just one more encounter, one more skirmish to be won.

"I have spent my entire life fighting my way around Her Majesty's glorious dominions, Lucie," he sneered, "Eleven million square miles in all. I've fought mutinous Indians, Afghan tribesmen and the fuzzy-wuzzy Dervish of Sudan. I've faced sword, spear, rifle and even cannon, by God. So pray tell me; how do you now intend to defeat me with that lump of wood?"

Lucie pursed her lips and gripped the branch yet tighter.

"I have a proposition for you, Lucie," Sir Hugh went on, more reasonably, "Given to me by the Fates themselves. You are a handsome woman, a very handsome woman indeed. Not, perhaps, as classically beautiful as Igraine was, but very handsome nonetheless. You will soon be free of your current marriage. 'Until death do us part,' as we say. If you would then consent to become my wife, I will, in turn, be glad to spare you. Of course, as my wife, you could not testify against me in law, but you could very soon expect the very greatest of honours: that of becoming Igraine herself, brought back from the dead by the munificence of the Norns."

Lucie stared at him incredulously.

"You are quite, quite mad!" she exclaimed at last.

Lowther bristled.

"I am not mad! This is the will of the Norns, Lucie Fox. The Norns have willed that your spirit must be given up for Igraine's. Atticus must be killed, lest she comes back as his wife in your stead, and that, my dear, would never do. If you doubt me, ask them yourself."

"*He speaks the truth, Lucie Fox,*" Verthandi confirmed, "*It is your wyrd.*"

"There. Do you hear her?" Sir Hugh cried triumphantly.

"What the devil are you talking about?" Lucie retorted.

"My Lady Verthandi is explaining it to you. Listen to what she says."

"I heard what you said to my husband; that you hear the Norns actually speaking to you."

"Of course I hear them. I am a Northumberland Fusilier. *Quo Fata Vocant!*"

"Listen to me! Those voices are not real. They exist only in your mind. You have a terrible, terrible illness. It's an illness of your brain. Sir Hugh, you must believe me. I was an asylum nurse and I've seen this before, many times."

"Stuff and nonsense," thundered Lowther. "Of course they are real. How else could they know the things they do – private things? They've been speaking to me since I was a boy, so don't go telling me they aren't real. And they say that you will be married to me."

He lashed the blade through the air in anger.

"And I say I never will."

"*She rejects you,*" Verthandi sneered.

"*Then she rejects us too,*" Skuld returned. "*Kill her; she is unworthy of the honour after all.*"

"But we will still owe Lowther a gift, Sisters. He has paid us six parts of the wergild already and there will soon be a seventh." Urth was emphatic.

"If not Lucie Fox, then whom?" Verthandi asked.

It was Skuld who answered her. *"Give him Jennifer. He can have the bastard in her belly given the iron and then he can marry her somewhere where no one will know she's his daughter."*

"Very well, Lucie," Sir Hugh growled. "Then you shall die with the husband you've chosen. Igraine can take Jennifer's place in this world instead. I will marry her."

Jennifer gasped. "Father, what are you saying? You're jesting, surely? I'm your own daughter."

"Only my daughter by Victoria, and you won't even be that once Igraine's spirit possesses you."

"So the finest swordsman in England, the great hero of the Empire, makes war on women does he?"

Artie stepped forward now and stood defiantly before Sir Hugh.

"Damn you, Arthur; it is the will of the Fates."

"This has nothing to do with fate. It is simply about a murderer; a brutal multiple-murderer, who cannot accept the truth that his wife loved another. I am ashamed I ever called you 'father'.

"Do as Mrs Fox says, Colonel Sir Hugh Douglas Lowther, Knight Commander of the Order of the Bath; drop that sword and face your accusers like the man I thought you were. *Magistratus indicat virum.* For honour's sake, drop your sword!"

"Even the madman's bastard knows what you are, Lowther!" Verthandi exulted, *"Even he can see you are a coward."*

"Or perhaps he can smell the piss in his breeches, Sister," said Skuld wryly.

Somewhere deep within Sir Hugh's soul, Artie's words seemed to have struck home. His head sagged forward and the sword tip dropped towards the floor.

Lucie saw it. She hesitated for only a moment, then lifted the branch high above her head and hurled it ferociously, straight at his breast. He glanced up, too late to duck or parry and it caught him full in the chest, the shock more than the force of the blow throwing him back against the wall. Lucie ran forward, darting between him and his shadow and fell into Atticus' reaching arms.

But the blow served only to enrage the great dragon that was Sir Hugh Lowther. He roared in shock and indignation and leapt forward, sweeping the heavy blade of the cutlass viciously through the empty air, where Lucie has been just an instant before.

"You missed her," Urth taunted, *"A woman beat you with a lump of wood after all."*

"Again!" screamed Skuld, *"Kill her this time. Kill her; kill her; kill her. Kill her like you killed that Sepoy's whore in Cawnpore. Do you remember Cawnpore, Lowther?"*

Atticus drags Lucie back, away from Sir Hugh's swelling wrath as he begins, once more, to advance on them. He raises his empty cane and tries to remember what he has read about singlestick. He thinks of David and

Goliath. He is suddenly aware too of Uther Pendragon standing next to him and beginning to stir.

A rush of movement, and a shape, black and heavy, catches Sir Hugh Lowther full in the face, smashing him back. The cutlass clatters from his grasp and the shape drops to the floor with a flat, heavy crump. It is one of the kegs. A dark liquid gurgles steadily from one shattered side and spreads across the floor, turning the dust into a glistening black pool.

Uther Pendragon snarls and in one fluid lunge, sweeps up the cutlass from beyond Lowther's scrabbling fingers. Sir Hugh springs to his feet, agile as a cat, and in the same movement draws his own sword from its scabbard.

They stand, sword tip to sword tip, measuring each other anew like two strange dogs.

Sir Hugh strikes, thrusting low, almost lazily, towards Uther's unprotected hip and Jenny screams. Uther catches the blade easily – too easily – and tips it aside. But it was a feint, and Sir Hugh follows instantly with a lunge, fast and high, and aimed straight at Uther's face. Uther jerks back his head and the tip of the blade sears a thin, bloody line across his cheek and plunges behind into his long, flailing hair.

They fall back *en-garde*, face to face, watching, waiting, alert now to lunges or feints. Uther, his forehead running with sweat and his cheek with blood, is wide-eyed with fear and concentration. Lowther is relaxed, almost amused by the encounter. He is a natural, practiced swordsman who has devoted his life to the art of the blade. He knows that he can deal with Britton as easily as he might swat one of the many rock spiders that scuttle incessantly back and forth across the cavern walls and, for now, this is merely a game.

He feints again, and then snorts derisively when Uther hurls himself to one side. Stung by the mockery, Uther cuts back, slashing wildly at Lowther's chest but, still laughing, Sir Hugh meets his blade, easily turning it away. His own riposte is an explosion of fury. It catches Uther Pendragon full and hard in the centre of his chest, directly on the dragon of the breastplate he still wears.

Uther grunts and staggers back from the blow. But the smith who forged that steel understood the art of his forbears well. A chip of red enamel flutters gently to the floor.

"You are out of practice and out of condition, Pendragon," Lowther taunts, "And now, you are out of time. That was merely a warning. My next blow will kill you."

"You cannot win, Sir Hugh."

Uther speaks quietly, timidly even, seeming to force each word out in turn. "Merlin has prophesied; the Red Dragon must prevail in the end."

"What?" Sir Hugh bellows incredulously. "*Merlin prophesied?* Do you hear him, my ladies? What heathen nonsense is this? Pah! Let me tell you of another prophesy, Pendragon, that of St John in the Book of Revelation. Let me tell you of a fiery red dragon that is seized and bound and shut into an abyss for a thousand years."

He makes a gesture of flourish around the vault with his free hand.

"Behold, Uther Pendragon, your own abyss."

"We will see." Britton wipes his hand, slippery now with sweat, on his trousers and falls back *en garde*. He is panting heavily, his eyes fixed intently on the tip of Sir Hugh's gently swaying blade.

Lowther's expression changes as he too presents to meet his old enemy. It changes from mocking amusement to deadly determination.

"Uther Pendragon," he growls, "It is time to make your peace with your god, and to say your farewells to your son and your unborn grandchild. *Prêt, allez!*"

With the speed of summer lightning, he strikes. It is a powerful lunge, deadly accurate, and aimed directly at the soft flesh below the steel of the breastplate. Uther has no time to parry and instinct alone hurls him back.

The worn, leather soles of his boots slip on the cavern floor, slick now from the spilled nitrate, and he falls heavily onto his back, gasping explosively as the air is driven from his lungs.

Sir Hugh steps forward and plants the sole of his boot onto the wrist of Uther's sword arm. A thin smile curls the edges of his mouth as he brings his sword tip down over his enemy's exposed throat.

"Farewell, Uther Pendragon," he says. "I have waited twenty long years for this moment. You are humiliated. Now you will repay your debt of life to the Sisters."

Uther's whole body is trembling and with his free hand he clutches desperately at his hurt. In the lamplight his fingers glisten red and wet as his heart pumps away his lifeblood.

Sir Hugh reaches into his tunic pocket and pulls out a long, golden-yellow fragment of silk.

"Does the great King Uther Pendragon have anything to say before I stop up his worthless mouth for all eternity?" he mocks. "Before I stop him inciting any other man's wife to stray beyond the sacred vows of her marriage?"

Uther stares up at him. He lifts one trembling, blood-drenched hand from the wound in his belly and, gasping with the effort and the pain, reaches high to the shelf above his head. His grasping fingers find the cold brass of the bugle horn and close around it.

Sir Hugh cackles.

"Do you see it?" he jeers. "But this is worth a Maharaja's ransom! As his final act, Uther Pendragon intends to summon up King Arthur. Go ahead, Britton, die as madly as you lived. Blow the bugle if you have breath enough left in your body. See if anyone comes to your aid."

Uther pushes the trembling mouthpiece to his lips. He blows a single short, gasping note and falls back, utterly spent.

Lowther stares at him with a countenance of pure scorn. He reaches down and forces the length of yellow cloth roughly into Uther's gaping mouth. Uther turns his head and feebly tries to lift his hand to resist. But he cannot.

Sir Hugh raises himself to his full height once again and draws back his sword.

"No!"

The scream fills every part of the vault. A shape erupts from the floor in front of the watching skeleton and hurls itself at Sir Hugh, who seems somehow to be frozen in shock and horror.

Arthur Lowther and Sir Hugh stand locked together, straining face to straining face, Arthur gripping the wrist of Sir Hugh's sword arm and Sir Hugh's fingers clenched around Arthur's throat.

One, two, three seconds pass.

Then, all at once, Sir Hugh's whole body seems to sway and to slacken, his hand drops from Arthur's throat and his sword falls from his grasp.

Urth's words carry through his rattling, gasping breaths.

"The bastard defeated you, Lowther. So in the end you have given yourself as our seventh part. So be it. We accept. Your debt is repaid."

And it is fitting that the very last voice he hears in this life is Skuld's, a voice so very, very much like Igraine's.

"You are reunited. Your and Igraine's spirits will live here, forever."

His eyes, filled with the relief of a struggle now passed, slowly drain of life.

Arthur stares down in bewilderment at the warm blood spilling over his hand and the pewter hilt of the swordstick he has plucked from the floor, and which he now holds tight against Sir Hugh's chest.

Sir Hugh Lowther's legs buckle and slowly, like a dear mama slipping through the twisted branches of a rowan tree, he slides away down the length of the slender blade and topples to the floor. His mouth twitches as if to speak, but instead of words, a trickle of blood bursts from the corner of his lips and snakes down his cheek. His jaw falls slack and he moves no more.

It was several long seconds later when Artie turned to kneel by Uther Pendragon. Gently he pulled the gag from his father's mouth and slipped his hand into the tangle of matted, bloody hair behind his head.

"You'll be safe now, Uther," he murmured, "The White Dragon is gone. He is dead. He cannot hurt any of us any more."

"Arthur, is that you?" Uther whispered.

"Yes, Father, it is me."

"You came?"

"Yes, Father."

"I woke you…in the Hour of Need, at the End of the Days?"

"Yes you did. You awakened me. You did very well."

"Then the Red Dragon has finally prevailed?"

Arthur smiled bleakly and said: "The White Dragon has been vanquished and the Red Dragon has prevailed, just as Merlin prophesied it surely would."

THE EIGHTH CIRCLE OF HELL

In the 19th century, when the British Empire was approaching its zenith, the Victorians began to believe that, with their power and with their fabulous wealth, they could do almost anything. Some gentlemen in particular were convinced that they could indeed do anything…and get away with it.

A noted Harrogate philanthropist is discovered murdered, the victim of a brutal and frenzied attack. The apparent killer, a frail and elderly imbecile, had fled his house as a child.

The Eighth Circle of Hell follows strands of love, lust and revenge as they twist together across that most infernal of times: the Victorian Defloration Mania.

A chilling and utterly gripping tour de force inspired by real events in 19th century England.

This is the type of book that will stay with you for many years. Readers will be distressed, captivated, and awestruck by this tale. The author's writing style is powerful and adds to the thrill the book provides. This book is more than memorable – it is an important expose on the cruelties faced by the sexual slave trade that still exists today.

-GREAT HISTORICALS

THE SATYR'S DANCE

Harrogate, 1892, and a string of savage attacks in the town appear to coincide with the arrival of a travelling freak show. The victims all swear that their attacker was a monster.

The Satyr's Dance takes us into the Esoteric Revival of Victorian England and lays bare the greatest and most ancient secret of all – the fall of the divine, and the ascent of man.

www.garydolman.co.uk

Lightning Source UK Ltd.
Milton Keynes UK
UKHW021225200720
366842UK00012B/3051

9 780993 420825